Not your
PUCKING
GIRL

Sheridan Anne
Not Your Pucking Girl - Kings of Denver (Book 1)

Anne, Sheridan
Kings of Denver (Book 1) Not Your Pucking Girl

Cover Design: Sheridan Anne
Editing: Fox Proof Edits
Formatting: Sheridan Anne
Beta: Holly Swain-Harvey & Kat Uluave

DISCLAIMER

Not Your Pucking Girl was previously published as Miller - Kings of Denver (Book 1) 2017-2022

The content of Not Your Pucking Girl remains the same with new edits and tightening up of each chapter. The story within has not changed. Simply received a facelift plus new interior formatting, title, and cover.

PROLOGUE

DANIELLE

I stand at the crowded bar, scowling as the bartender skips past me for the third time. Damn him. Am I really not that noticeable? I know my tits could be a little bigger and my hair is on the wild side, but at least I have an ass to kill for. Well, an ass that this douchebag can't actually see past the high bar he works behind. But if he could, I would've had my drinks fifteen minutes ago. Maybe I should get up on the bar and give it a shake. I'm sure that would get me service.

"Finally," I murmur when his eyes land on me. I give him my show-stopping smile. "Two vodka sunrises, please," I tell him, hoping he hears me over the impressive crowd. He nods and sets on his way to get my drinks. Once he's returned, I hand over a twenty and drop the change into the tip jar. Not that he really deserves it tonight, but my momma raised me right.

I push my way through the throng of students who I assume are here to watch the championship ice hockey game for the famous Denver Dragons. The crowd roars around me, pushing me left and right, causing me to spill both drinks down my arms as I try to save myself from landing on my ass and making a fool of myself.

Just my luck.

I make it back to the table and place what's left of our drinks down. "What took so long?" Sophie questions, leaning over the table to pick up her drink, "Ugh . . . gross. It's sticky."

"Shut it. You're lucky you even got a drink. Have you seen how crowded this place is?" I ask, reaching under the table for my oversized purse and rummaging through until I find my trusty packet of wet wipes. One can never be too prepared.

Pulling out two wipes, I hand one to Sophie and get to work cleaning up the spilled juice dripping down the side of my arms and glass. I glance up from my task to find Sophie raising her drink to me. "Here's to you, Dani girl—for finally dumping that sorry-ass boyfriend and agreeing to move in with me and Jared."

I beam at her excitement and pick up my glass before clinking it against hers. We drink what's left and get back to gossiping about her brother, Zac, and his latest conquest. Although nothing surprises me at this point. He's possibly the biggest man-whore on earth. If I have to hear *any hole's a goal* one more time from that big asshole, he and I are going to have problems.

The crowd of eager Dragons fans surrounding us begin to shout in outrage, and I take a moment to glance at the screen to see what all the fuss is about. Ahh . . . a fight has broken out, not only during the championship game but during the last few minutes.

Those morons. Why am I not surprised?

I squint at the small screen. Yep, just as I thought, the Dragons are behind by two points and are going to throw their hard work away just to prove to the world that their balls are so big they can barely fit into their itty-bitty jockstraps. What a bunch of dickheads. No wonder they haven't been able to win the championship for the past three years.

The buzzer sounds, ending the game with the Dragons still pounding on the other team, though I'm pretty sure the commentator just said something about the teammates beginning to fight one another. The camera zones in on the guy who must be the coach, and man does he look pissed. I would hate to be in that locker room . . . Actually, on second thought, being a fly on the wall might just be the most entertaining thing I've ever seen.

Sophie pulls me out of my thoughts when she grabs my hand and drags me out of my chair. "Come on," she says, already halfway across the bar, glancing back at me over her shoulder. "We need to find you a hot piece of man-meat to dance with."

I smile at my best friend. Where would I be without her?

After spending the next hour out on the dance floor, I call out to Sophie that I'm heading back to the bar for another drink. I start walking, squeezing through the raging crowd, and get halfway there when my elbow is yanked back, and I'm forced into a hard body. A gasp sails through my lips before the sound of his voice sends fear rocketing through my veins. "What the fuck do you think you're doing shaking your ass like a cheap fucking whore? No girl of mine is going to make a fool of me."

Fuck, fuck. FUCK! How did he find me?

My eyes widen, terror gripping me. "What are you doing here?" I demand, trying to pull my elbow free, but it's no use. He's too strong for me to fight off. I glance around, hoping to catch someone's eye. Maybe I could scream, but I know for a fact that will only make things worse.

As if reading my mind, Brett smirks down at me. "Try it. I dare you, but you'll fucking pay for it when I get you home. I promise you that."

CHAPTER 1

DANIELLE

"Get up," I say, grabbing the edge of Sophie's blanket and ripping it off her bed. As the chilly air rushes her body, she gasps and squints into the morning light, her left tit half hanging from her sleep shirt.

"What the hell, Dani?" she groans, turning to check the time on her bedside table as she reaches for her blanket and attempts to pull it back up. "It's barely six thirty in the morning."

"Nope, sorry, Soph," I say, fighting the blanket back off her. "You said you were going to start working out with me. It's a new semester and we're starting it right."

She digs her face into her pillow. "Fuck off."

I steal that too and get an odd satisfaction out of the way her face bounces off the mattress. "You promised," I remind her, giving my best puppy dog eyes and knowing damn well she can't resist.

Sophie glares at me, and I wait a moment, the seconds ticking down until her resolve finally breaks. Her lips press into a hard line before she lets out a frustrated huff. "Fine," she grumbles as she forces herself into a sitting position. "But you're buying me breakfast after."

"Thank you, thank you, thank you," I grin, feeling as though I've just accomplished the impossible. "Trust me, you won't regret it."

"I'm already regretting it," she murmurs under her breath, her heavy pout only making this so much better.

Turning on my heel, I laugh and make my way out of her room to give her a bit of privacy. Not that she's ever needed it. "You'll be thanking me when you're rocking the hottest bikini body on campus," I call through our paper-thin walls.

"I already have the hottest bikini body on campus, you bitch."

Heading into the kitchen, I grab our water bottles out of the fridge before taking a seat on our couch. Waiting for my roomie to come striding down the hallway, I get busy tying my laces, and a few minutes later she emerges, looking much more awake as she pulls her long blonde hair into a messy bun.

"We'll take my car," she says, striding to the front door and pinching her keys off the hallway table.

I shake my head, knowing this isn't going to go down well. "Uhh . . . no. We're walking."

Sophie's face drops as she turns to glare at me. "You've got to be kidding. It's the first day of the semester. Are you trying to kill me?"

"Don't be so dramatic," I tell her, joining her near the door to check my reflection in our hallway mirror. "It's only a ten-minute walk. It'll give you a chance to wake up properly."

Sophie lets out a frustrated huff. "I wouldn't need a chance to wake up properly if I was given the chance to wake up when I was good and ready," she grumbles, taking her water bottle from me and tossing it into her bag.

I've lived with Sophie and Jared for the past four months in a beautiful little cottage-style house, which we rent for next to nothing. Seeing as though each of us only hold part-time jobs, we consider ourselves pretty damn lucky. Most college kids around here are paying double what we do, but fortunately for us, Sophie has a killer rack and knows how to work it.

Pushing out the door, we walk the ten minutes it takes to get to the Denver campus gym and swipe our student passes to gain access. After getting through the oversized entrance, we head straight to the lockers and throw our things in.

Sophie turns and studies the gym as I dig through my bag for my AirPods. "Wow," she purrs. "It's a sexy sausage fest in here."

I smirk, knowing she's currently living the dream. "Yeah," I laugh, closing up my bag and shoving it back into the locker. "Why do you think I come?"

Soph laughs and leads the way over to the small floor space where we sit and stretch for a few minutes before our workout. "Are you ready for your classes?" she asks as she reaches for her toes, trying not to make a face at the stretch in the back of her legs.

"I think so," I tell her. "I'm pumped for our communications class. That should be crazy."

She nods back at me with the same enthusiastic smile. We're both in our last year of college and are in a few of the same classes this semester, including the communications class. Sophie is working on a degree in journalism, and I must be out of my mind trying to get through a degree in media and communications while minoring in a photography course on the side, but it's worked out for me so far. A lot of our studies go hand in hand, which is how we became such good friends.

Sophie and I met in our first year of college, both newbies living in dorm rooms. Neither of us knew a living soul on campus and were fumbling around without a clue of what to do. We were paired up for a project in our first week and quickly became inseparable. Now, I can't get rid of the bitch, and I wouldn't have it any other way.

Finishing our stretches, we get up off the floor and head over to the squat rack, which I'm surprised is actually available considering all these guys crammed in here. We get to work loading up the bar, taking turns completing our sets while trying our best not to embarrass ourselves.

"Hey," a low, husky voice says from behind us as Sophie rises out of her squat and racks the bar. I turn to look at the newcomer while Sophie watches on from the reflection in the mirror.

The largest man I've ever seen stands before me. He's good looking and most certainly an athlete with a body like that. The guy's got to be at least six four, with beautiful, tanned skin and a sexy smirk that is enough to knock any woman off her feet. He glances in my direction, but it is Sophie who has his undivided attention.

A seductive smile comes over Sophie's lips as she takes in the huge man behind her. "Hi," she grins to Mr. Tall-dark-and-handsome, knowing all too well she's got him hook, line, and sinker.

His eyes flare at her cheeky smirk, but I'm not surprised. Sophie is drop-dead gorgeous. She has the body of a model, blazing blue eyes, and thick blonde hair. She's a showstopper. If I was the casting guy for Victoria's Secret, I'd be hiring this girl.

He nods toward the bar. "Need a spotter, babe?" he questions, coming on strong. Lucky for him, Sophie eats that shit up.

Her gaze sails up and down his body, the interest in her eyes like nothing I've ever seen from her before. "What's your name, big guy?"

His eyes don't leave hers as he answers. "Name's Tank, but you can call me whatever the fuck you want."

She smirks at him once again. "You know, I think I might need a little help."

Yep. That's my cue to leave. "I'm heading to the treadmill," I tell her, though I'm not entirely sure she hears me.

Sophie glances back at me and gives me a cheeky smile that tells me she won't be coming home in a rush. She nods. "K."

I give her a pointed stare. "Don't be late for class."

As soon as she's acknowledged me, I turn in the direction of the treadmills and take a few steps before stopping and glancing back. I catch Sophie's gaze. "Be safe," I mouth to her. She covers up another smile but focuses her attention on Tank as he steps up behind her and places his hands on her hips. She settles the bar back in place on her shoulders.

Finding the perfect treadmill that allows me a good view of Sophie, I step up onto it and fiddle with the buttons until I'm in a comfortable jog. Popping my AirPods in, I press play on my favorite upbeat playlist and try to focus on my run.

Watching Sophie out of the corner of my eye, she gets through half her set with the too-forward, cocky monster behind her before I recognize the look in her eyes. I shake my head in mirth, watching as she puts the bar back on the rack and turns to face Tank.

Sophie grabs him by the shirt and pulls him in, and I'm not surprised when he goes willingly. Grabbing her ass, he effortlessly picks her up and she winds her legs around his waist. He walks them in the direction of the bathrooms, neither of them caring one bit about the people staring at their display.

Bewilderment slams through my veins. Days like this just don't come along—for the first time ever, Sophie's met her match.

"**Y**ou better get going before you're late," Jared calls through our small cottage as I run around collecting my books, certain that a small hurricane must have spread them through the entire house.

"I know, I know. I'm going," I say, shoving them into my bag and rushing to the door before blowing him a kiss. I pass my camera on the hallway table and double back a step, grabbing that too. "Love you."

"Love you too, Dani girl," his voice rings out, just moments before I slam the door shut between us.

Fiddling around in my bag, I search for my phone as I hastily make my way down the street to the college campus. I quickly hash out a text to Sophie, who I haven't seen since her departure to the gym bathroom.

Dani - You never came home. Are you okay? Class starts in twenty minutes.
Sophie - HOLY SHIT, BATMAN! Best morning EVER! I'm on my way. I'll tell you all about it.

Making my way into our communications class, I find a seat in the back and drop my bag onto the chair beside mine, saving it for Sophie. The first class of the semester always seems to be a slow day when it comes to Professor Whitaker, and I know Sophie has got a lot to spill.

A few minutes have passed when I see that familiar wave of blonde hair making its way up the stairs. A cheesy grin cuts across my face, noticing she's positively glowing from her morning activities while still strutting around in her workout clothes. She smirks back at me, shoving my bag out of the way as she flops into the seat beside mine with a satisfied sigh. "I told you. I knew you wouldn't regret coming to the gym with me," I remind her.

Sophie scoffs but agrees all the same. "Oh, I never regret coming," she smirks before jumping straight into her story. "You should have seen the size of him, Dani. He was a beast and a god, he knew what he was doing," she beams, not skipping out on a single, dirty, detail. "We got kicked out of the gym, so he took me back to his place for rounds two, and three, and fuck, don't get me started on his tongue. He was a machine."

I laugh at her enthusiasm. "Wow, so, I take it he was pretty good then?"

"Hands down. Best sex I've ever had."

My brows shoot up with intrigue. "Geez, he must have been really good to deserve a title like that," I laugh while glancing across the room, making sure we still have time to chat. "Are you sure, though? Because you said the same thing about that guy you met during the photography exhibition a few weeks ago."

"Oh yeah, Jack," she laughs with a fond sigh. "I forgot about him. He was great, but compared to Tank, he's got nothing."

My cheesy smile returns. "So, when are you seeing him again?"

Her lips press into a hard line as she gives me a pointed stare, as though I should know better by now, and honestly, I do. I know exactly what's about to pour out of her mouth. I just really wish it wouldn't. "You know that's not how I roll," she says. "I never go back for seconds. No matter how amazing it was."

"Are you—" My response is cut off when Professor Whitaker walks into the room, calling the class to silence. She stands front and center, looking extremely professional in her gray pantsuit and low heels. She slides a pair of glasses up her nose and welcomes us all to our first class. "I trust you've all had a great break and are motivated for a challenging semester," she says, jumping straight into her lecture.

An hour later, I'm madly scribbling notes in my notepad when Professor Whitaker goes ahead and drops a bomb on us. "Alright, your first assignment is going to be a big one. In fact, it will last the duration of the semester and count for fifty percent of your grade. I trust you will take this assignment seriously."

We listen intently as she continues. "We're roughly fifty-fifty between journalism and PR students, so you need to partner up, one from each area. There may need to be a couple groups of three. Your brief is to follow one of the college's sporting teams throughout the year, specifically their training and games. You are to promote them in new ways and write an article each week on their progress and events. Your article will then be published in both the university's online and physical newspapers, so make it good. There are specific sections of the assignment that are solely for the PR students, and some for the journalism students, but the majority of the assignment will involve your combined skills. All the instructions you need will be found in the brief, and the rest you will have to work out for yourselves."

The room falls into hushed whispers of excitement while Sophie reaches for my hand, instantly claiming me as her partner. As if I would have chosen anyone else. "You should have all received an email with a detailed outline of the assignment, so take a moment to read over it and get an idea of what will be required of you."

Grabbing my phone, I open my emails and sure enough, the brief is right there waiting for me. I begin reading over it as Professor Whitaker grabs a hat from the boy sitting in the front row and takes a seat at her desk. "You have a few minutes to figure out who you would like to partner with and then we'll work out who's taking what team," she explains as she begins tearing up little pieces of paper and placing them in the hat.

Five minutes later, she stands and begins calling students to the front of the room, and one by one, they slip their hands into the hat and choose their team. The baseball team, the swim team, the football team, even the cheerleaders get a mention.

When I hear my name called out, I get up and shuffle past Sophie. She gives my ass a good luck spank as I pass her, and I cross my fingers, hoping to God I pick out a good team. After all, this is fifty percent of our grade.

Professor Whitaker holds the hat up high, and I reach up onto my tippy-toes and begin shuffling the leftover teams between my fingers. Then finally, I select one, feeling my stomach knotting with anticipation.

Pulling the small piece of paper out of the hat, I nervously glance up at Sophie and open it. My stare drops to find Professor Whitakers' perfect, cursive handwriting, and my world burns to ashes at my feet.

Oh shit.

How do I break it to Sophie that we just got stuck with the worst team on campus?

Well, I suppose that's not fair. They're certainly not the worst. They're extremely talented, but they waste it on alcohol and parties. Maybe that could be a good thing. I'm sure we could get a lot of great stories that we could exploit. I'm almost certain there are secret pregnancies and drugs surrounding all of them. I can't say it would do any good for the promotion part of the project, but after last year's epic fail during the championship game, they are easily the most hated sporting team on campus. Their plummet from stardom happened after their last game, and now, I guess it's our job to return them to the previous gods they were once known as.

I look up at Sophie, who is watching me intently from the back of the room, before begrudgingly making my way back to her. "Well?" she prompts.

"We've got the Dragons. The ice hockey team."

CHAPTER 2

MILLER

"Come on. Quit skating like a bunch of pussies and show me what you've got," Coach Harris yells from the barriers, his face turning a nasty shade of red. "You've had a few months off and you all come back looking like this. I may as well replace the lot of you with the Figure Fairies. Get. Your. Asses. Moving."

I push myself harder. I've got to be my absolute best and show the team what a great captain I'll be this season. After all, it's the only way to win us the championship this year and get a one-way ticket into the NHL. But that isn't going to happen without a shitload of hard work and dedication. Not just from me, but from the whole goddamn team.

My blades cut into the ice as I continue my sprints. Up. Down.

Up. Down. Spraying an avalanche of ice shavings as I stop at each end before pushing myself even harder. The ice beneath my blades numbs my feet inside my skates, a welcome feeling I've long since gotten used to, and I use it as fuel to push myself harder. No achievement was ever made without self-sacrifice.

I glance down the line, noticing a few of the boys lacking, and I slot myself between them. "Come on, Bobby," I encourage, giving the newbie junior a slap on the shoulder and smirking as he picks up his pace. Now that's more like it.

We complete our sprints and move on to the next set, doing what I can to push these guys to their absolute limit. After last season's shit show, they really could use the win. We haven't won the championship for the past three years. Each season we've made it to the finals, only to let it slip right through our fingers. But that shit isn't going to fly this year. Not on my watch. I'm going to bring it home for us. I'm going to show these new guys what hockey is all about and repair our reputation if it's the last thing I do. Especially after last year's fuck up.

It's our first session back, and to say the guys look like shit would be an understatement. They've spent their time off partying and fucking around, probably with the same bunch of whores they recycle between them. Me? I've spent my break on the ice and in the gym. I know where I'm going and there's no way in hell I'm letting it out of sight.

"Cain," Coach bellows. I turn and make my way over to the man who's become so much more than just a coach. He's my mentor, friend, and an all-out ball-buster.

"Yeah, Coach?"

"Looking good out there," he grunts, barely sparing me a glance, but I don't expect anything more from a guy like Harris. I don't think I've ever seen him show an ounce of emotion. "Get the goals out and run some drills."

"Yes, Coach." Heading back into the center of the ice, I call for them to stop their sprints before giving a few simple orders, and the team splits into groups. A few freshmen grab the goals while others scoop up the box of pucks and empty them onto the ice, letting them spill in every direction. We skate around, each collecting a puck and getting straight into our drills.

We're a good half hour into training when two girls walk into our closed session and take a seat up in the grandstands. They're probably one of the guys' current hook-ups wanting to see us mighty Dragons in action. I ignore them as best I can until a bright flash draws my attention. I glance up at the grandstand to see one girl standing with a camera raised to her face and the other scribbling furiously in a notepad.

What the hell? Who are these girls? We couldn't be getting reporters sneaking in already. Usually that only happens toward the end of the season, or if one of the guys has fucked up real bad. Considering it's only the first day back, I can't imagine that one of my guys would've been idiotic enough to fuck up already.

I skate over to Coach Harris, who has his back to the grandstand. "Have we got an interview today?"

His brows pinch together in confusion. "No. What are you talking about?"

I indicate with a nod up toward the grandstand and Coach turns around, following my gaze. He zones in on them, taking in the notepad and camera, and his face darkens with frustration. If there's one thing this man despises, it's reporters. Though, it wouldn't be the first time he's booked an interview and then completely forgotten about it. "Hey," he hollers, gaining their attention along with the rest of the teams'. "Get down here."

"Shit," I hear my best friend, Tank, grumble under his breath as he comes up behind me while watching the girls make their way down the grandstand. "Wouldn't want to be them right now."

The other boys gather around to see what's going on as the girls get closer. "Fuck," Tank laughs a moment later, indicating the taller girl as they clear the bottom step. "That's the chick from the gym."

"No way," I laugh, taking her in. "She's hot."

"Yeah, you should see what that girl's willing to do, man. She's fucking wild," he says, lowering his voice as they reach the team, and I finally get a chance to take the girls in. The girl from the gym is exactly Tank's type. Blonde, tall, and toned, with a hint of crazy in her eyes.

But the other, fuck. She's stunning. Long dark golden hair is pulled back and begging for me to wrap my hand around it. She glances around the group of men before her, and I expect her to be shy or intimidated, but instead, she smiles the most breathtaking smile I have ever seen, making her green eyes shine like two beacons drawing me in.

My dick hardens at the sight, twitching painfully.

"What the hell is this?" Coach demands, indicating the camera and notepad. "This is a closed training session. Who are you?"

"Hi," my little Golden Girl says, sticking her hand out. "You must be Coach Harris? I'm Dani and this is Sophie. We're students in Professor Whitaker's communications class," she explains as if that should mean something to him. He takes her hand and gives it a quick shake, purely to be polite.

"Okay, that's wonderful for you, but we have a lot of work to get through. I'm sure you can see yourselves out," he says dismissively.

The girls glance at each other in confusion before focusing on Coach once again. "Um . . . We were given an assignment to promote and write weekly articles on the team. We were under the impression you were on board," Dani says.

"I . . . ahhh, shit," he mutters, letting out a frustrated sigh, making it all too clear he forgot all about it. "Look, I don't mean to be rude. I agreed to this toward the end of last season, but you need to focus your energy on another team. I don't have time for this."

Sophie shakes her head and captures Coach's gaze. "Unfortunately, we can't do that, sir. Professor Whitaker has assigned us the hockey team, and she won't accept any changes. Believe me, we tried," she says, rolling her eyes. That last comment hit me like a knife through my spine. "This assignment counts for fifty percent of our grade."

Coach Harris begins to fume, and Dani takes a step forward, placing a hand on her friend's arm to cut her off. "Coach, with all due respect," she starts, softening her tone. "Sophie and I are really good at what we do. It's no secret that you guys have lost a lot of respect after last season's championship blunder, and I hate to say it, but your reputation has seriously gone down the toilet. Honestly . . . maybe we're exactly what you need right now."

Coach lets out a loud huff and studies the girls before sparing his team a glance, knowing they're right. We could use all the help we can get. "What exactly does all of this involve?"

"Not much," Dani says. "We only received the assignment this morning, so we haven't planned it all out yet. But most likely, a few charity fundraisers and interviews with the guys. You know, those types of things."

He presses his lips into a tight line. "What kind of fundraisers? That sounds like a waste of their time. These boys have a strict training schedule. There's not a spare moment in their day between training, gym, and classes."

"No, no. They won't need to do a thing, only show up. But we'll ensure it doesn't conflict with their training or games. All we need from them is a waiver, giving us permission to photograph them and use those images for social media purposes and in print."

He huffs once again and turns toward us. "You boys on board with this?"

The boys begin grunting their approval, but I speak up. There are a few things Golden Girl hasn't answered. "What kind of fundraisers and events are we going to have to be involved in?"

Her beautiful green eyes land on mine, and she takes me in, sucking in a shallow breath as she fumbles, almost dropping her camera. Her cheeks take on the sweetest shade of pink, mesmerizing me until my mind goes blank and I forget what I even asked her. I become so focused on her lips that I barely even hear what she says next.

"Well, we're hoping you guys would be cool with this, but we were thinking that sex sells," Dani continues with confidence. My dick hardens even more hearing those words come from her sweet mouth.

"What?" Coach sputters out, clearly not impressed by their approach. "That's ridiculous. My boys are not whoring themselves out."

The boys begin to snicker at their coach's misunderstanding. "No," Dani quickly clarifies, looking equally as horrified at the idea. Though, I know some of these guys honestly wouldn't mind. "What I meant was, we could do things like a *Boys of Ice Hockey* calendar that we could sell, and all proceeds would go to a charity," she continues before one of the boys cuts in.

"No offense, but a calendar sounds pretty shit," Brody smirks, unapologetic.

Sophie scoffs at him. "Very unimaginative," she mutters. "We were thinking more along the lines of you guys would be naked and oiled up with say . . . I don't know, a strategically placed puck covering the goodies, for example. Although for you, all you'd need is a few ice shavings." The guys laugh at Brody's expense, but Sophie is quick to continue. "Take it from a female perspective. Every woman on this campus, and probably in the state, would want a copy of that calendar. Sell it for twenty dollars apiece and suddenly, you're raking in the cash. You make a big show of donating the money to a charity at one of your televised games, and you've instantly restored your reputation. Assuming you guys can manage a game without beating the shit out of each other."

I ignore her snide comments as I nod along. I like where this is going. "So, the calendar sounds good, but there's got to be more. The good publicity from a single charitable donation won't last the whole season."

"Don't worry, we've got it covered," Dani says with a beaming smile that makes my stomach clench. "We were thinking of auctioning you all off. Possibly something along the lines of 'A night with a Dragon.' Which . . . no. Before you ask, it does not mean a night in bed, but simply a respectful date at a restaurant of the winner's choosing. We could also have a small bio in the article we write highlighting a hockey hottie of the week to keep you guys relevant. Obviously, on top of all this, we will be keeping on top of your social media pages as well. Though from what I can find, they haven't been updated since the stone age."

"Okay, sounds like you've put some thought into this," I say, unable to take my eyes off her. Noticing my attention, her cheeks start to flush in the most breathtaking shade. "Seems like you girls are going to be spending a lot of time around here."

"It looks that way," Dani says, glancing at Coach. "If that's okay? We're all going to know each other pretty well by the end of the season."

"Some of us already know you pretty well," Tank mutters, winking at Sophie who finally looks in his direction, making her eyes pop out of her head.

She recovers within seconds, a sly grin stretching across her lips.

"Oh, hey there, big guy," she purrs, her eyes becoming hooded as she obviously reflects on their time together.

"You let me know if you need anything," he tells her, though we all know he's no longer talking about this project.

"Right," Coach says, moving this along. "As long as you girls stay out of the way while they're training, there will be no problems."

"Got it, Coach," Dani says. "Do you mind if we take a few photos after training?"

Coach shrugs his shoulders as if to say he really doesn't give a fuck, as long as it doesn't impose on his schedule. "Sure," he grunts, turning his attention back to us. "Get on with it."

Not wanting to earn his wrath, we break away and get straight back into our training, but I find myself watching Dani every chance I get. My gaze is transfixed on her movements, the way she flicks her hair over her shoulder when it falls in her face, the way she stands and focuses the lens of her camera with such precision it could knock me over.

I know one thing—I won't stop until I have this girl in my bed.

An hour later, we wrap up the most enjoyable training session I've ever suffered through, and I head into the locker room. The boys are a mess, dripping with sweat and grumbling non-stop after I kicked their asses on the ice. They all talk animatedly about Dani and Sophie, naturally making bets on who's going to tap that fine ass first. We all know Tank has already been there, but what I didn't expect was to hear him tell them all to knock it off. Maybe this chick was a better lay than he let on, or worse, she's already set up shop in his head.

I take my skates off, and after ridding myself of my sweaty uniform, I grab a towel and head into the shower with one thing on my mind.

CHAPTER 3

DANIELLE

"Holy shit," Sophie laughs as the boys file off the ice and head toward the locker room. "I knew Tank must have been an athlete, but the hockey team? Fuck! There's no way I'm going to be able to keep it to a one-time thing now."

I laugh at her misery. "I think we have bigger problems," I say, glancing down at Coach Harris. "He hates us. He's probably waiting for us to screw up so he can kick us out of here."

"He'll come around. Once this gets going and he sees some results, he'll be all for it," she promises. "Now get your ass downstairs and get a photo of them in the locker room."

My eyes bug out of my head. "What?" I squeak, slightly panicked.

The thought of going into that STD-infested locker room makes my skin crawl. "No way. I'm not going in there."

"You have to," she encourages. "You're the photographer. I mean, don't get me wrong, I'm coming with you, but you're the one with the skills, Missy. Now, get off your ass."

"Fine," I grumble as I get up. "Why do you need a photo of them in the locker room?"

Sophie scoffs and mutters under her breath. "So I can add it to my spank bank."

"Be serious," I scold, swatting her shoulder.

Soph lets out a sigh and glances back at me as we trail back down the stairs of the grandstand. "I think we need something exciting to kick it off, and the boys' locker room has always been taboo, prohibited, dark, and downright disgusting. But we have a chance to break that stereotype. It's the Garden of Eden and all the ladies will be dying to know what kind of fruit it holds. So, we're going to give them exactly what they want."

I smirk at her reasoning, but I can't dispute her. The girl has a point.

We make our way downstairs and search out the boys' locker room, but it's not hard. We just follow the scent of man-sweat until we find ourselves cowering in front of the door.

I go to knock to warn them we're here, but Sophie barges straight by me, not hesitating even a bit. "Cover up, boys. We're coming in," she announces, pushing her way through the door.

Ahh, fuck.

I hastily follow behind, and I feel the heat rise to my cheeks. I don't know why I feel so embarrassed about being here, but damn it, I am.

Keeping my eyes down, I try to give them a little privacy, but as Sophie chats and giggles away, I realize these boys don't have a single fuck to give. They're all confident in what they've been blessed with, and from what I can see, they damn well should be.

Sophie begins to explain what we want to the half-naked boys, so they huddle around, ready for a photo with their ripped bods on full display. "Hold on," Tank calls. "We're missing Miller."

A few of the boys moan and tell us to get on with it, but Tank insists we wait. After all, Miller is the captain, and what locker room photo would be complete without him?

Not two minutes later, Miller walks out of the bathroom, freshly showered with his towel wrapped loosely and dangerously low on his hips, giving me the perfect view of his toned chest and abs that lead down to that mouth-watering V.

Drops of water glisten on his body, and heat begins to flood me as an intense desire rocks me to my core. I raise my eyes, locking on his, and I realize I've been caught checking him out. He smirks as though he's just won some kind of game, and easily slots himself into the herd of boys.

I raise my camera and take a few shots, some with the boys posing and some natural, which to me, comes off a lot sexier. "Okay, thanks, guys," I say, placing the cap back on the lens. "We've got what we need. You can get dressed now."

I scramble as I try to flee the locker room. "Dani."

Fuck.

I stop in my tracks and turn to figure out which of these sexy men is pining for my attention. Looking around, I find none other than the captain's eyes on me, indicating with a slight jerk of his head for me to join him. I hesitantly walk over and stand before Miller, very aware that he's wearing nothing but a very loose towel and still glistening with water that's slowly dripping from his dark hair.

"Like what you see?" he smirks as he reaches into his locker and pulls out a sharpie.

I make a show of looking him over, then give a non-committed shrug. "Nah . . . seen better."

"I doubt that," he grins, his dark eyes flaming with excitement and desire. He takes my arm, and his touch sends shivers sailing through my body. I watch in confusion as he uncaps his sharpie with his teeth and begins scribbling a random number right down the length of my arm.

"What the fuck do you think you're doing?" I yelp, pulling my arm out of his firm grasp and fixing him with an unimpressed look, while pointedly ignoring the way his intense gaze bores into mine. I look down at my forearm to see the first half of what I can only assume is his number, taking up all the skin on my forearm.

A smug expression crosses his face. "What does it look like I'm doing? I'm giving you my number."

"You know, there are much more conventional ways to give a woman your number," I explain.

"Yep, but this way you can't tell me you lost it," he smirks, then reaches out, waiting for me to place my hand in his so he can complete the number. "Call me," he says once he has branded my arm with his mark.

Oh God, this guy is trouble, but that doesn't mean I won't enjoy playing with him before completely shutting him down. "Don't think so," I say, enjoying the way his eyes dance as he watches me.

"You will," he smirks, the confidence radiating off him like nothing I've ever experienced before. I give him one last smile and turn my back—before I do something stupid—and hastily make my way out of the locker room. I hope to God he can't see the way my cheeks flush at just the thought of what he could do to me.

"Hey," Miller calls.

Glancing back over my shoulder, I catch him just in time to see his towel drop, showing off exactly what he's working with, and a devilish smirk crosses his handsome face. My jaw goes slack as my eyes bug out of my head. He's huge.

"See you around," he says, acting as though he was merely trying to get dressed.

That fucker.

My cheeks flame and intense need rushes through me once again. I find myself stuttering like a fool. "Y-yeah," I say, which comes out all too breathy, and I swear there might have been a slight moan in there somewhere.

Crap. I need to get out of here before I jump him and end up with a little something more than an ice burn.

Miller's laugh echoes through the locker room as I scurry out the door and run headfirst into Sophie. "Watch it. What's the hurry?" she says. "I'm dying to get back in there."

"Oh, shut it. I just got flashed by the captain and he branded me with his number," I say, holding up my arm, still feeling the overwhelming heat in my cheeks.

"Damn, you work fast. He's hot." Sophie grabs my camera and begins flicking through all our photos before going back to the locker room ones and zooming in. "When are you calling him?"

I gape at my best friend. "I'm not. He's the biggest player on campus."

"What? That's ridiculous," she says, then her eyes widen as if she has just discovered a secret. "Did he not have a lot to show for himself? I'm surprised. You know, maybe he's a grower, not a shower."

"Oh my God. Shut up," I groan, wanting to talk about anything but this. "But for the record, I was extremely impressed with what I saw. I'm just not ready to date yet. Not after what happened with Brett."

"Woah. Slow down, cowgirl. Who said anything about dating? Whatever happened to just all-out, down-and-dirty, fun sex? I'm sure he would be down for that. Actually, I'm certain he'd be down for that. I bet he's a bomb in bed."

"No, you know I can't do that," I tell her. "Sex for me is more than just a quick pump and dump. There has to be a connection. I'm a relationship girl, not a one-nighter like you."

"Hey, don't knock it till you've tried it," she grins.

"Yeah, that's never going to happen," I scoff. "Now, what do you think of the photos? I think we have enough to get the first story out. I liked the idea of the 'Hockey Hottie of the Week' bio."

"Yeah, I liked that too," she says as we make our way out of the ice rink. "Did you just come up with that? I don't remember talking about it before."

"Yeah, it just kind of popped into my mind so I rolled with it," I tell her, getting all too excited about the prospects of how we can do this. "Maybe we should start with the juniors, so there are some familiar faces from last season before moving on to the newbies and finishing it with the popular guys."

"I agree," she says. "Now, let's get home so we can show Jared these pictures. He's going to die when he sees this."

Getting back to our small cottage, I make my way down to my bedroom while digging through my bag to find my phone. After barging through my bedroom door, I drop down onto my bed and get comfortable as I bring up my mother's number.

"Dani Bear, how are you my sweet girl?" my mother's high voice beams after the second ring. "When are you coming home? We miss you," she says as I hear Dad calling out "Hello" in the background.

God, I miss them. It must have been Christmas when I last saw them, and that nearly sent me broke. I'd do anything to be able to afford another trip home, even if it's only for a day or two.

"Hi, Mom," I smile, feeling something warm within my chest. "I miss you too. Hopefully, I can make it home in the next few weeks."

"That would be great, darling. How are your classes going?" she asks, falling into our usual weekly conversation.

"So far, so good," I tell her. "We got this huge assignment in communications that's worth fifty percent of our grade and I'm paired with Sophie, which is great. The only downfall is that we're stuck being the hockey team's groupies for the season."

"Really?" she questions, a little too interested. I can practically hear the smile in her voice. I imagine her flopping down on their old couch, her dark hair high up on her head. "Why do you make it sound like such a bad thing? I bet there are a lot of good-looking boys on that team. Have you met them yet?"

"Mom, I'm not interested," I groan, fibbing through my teeth. I haven't been able to get the image of Miller Cain dropping his towel out of my head. "I told you, I'm not interested in dating anyone. And even if I were, it's not going to be one of those guys, no matter how hot they are. I'm not about to mix business with pleasure."

"Come on, darling. Don't you think it's about time you got back on the horse?"

I put my phone down and hit speakerphone as I make my way across my room to pull out my nail polishes. "No Mom, I don't. Why are we having this conversation again? You know how I feel about all of this."

"Baby," she scolds. "It's been months since you left Brett. Maybe finding someone new will be good for you. Dating is healthy, and I'm not sure if you're aware, but sex is fun. At least, it is with your daddy."

Holy shit, this woman is going to be the death of me. Unfortunately, I'm all too used to her comments. I just wish she wouldn't go and bring up Brett.

Letting out a heavy sigh, I ignore her *sex is supposed to be fun* jab and concentrate on what's important. "I'm not looking to date, Mom. It's way too soon. I just want to enjoy being single. Besides, if the right guy comes along, then he comes along. But until then, I'm not actively searching for him."

Glancing through the polishes and pulling out my favorite red, I listen as she goes on. "Why do you have to be so difficult? You get that from your father, you know?" she laughs as I prop a foot up and start painting my nails. "But one day, whether you like it or not, some amazing guy is going to come along and sweep you off your feet. I just hope you're open to him when he does."

"I know," I grumble with an eye roll.

"You better not be rolling your eyes at me."

"I'm not," I laugh as I move onto my other foot.

We chat for another half hour discussing classes, the assignment, and life in general before I hear Jared getting home.

Mom doesn't allow me to hang up until I've promised to send her the pictures from the boys' locker room with some ridiculous lie about wanting to help me decide which photos to use. In reality, I know she's a little more interested in checking out the man-meat and figuring out which player she'd like to see me with.

I hop up from my bed, hoping my nails have fully dried, and follow the enticing smell of Chinese food into the kitchen.

"Yummm," I moan as I make my presence known, noticing Jared and his boyfriend, Ashton, sitting up at the counter. "God, I hope there's enough to share."

"Girl, I know better than to come home without bringing you ladies dinner," Jared smirks, knowing us all too well.

"I thank God for you every day, Jared," I say, crossing the kitchen and wrapping my body around his in the tightest hug.

"Shut up and dig in," he laughs, leaning back and pulling a clean plate out of the dishwasher behind him.

"What's that smell?" I hear Sophie call from her bedroom.

"Get your skinny ass out here," I yell back. "The boys bought us Chinese."

She comes rushing down the hallway in nothing but her pajama shorts and a hot pink bra and smirks when she sees the plate Jared has just retrieved for her. She grabs it enthusiastically before reaching up on her tippy-toes and pressing a kiss to his cheek. "What do you say to a movie night?"

"I'm in," Ashton pipes up, hopping off the counter and making his way into the living room, being sure to smack Jared on the ass on his way past. We all follow behind with our dinner and flop down around the TV, Sophie and I sprawled out on one couch while Jared and Aston claim the other.

"This is amazing," Sophie grumbles as she stuffs a forkful into her mouth, her eyes rolling in delight.

"Mmmm," I agree, shoveling my own food in like I've been starved for a month.

Jared places his plate down on the coffee table and heads down the hallway, coming back a minute later with pillows and blankets for all. "Alright," he says, glancing over our selections. "It's either *The Notebook* or *Burlesque*."

"*Burlesque*," we all say in unison, though Sophie and I grumble it with full mouths.

Jared laughs and hits play as we all settle in for a perfect night. "You bitches are going to give yourselves muffin tops if you keep eating like that."

"Don't stress," Sophie smirks. "I get enough action. I don't have to worry about a muffin top."

"Oh, and what about you?" Ashton asks me with eyebrows raised.

"I'm fine," I huff, earning a scoff from both Sophie and Jared. "What? I am."

"You're not, babe," Sophie says. "But you will be if Miller Cain has anything to do with it."

Ahh, shit.

CHAPTER 4

MILLER

Why hasn't she called me yet? This is getting ridiculous, and it's definitely not how this game is played. I give a girl my number, she calls me. Simple. But I haven't heard a peep from this chick, and it's killing me. Miller Cain does not get rejected. It's just a fact. She hasn't even sent a text telling me to fuck off. I can work with that, but what I can't work with is radio silence.

It's been a few days since Dani first graced me with her presence, and so far, the girls have come to a few of our training sessions. I must admit, I'm enjoying their audience, and I know the rest of the guys are too. They've been killing it during practice, giving one hundred and ten percent, and I know for a fact that's not because they're listening to Coach's demands.

The girls have been keeping to themselves, sitting up in the grandstand, taking photos, and scribbling notes before packing up and heading out. They asked Johnny for an interview for their "Hockey Hottie of the week" bio, and man, I have never seen a kid look so stoked about chatting with a bunch of girls. They really must have worked their magic on him.

I know I've got Dani's attention, but whenever I glance her way, she makes a show of being busy, searching through her bag, or taking another picture. I don't get it. She didn't strike me as shy that first day, so there must be another reason she's avoiding me, and I don't doubt that I will figure it out.

I sit with Tank as our business professor wraps up his lecture. I grab my bag from the floor and begin to stuff my pens and notepad inside. "What's the plan for tonight?" Tank asks, getting up from his seat and trailing toward the exit.

"Don't know," I say, following him out of the room. "Maybe a few drinks at Micky's. I was planning on hitting up the gym early in the morning," I add, thinking a quiet drink at our local bar would probably be the best idea.

"Cool. I might hit the gym with you."

My brows furrow as I glance at my best friend. "The fuck? You never go to the gym on a Saturday. What's the deal? No date tonight?"

He shrugs a shoulder. "Nah, man. Not tonight."

We walk out of the building and across campus in search of some lunch, when a head of thick golden hair darts into a café, and something stirs within me. "Let's go in here," I tell Tank, turning into the café without a backward glance.

Tank grunts in disapproval behind me. I know he hates this café after he spent four days hunched over the toilet when he ate one of their chicken sandwiches last year, but fuck him. I'm not letting this opportunity go to waste.

We enter the café, and I watch as Dani gives her order and then steps off to the side to wait. I make my way up to the counter and order a coffee and a salad, hoping that shit won't make me sick. I pay my bill while I watch her out of the corner of my eye and notice the exact moment she realizes I'm here. She gasps and quickly turns away, making a show of studying the artwork on the wall, as if she hasn't seen me.

I laugh as I make my way over and notice how her jeans are perfectly plastered to her firm ass. I come right up behind her, close enough that she can feel the heat from my body, and gently place my hands on her hips. I slide them up under her shirt, letting them rest against her toned waist. Giving a little squeeze, I watch as a shiver takes over her body, leaving goosebumps across her creamy skin. God, I've been needing to touch her, to feel her smooth skin under my fingers.

I gently pull her into me and whisper in her ear. "You never called."

Dani takes a slow deliberate breath as a satisfied smile rips across my face. Yeah, she wants me. "I lost your number."

Nah, there's no way. I made sure that number wasn't coming off. Hell, I used a permanent marker just to be sure.

Reaching around her sexy body, I take her hand in mine, holding it out while I use my other hand to slide her sleeve up to her elbow.

"You're a liar," I tell her, as I see a slightly faded version of my number, still clear as day.

"Oh, I didn't see that there," she smiles, knocking me right off my feet with her beauty.

I tug her sleeve back down into place and turn her in my arms. She looks up at me, her green eyes confused and unsure. Dani lowers her gaze to my lips and then darts it straight back up to my eyes.

I grin, knowing I have an effect on her, and lower my face, stopping an inch from her lips, an open invitation if she wants it. All she has to do is take it. She catches her breath, "Come to my place tonight. We're having a party."

She bites her bottom lip and gently shakes her head. "I don't think that's a good idea," she tells me.

"Baby, it's the best idea. Besides, the whole team will be there. It would be good for your assignment if you knew us all on a more . . . personal level."

Dani cringes as she realizes I'm right, and I know I've drawn her in. She gazes at my lips once more, and just as I'm sure she's about to kiss me, the barista calls her name, making her jump in my arms. Damn it, what I wouldn't do to feel her lips on mine.

She lets out a small huff. "Fine, we'll be there," she says, stepping out of my arms before turning her back on me, grabbing her coffee, and hastily making her way out the door. Probably in an attempt to avoid something she doesn't want to do.

My coffee and salad come up next, and I grab them and turn to find Tank staring back at me, his brow arched and gaze full of suspicion. "What the fuck was that?"

I shrug my shoulders and pull my phone from my pocket to send a group text.

Miller - Party at my place. Get your asses there and help me clean up. Bring booze.

Tank pulls out his phone and reads over the message, shaking his head at the same time. "You've got it bad for this chick."

"I don't," I tell him. "I just want to get her in bed."

"Nah man, that's bullshit," he scoffs, not one to hold back when calling someone out on their shit. "I haven't seen you try this hard for a woman's attention since we were freshmen. You've had your eyes glued to the grandstand all week."

"You're one to talk. You haven't even looked at another woman since you were with Sophie."

He shrugs and continues forward. "She's in my head," he confesses.

"What do you mean *she's in my head?* You like this chick?"

He scoffs at my question but grows serious a moment later. "Yeah, I think I do," he admits, sounding as though he can barely believe the very words coming out of his mouth. "I mean, don't you ever think about having a serious girlfriend?"

"Girlfriend?" I ask in shock. "That's not how we do things, bro," I say, slapping him on the back. "We're heading to the NHL. We don't need chicks holding us back."

He shakes his head at me once again. "I think you're wrong. I think things are changing, and I think this thing with Dani is about more than just sex. You just haven't realized it yet. As for me, I'm going after Sophie."

"Alright man," I laugh in shock. "Tonight's your night then. Dani is bringing her along."

He nods in understanding, and after finding something for Tank to eat, we walk the rest of the way back to my place in silence. I contemplate what Tank has just told me. More than just sex? There's no way. I did the whole girlfriend thing, and to say that was a major fuck up would be an understatement. I don't need that shit holding me back. Besides, I'm heading to the NHL. Who even knows where I'll be next season.

When we get back to my place, we find a few of the boys already waiting for us, their arms overflowing with booze. "Alright, fuckers. We've got a few hours to make me not look like a lazy ass slob. Get to work." I unlock the door and let everyone in. "Oh, and get the word out. This has got to be the best party this campus has ever seen."

I sit out back surrounded by my teammates as the party rages around me. Bodies fill every spare corner of my place, inside and out. Girls dance up on each other as the guys kick back with beers, watching the show. Empty red cups litter tabletops and benches as the music vibrates through the walls and into the ground.

Heading into the kitchen, I grab a few beers when a hand shoots out to my chest. "Hey, baby. Come and dance."

I look up into the pleading eyes of Natasha Wilkins, the beautiful, leggy blonde that I may or may not have slept with in a moment of weakness. Though, I think it's fair to say that every guy in the room has too. I shake her off and smirk as she pouts for my attention. "Sorry, babe. Not tonight."

Sliding away, I make my way back outside and take a seat beside Tank, who's trying to shoo away some chick from taking possession of his lap. He takes the beer I offer as he pretends to listen in on the guy's conversation, but I recognize the look on his face. He couldn't care less about what they have to say right now.

I sit across from Jaxon, a junior, and assuming he can get his shit together, he'll be the guy most likely to take over as captain next year. He has a promising future ahead of him, but he needs to pull in the reins a little.

Jaxon's eyes light up as he looks over mine and Tank's shoulders, his intentions crystal clear. "Ah, there's our girls," he smiles before rising out of his chair. "Fuck, Dani is hot. I'm going to tap that tonight."

Rage fills my veins and my fists clench beside me. This little prick better watch his next words. "Sit your ass down," Tank tells him, noticing my fists.

Jaxon stops in his tracks and looks at Tank in confusion. "What's the big deal? Those girls are too hot to pass up."

Tank stands up and gets in his face. "I told you to sit the fuck down," he growls with the type of authority that can't be ignored. Jaxon's face turns a sickly shade of white in response. "There are hundreds of chicks here more than willing to suck your dick. Go after them. Sophie and Dani are off limits," he looks around at our rowdy group. "That goes for all of you."

The boys nod in understanding, not one of them willing to go up against Tank, but Jaxon apparently still has a bit to learn. "Don't be greedy, man. Aren't you already messing around with Sophie? Share her around," he smirks as he casually falls back into his chair.

"I don't share. The girls are spoken for," Tank says finishing the conversation.

Tank turns back to me with a knowing smirk on his lips. Yep, he just staked our claim. Well, sort of. But damn, it feels good to know that none of these idiots are going to try and mess things up for me. Dani is mine.

A few of the guys send me curious glances as they try to work out who has claimed Dani, but they're not stupid. They all saw me get naked for her in the locker room. Hell, they've been giving me shit about it since it happened. But it was worth it to see the look on her face.

Tank and I hang back for a while, letting the girls get themselves a drink and look around. Dani can come to me tonight.

Twenty minutes later, Sophie makes her way into our circle. "Well, hello boys," she purrs, making it clear that she's a few drinks in already. A smirk comes over Tank's face as she flops herself down onto his lap. His arm immediately circles her waist, and she relaxes into him, the two of them fitting together so perfectly.

"Sorry about her," Dani says from above Tank's shoulder. My eyes immediately take in her sexy curves covered in nothing but a little black dress. "She gets a little too relaxed when she's drinking." Dani's eyes go around the circle and stop when they land on me. I can't help but love the way shyness creeps into her gaze.

"No problem at all," Tank murmurs as Sophie readjusts herself on his lap so she's straddling him.

Dani scoffs at her friend's performance. "So much for that," she grumbles to herself.

"So much for what?" I ask, forcing her eyes in my direction once again.

She begins to fidget as she feels the force of my gaze on her but remains strong. "Before we got here, Sophie made a big declaration about no repeat performances," she says, indicating her friend who currently has Tank's tongue down her throat while she grinds on him.

"Yeah, I'm not sure she meant it," I say, getting up and offering my chair. "Why don't you sit down and meet the boys properly?"

Dani moves into our circle and takes my seat. "Thank you," she smiles as I notice her drink is nearly empty. I swipe the beer that Bobby's struggling to open and offer it to Dani.

She twists the cap off effortlessly and smirks at Bobby as I go around the circle introducing a few of the guys. "This is Bobby," I start, pointing to my left and making my way around. "Shorty, Jaxon, Johnny who you already know, Aaron, and of course Tank. I'm sure you'll probably meet the rest of the guys at some point tonight."

"Right, okay. I'm not going to remember any of your names tomorrow, but hi," she smiles sweetly, instantly getting the approval of the guys. I steal a chair on the opposite side of the circle and drop down so I can keep my eyes trained on her. We fall into an easy conversation, mostly with Dani asking us questions about hockey and classes. The boys practically fall at her feet with answers. She's just that kind of girl.

I watch as she talks with the guys, noticing her eyes keep coming back to mine. "Tell me more about this calendar thing," I request, to selfishly keep her attention.

"Oh," she says, her cheeks flushing pink. "I don't really know too many details yet, but basically, you'll be butt naked and getting cheeky for the camera. But it can't be too bad because we don't want to cause issues with administration or get you guys in trouble. Also, we'll probably need to have the Dean sign off on the whole project."

"And who'll be the photographer?" I ask.

Jaxon cuts in. "Yeah? I'm not getting naked for a dude."

Dani lets out a laugh that wraps right around me. "Don't stress. I'm studying photography, so I'll be doing it," she pauses as if second-guessing herself. "If that's okay with you guys, of course."

They all nod and give enthusiastic agreements that have her cheeks flushing all over again, and I can't help but like the idea of getting naked for her once more.

"God, you guys are boring. Let's go dance," Sophie says, jumping off Tank's lap and grabbing a few of the guys before dragging them inside. Tank gets up and follows, shooting death glares at the guys who look back at him nervously.

"Guess we're all dancing," I say, getting up. I grab Dani's hand, pulling her to her feet before she has the chance to decline. I walk inside with her trailing behind me and find the rest of the hockey team.

Tank dances behind Sophie as she grinds her ass into him, and I laugh at the sight. Match made in porn star heaven.

Making our way toward them, I grab Dani's hand and pull her into the middle of the circle, listening to the sweet sound of her shrieking laugh. She tries to scurry away, but the boys are too quick, chanting her name and keeping her the center of attention. She's had just enough liquid courage to keep moving. I find myself mesmerized by the way she moves, but it's nothing compared to the feeling I get when those stunning green eyes lock onto mine.

Tank's right. I'm in fucking trouble when it comes to this girl.

CHAPTER 5

DANIELLE

The makeshift dance floor is packed, and I'm surprised to find I'm actually having a great time. Who would have known these hockey boys would know how to throw such a good party?

The guys crowd me, and I absolutely love it. Jaxon reaches out and attempts to pull me into him, but I squirm out of his grasp and back up as another set of arms circle my waist and pull me in tight. I stiffen in his hold. "Relax," Miller says, his soft tone in my ear. "It's me."

I relax into his hold and continue dancing with his hard body pressed against mine, a thrill shooting through my veins. Everything about him is a red flag, warning me to pull away, but I can't find the strength to run in the opposite direction. He's drawing me in, and it's the scariest thing I've ever experienced.

Miller turns me in his arms as we continue dancing. When the music slows, things become hot. He pushes his knee between my legs, and as my gaze raises to his, I find myself grinding against him.

I suck in a breath as Miller lowers his face to mine, and I watch as his eyes dip to my lips. God, I desperately want to feel them against mine, but I can't let that happen. "Don't even think about it, hotshot," I tell him, bringing my finger up and pressing it against his warm lips, gently pushing his face away.

He nips at my finger, and an excited gasp slips out of me, which of course, he hears loud and clear. Miller smirks down at me, and I see the hunger in his eyes.

Damn. I have to put a stop to this.

I turn back around in his arms and feel him pull me even closer against his strong body. His excitement is evident as he moves his hips against my ass, and good God it feels incredible.

We dance for what feels like hours when he takes me by the hand and pulls me off the dancefloor. "Want a drink?" he asks as he heads into the kitchen. My eyes study his firm ass through his dark jeans, and the urge to grab it rocks through my body. Miller turns and smirks at me. "Were you looking at my ass?" he questions.

Crap. Sprung. "No," I lie.

He stops in the hallway and pulls me into him, once again catching me around the waist. "You're a terrible liar," he says, his eyes sparkling as he watches me.

I smile up at him, completely consumed by this man. Oh well, I may as well own it. "Okay, so what? I was looking at your ass. I'll be seeing a lot more of you at some point. Why not start now?"

Miller laughs, and the sound wraps around me like a warm caress. Then, letting me off the hook, he lets me go and continues dragging me into the kitchen. "So, what do you think?"

"It's a nice ass," I tell him, not bothering to hold back anymore. Hell, he knows it. I know it. Everyone in the room knows it. There's no point in lying.

He looks back over his shoulder and smirks once again, doing things to me that I'm really not ready for. I watch as he makes his way around the kitchen and opens the fridge, pulling out a beer. "Want one?"

"Sure."

He twists the cap off and hands me the drink in his hand before turning back to the fridge and grabbing one for himself. Placing the bottle caps onto the counter, he leads us outside. I glance around at the state of the house, seeing nothing but littered bottles, knocked-over cups, and tables upturned. I would hate to be the guy responsible for cleaning up this mess.

"Whose place is this?" I ask as we step out into the breeze.

He glances across at me with a guilty expression. "Mine," he says.

"Really?" I laugh, taking another look around. "It's going to suck being you in the morning."

He grins and grabs my hand, leading me around the side of the pool, and just as I go to take another step, he spins me to face him, pulling me in hard as those deep eyes seem to stare straight into my soul. I see his lips and suck in a breath, the need to kiss him is the only thing on my mind. His eyes become hooded, and just as I go to push up onto my tippy-toes, some drunken idiot bumps into me and sends me flying right into the deep pits of the freezing water.

Shock grips me as I hastily swim up to the surface, shivers rattling through my bones. I resurface to find the drunken idiot knocked out on the ground and a concerned Miller looking down on me with wild, crazed eyes. "Fuck, babe. You okay?"

I nod as my teeth begin to chatter and make my way over to the side. Miller bends down and effortlessly scoops me out of the water, gently placing me back on dry land. He pulls his shirt off, putting his impressive torso on display, and starts to mop up the freezing water from my body. "Come on," he says, wrapping a hand around me as a violent shiver takes over my body. "Let's get you dried up."

He leads me back inside and takes me upstairs to his bedroom where he begins rummaging through his wardrobe, and I cringe, realizing I'm dripping all over his carpet. He pulls out a pair of gym shorts and a shirt and hands them to me, but he doesn't seem fazed by the mess I'm making. He's far too occupied by the way my wet dress clings to my body. "These are going to be huge on you."

"Do you mind if I have a shower? I don't think I'll stop shivering until I do."

"Sure," he says, then points across the room. "Just through that door."

"Thanks," I take myself across the room and into the bathroom before closing the door behind me. My dress is all but glued to my body, and peeling it off is a bigger pain in the ass than getting bumped into the pool in the first place. I have no idea what possessed me to wear this particular dress. Oh, that's right. Sophie did.

Reaching into the shower, I turn on the water and am surprised when I don't have to wait too long for it to heat up. I hop in straight away, letting the warm water soothe my shivering body as I take a deep breath and smell Miller all around me.

He's getting too deep inside my head.

I rinse my hair for a few minutes and attempt to get all the chlorine out of it, then give up and grab his shampoo. After washing my hair, I get busy washing my body and start lathering up, and as I do, I'm hit with a million dirty thoughts. All to do with Miller's hands roaming over my body.

My eyes flutter closed as my hands move down my waist. My fingers skim over my clit, and I gasp, picturing the way Miller would touch me. I do it again, this time rubbing slow, torturous circles and getting a thrill at the way I smell him all around me.

His name is whispered on my lips as my fingers push up inside me, gently massaging my walls as I continue my sensual torture on my clit with my thumb. My eyes roll as my body is worked right to the edge, my breath shortening, coming in gasping pants.

"Oh God," I whisper with a low groan, needing to brace myself against the shower wall, picturing the way Miller would touch himself in this very shower. Hell, maybe he's even thought about me while he's been in here.

That thought pushes me over the edge, and I come hard on my

fingers, doing what I can not to cry out. I gasp for air as my high rocks through me, and I open my eyes, unable to believe what I just did here.

After realizing I've been in here suspiciously long, I climb out of the shower and wrap his towel around me. Glancing down at his clothes, I try to figure out how the hell I'm supposed to make this work. Picking up my underwear, I quickly realize they are way too cold and wet to put back on, and I have no choice but to go commando.

I slip on his gym pants, which I am thrilled to find have a drawstring, and I pull it as tight as it will go. Even though it's still a little big, I'll have to make do. Now for the shirt. I pull it over my head and find myself swimming in the soft fabric, so I bunch it up before knotting it at my waist. Finishing off my drowned-rat look, I roll up the sleeves a few times and hope I look somewhat cute. Though to be honest, I don't think he'll notice. Not with the way my nipples are protruding from the soft cotton like two little targets begging for attention, making it all too obvious that I'm not wearing a bra.

I look at myself in the mirror. Hmm, not bad. I do what I can to fix up my makeup, which has smudged under my eyes, and then search for a hairdryer. Which, of course, he does not have.

Brushing my fingers through my hair, I throw it up into a bun before collecting my wet things from the ground and stepping out of the bathroom. I find Miller still in his bedroom, sitting on the edge of his bed with his intense eyes on me. "You didn't have to wait," I say, my cheeks flushing as I realize he was just out here while I was going to town on myself.

"I wanted to." He gets up and makes his way over to me, his eyes greedily roaming up and down my body. "You look good wearing my clothes," he says with hooded eyes.

I make my way to the door before this goes somewhere I don't need it to go. "Thanks for the shower. I feel much better."

"Anytime," he says, following right behind me.

Glancing over my shoulder to give him a smile, I find his eyes locked securely on my ass and I can't help the wide smirk that settles across my lips. "You looking at my ass, hotshot?" I joke, throwing his earlier comments right back at him.

"Fuck, yeah," he grunts, then looks up to find my eyes. "Are you going commando?"

I can't help but laugh as his dark eyes dance with mirth. I ignore his question, knowing it must be driving him crazy, and hold up my wet clothes. "Do you have a bag I could throw these in till I get home?"

"Yeah," he laughs, stepping closer and placing his hand on my lower back as he leads me down the stairs. My skin burns from his touch, and I wish things could be different. That maybe I could be ready for someone like him. That maybe he wasn't such a playboy and that maybe he wouldn't break my heart if I gave him the chance.

Miller leads me back into the kitchen and pulls a bag out from under the sink. "Here you go," he says, opening up the bag so I can dump the clothes in. "Do you want another drink?" he asks with a hopeful smile.

"No, thanks," I say, taking the bag from him. "I think I'll find Sophie and get home. I'm not really dressed for a party anymore."

"Okay, but you're not going to find Sophie anytime soon," he tells me.

My brows furrow and I glance around at the guests flooding the living room. "What do you mean? Where is she?"

Miller smirks. "I saw her sneak upstairs with Tank not long ago. She's most likely impaled on his cock right about now."

"God, I can't trust that girl to keep her legs closed," I laugh as I make my way to the door.

Miller hurries behind me and catches my elbow. "Hey, where are you going?" he asks, stepping out the door with me.

I nod out toward the street. "I'm ordering an Uber."

He looks at me as though I've lost my mind. "You can stay here," he suggests.

"Nice try, but no," I laugh, pulling out my phone to search for the Uber app.

He pinches my phone from my fingers. "If you insist on leaving, then let me walk you home."

"I don't know," I say watching him, looking for any clue that this is just another trick to get in my pants.

Miller holds up both hands in a show of innocence. "I swear, I'll be the perfect gentleman."

I narrow my eyes in suspicion. "Promise?"

"Cross my heart and hope to die."

I watch him a moment longer before finally giving in, despite my better judgment. "Okay."

A beaming smile crosses his face, and he instantly leads me down the path. When he doesn't return my phone and begins playing around on it, my suspicion only grows. "What are you doing?" I ask as I attempt to grab it from his hands.

"Putting my number in your phone, so you can't pretend you lost it," he tells me. "And I'm sending myself a message so I've got your number too. You know, just in case you accidentally delete your whole contact list."

I laugh as he passes my phone back to me. "I swear, you've got to be both the most confident and relentless guy I know."

He looks down at me, his eyes softening with something I can't quite place. "Is that a good thing?"

I study him for a moment, watching how he waits intently for my response. "Yeah, I think it is," I tell him as the corners of his lips lift into a small, satisfied smile.

"Tell me about yourself," he says, placing his fingers on my elbow and slowly sliding his hand down, sending goosebumps all over my skin. He laces his fingers through mine and continues walking as if he hadn't just made a move on me.

Real smooth, Miller Cain. Real fucking smooth.

"There's really not much to know," I say, skipping right over the hand-holding thing because let's face it, not only does it feel so damn good, it also feels right.

"Bullshit," he argues. "I've known you less than a week and you're already the most interesting chick I've met."

"No, really. I'm an only child. I grew up in a super small town that I'm sure you've never heard of. I came here, fell in love with the wrong guy, and here I am now. The story of my life."

"Tell me more about the guy. What happened to him?" I cringe away from his question and go quiet, suddenly not sure what to say. "Sorry," he says. "I didn't mean to pry. It's none of my business."

"No, it's not that," I explain. "It's still just a bit fresh, you know? I don't really like talking about it."

"Ahh . . . just answer me this," he says. I give him a smile and a small nod, encouraging him to continue. "Is this guy the reason you're not giving me a chance?"

As I study him for a moment, a million different cheeky comments come to mind, but I settle for the truth. "Honestly, yes and no," I say. "I'm not ready for anything, not so soon after what he put me through, and no offense, but you have the worst reputation as a player, and I'm the kind of girl who falls hard and fast. I can't let myself do that because you'll one hundred percent break my heart, and I'm not sure it can take another beating."

He nods as he takes in everything I've just told him, and I know he's considering every last word. "There's something about you, Dani," he says. "I don't know what it is. But I need to figure it out."

Well, shit just got real.

"Can we put the spotlight back on you now?" I ask, feeling a little shy.

"Alright," he laughs. "What do you want to know?"

"Um . . . why hockey?"

"Geez, go straight for the kill," he mutters.

"Sorry," I mutter, hoping I'm not crossing a line.

He squeezes my hand and tugs me closer to him. "It's okay. I haven't told anyone this for a long time," he says, then takes a breath. "My dad died when I was seven, and I went through this phase of hating the world and everyone in it. I was angry and didn't know how to deal with it. Dad was a huge hockey fan, so Mom put me in lessons as a way of being closer to him and as a way to use up all my energy. I fell in love with it. I'd stay at the rink for hours practicing, come home, and do it all again the next day."

"Wow," I say, a little unsure of how to respond. "That's kind of amazing and tragic at the same time. I guess hockey was your dad's last gift to you."

He's thoughtful for a moment. "I've never thought of it that way," he murmurs. "I like it."

"Do you miss him?"

"Yeah. I mean, I was seven, so I only have a handful of memories and a few photos, but I wish he was around." I give him a sad smile, not knowing how he does it. How anybody does it. I couldn't imagine losing a parent. I haven't seen Mom and Dad since Christmas, and I'm already going crazy.

"I bet," I respond as we head down the small path leading to my front door. "This is me," I tell him, indicating my house.

As I go to find my keys, I let out a soft yelp as Miller's hands find my waist, and before I know it, he has me up against the locked door, his darkening gaze locked and loaded on mine. "What happened to being a gentleman?" I ask him, my lips kicking into a seductive smirk, the feel of his body pressed against mine doing wicked things to me.

"Even a gentleman hopes for a goodnight kiss," he says, slowly dropping his face to mine, giving me the chance to pull away.

Oh, God.

I know I shouldn't, but the invitation is quite literally staring me in the face. I reach up and hover my lips before his, the hesitation all too real. Letting myself take a leap, I press my lips to his.

Miller's lips move against mine, kissing me with intense passion, enough to drive a woman wild. He slips his tongue into my mouth and I moan against him.

God, this is good. Too good.

My hand slides up his hard chest and over his broad shoulders, tangling in his hair as my other slips around his waist before lowering down his strong back. His hands begin exploring my body and come to a stop on my ass, gripping me tighter. Miller lifts me and my legs automatically lock around his waist as he holds me against the wall, and I feel him there, his cock raging and ready to go as he grinds against me. My eyes roll with pleasure, more than ready to let him take me right here on the fucking doorstep.

I gasp for breath and his lips find the soft skin of my neck. "Fuck," I moan. I know deep down I need to stop this before it gets too far, but it feels too damn good. He slams his lips back against mine and we continue our sensual dance against each other, his slow grinding driving me wild as the sexual tension skyrockets between us.

No, no, no. I've got to stop.

I pull back from him and rest my forehead against his. "Stop. We can't," I tell him as I try to catch my breath.

"Stopping would be considered criminal," he informs me as he attempts to pull me in again.

"No," I say more firmly. "You're going to start something that you can't finish."

A wicked grin rips across his handsome face. "Oh baby, you've got me wrong. I can definitely finish this. And in fact, I'll probably finish it a few times," he winks.

I smirk at him and shake my head, hating just how much I crave his attention. "That's not what I meant and you know it."

"I know," he sighs, allowing me to untangle my legs. He gently places me back on the ground but keeps me right up against the wall.

"I'm a relationship kind of girl. I can't do one-night stands. It's not me," I tell him.

"What if I want more than just one night?" he questions.

I reach up and gently kiss the side of his mouth. "Then I'd say you better be damn sure before you come and promise me something like that."

He studies my face searching for something in my eyes, then nods. "Okay," he says, taking a step back and giving me room to think.

"Thanks for walking me home," I tell him. "And for the clothes," I add, tugging on my shirt.

"Am I ever going to get those back?" he asks smugly.

I laugh. What a fool. "Miller, you should know you never offer your clothes to a woman and expect to get them back."

He shakes his head in exasperation then steps forward, pushing me up against the wall again. "I bet you're going to sleep in it, imagining it's me curled around you instead," he says with hooded eyes.

I don't respond because that's exactly what I was planning on doing, and he knows it. He takes my silence as a big fat whopping *yes* and smirks at me with the sexiest smile I've ever seen. A smile that I'd love to see again, maybe looking up at me from between my legs.

Shit.

I put my hand on his chest and gently push him away. "Goodnight, Miller," I say softly.

"Goodnight, Dani," he answers in the same hushed tone. I reach up and give him one last kiss on the cheek before slipping through my door and practically running to my room. I let out a sigh, which could very probably be misinterpreted as more of a moan, before flopping on my bed.

Once reality has finally come back to me, I slip off his gym shorts and find some underwear. I send a quick text off to Sophie, letting her know I'm okay, and slide in under my covers.

His shirt wraps around me, just as he had expected, and I fall asleep imagining that it's his arms wrapped securely around me.

CHAPTER 6

MILLER

I pinch the bridge of my nose as my head begins to pound. "Shut the fuck up," I groan into my pillow. Music blasts downstairs, and I swear I can feel the bass blasting right through my skull.

A loud knocking sounds at my door followed by Tank calling out. "Get up, man. Cleaning crew is here," he says, referring to the few freshman kids on the team who offered to help clean up for a few brownie points.

I glance over at the clock. 10 a.m. Shit.

Tank and I had only gone to bed a few hours ago after staying up all night, drinking beer, and talking about our big plans and dreams for the future. How we're going to the NHL and going to live it up big. Yet somehow, Dani kept popping into my head, and I'd bet that Tank was thinking the same about Sophie. Maybe he was right yesterday when he said things were changing.

Her words last night pulled at something within me. The moment she said she was a relationship girl, I knew immediately that I wanted that with her. But what if she's right? What if I'm not ready for that? I've done the relationship thing once, and it came back to bite me in the ass, which is why I only use girls for sex, earning myself the reputation I deserve.

But Dani. There's something about that girl, and I wasn't lying when I said I needed to figure her out.

She told me to be damn sure before I go searching for something with her, and that's exactly what I'm going to do because the last thing I want is to hurt her. She deserves more than that. She has already been hurt by some jackass, and I swear, I will find out what he did to her, and I will hunt the motherfucker down.

I groan as I climb out of bed and head into the bathroom. I walk up to the vanity mirror and take myself in. I look like shit. I reach into the shower to turn on the hot water and begin stripping off my clothes. The realization that Dani was the last one in this shower, standing in this very spot while butt naked, has my dick twitching to life.

I'm pulling my underwear down when I catch sight of something black sitting on the floor by the vanity. I stride over and pick up the material, realizing Dani left her lacy thong in my bathroom. My dick hardens as I hold the flimsy material between my fingers, thinking about the last place this material touched.

I can't help but laugh. The fun I'm going to have with this. But first, I need to deal with the fucking monster between my legs.

Getting in the shower, I immediately get to work, desperate for a release. I curl my fingers around the base of my cock, working my way up and down as her face lingers in my mind. Stroke after stroke, thinking about sinking my cock deep into her sweet cunt. I know nothing will ever come close to how amazing the real thing would be, but damn, if this is the next best thing, I'll fucking take it.

I picture her eyes looking up at me as she wraps her lips around me, teasing my tip with her tongue as she takes me deep into her mouth. She smirks at me, and that's enough to throw me over the edge. I find my release and groan her name as I come hard.

Fuck. I've got to have her.

After finishing in the shower, I pull on a pair of jeans and jam her lacy thong into my pocket like some kind of fucked-up stalker. But hey, it gives me another excuse to see her again. Grabbing a shirt, I head out into the hallway, dreading the clean-up that awaits me.

I shrug my shirt on as I walk into the kitchen and come to a startling stop as I find the place immaculate.

What the actual fuck?

I look around to find my house clean of beer bottles, no unconscious bodies sprawled throughout the living room, and nothing sticky lining the floor. All the furniture is back in place and a few of my teammates are hanging out by the pool, as though there wasn't just a raging party in this very house.

What the hell? How long was I in the shower?

I glance up at the clock to find the time. 10:23 a.m. Hmm.

I head over to the back door and slide it open. "Hey," I call out to the guys. "What happened to the mess?"

Tank looks up at me with a knowing smirk, something sparkling in his eyes. "I'll give you one guess."

No. No fucking way. I narrow my eyes at him, but all he does is smirk again.

"Good morning," the sexiest voice chimes from behind me.

Spinning around, I grab Dani and press her up against the wall beside the door, briefly noticing that she's still wearing my shirt. "You're too fucking good for me," I tell her, leaning in and breathing in her scent, my morning activities doing nothing to stop the monster hardening in my pants.

Her eyes glisten with satisfaction, more than happy to be in my arms. "I figured I owed you after you looked out for me last night," she explains, sliding her hands up my shirt and resting them against my chest, the feel of her hands on my body making me so desperate for more.

"You know, there are other ways you could have paid me back," I say with a wicked grin, knowing exactly how she's going to react.

"Oh, I know, but I figured I'd save that for when you really deserve it," she explains without missing a beat. Fuck, this woman is driving me crazy in the best possible way.

"Go out with me?" I ask.

"No."

"Just one date," I tell her. She shakes her head. "You're going to break one day, and when you do, it's going to be amazing."

Her smile lights up the room, and I lean in to give her a light kiss on the lips, knowing there's no way I'd get away with anything more this morning.

Knowing she needs her space, I step back from her and head into the kitchen. Dani remains right on the wall as she watches my movements. "Oh, hey," I say, making sure I have her undivided attention. She raises an eyebrow in question, and I pull her thong out of my pocket before swirling it around my finger like a lasso. "I think you left something in my bathroom."

Her face drops as her eyes bug out of her head, and one teasing smirk from me has her diving toward the kitchen. I shoot out of her reach and up the stairs with her following closely on my heels.

"Give it back," she demands.

"No way. Finders keepers," I sing, bolting down the hallway with her thong high above my head.

"What are you? Twelve?"

I push through the door at the end of the hallway and dive into my spare bedroom before coming to a screeching halt. Dani slams into my back as she dives in after me, and I quickly catch her before she stumbles back.

She looks around, takes in the room, and gasps at the three naked bodies in the bed.

"What the fuck, man?" I ask Jaxon, who's lying butt naked in the middle of two brunettes with his dick out for the world to see.

The girls startle at their sudden audience and immediately sit up. "Woah," Dani says, wide-eyed. "See the rack on that one?" she whispers, indicating the girl on the right.

"Yep. I see it."

"You need to burn this bed," she says, still in shock.

"You got that right, baby."

The girls go about getting dressed as Jaxon remains fast asleep. I turn and leave, heading into my room with Dani right behind me. I grab the glass off my bedside table and walk into my bathroom to fill it with cold water. Walking back down to the spare bedroom, I go to pour it over Jaxon when Dani stops me. "Can I do it?" she asks with excitement in her eyes.

God, how do I say no to that?

I hold out the glass for her and step back to give her room. I place my hands on her waist and watch as she takes absolute pleasure in tipping the water over Jaxon's face.

He gasps and shoots up out of bed with his dick windmilling around. Dani looks away but can't help laughing. "What the hell?" Jaxon grunts in shock.

"Get some clothes on and get out of here," I tell him.

He looks down to realize he's naked in front of Dani and does his best to cover himself up, but it's too late. We've already seen every angle he has to offer. We leave Jaxon to it and head back down the hallway. "So . . . Can I have my underwear back now?" she asks sweetly in an attempt to catch me off guard.

I scoff at her question, not falling for that innocent act. "Nope. It's mine."

"Damn," she says with a sigh. "That was my favorite pair."

"They're my favorite now."

"Hey, Coach," I say, stepping into his office on Monday afternoon before training.

"Cain," he says. "Take a seat."

I sit down awkwardly, unsure why he's called me into his office. I mean, I haven't fucked up yet, so it can't be anything bad. Well, at least, I don't think I have.

"What's up?" I ask, getting straight to business.

"Just checking in. We're kicking off the season next week, and I need to know that you're ready. You've got a lot riding on this."

"Yeah, boss. I'm good," I tell him with confidence.

"That's what I want to hear," he says gruffly, leaning back in his chair. "I want you putting in more hours at the gym, specifically on your fitness. I don't want anything holding you back. I know you're already putting in extra hours on the ice, but I want you to push yourself harder, give me more. You've got a real shot at the NHL if you keep your head in the game," he explains.

"No problem," I say, mentally working out how on earth I'm going to squeeze in another few gym sessions on top of my current training schedule. But hell, if it means raising my shot at making the NHL, I'll make it happen.

"I've already heard your name whispered as one to look out for in the up-and-comers," he says, fixing me with a stare that tells me to keep my shit together.

"Fuck. Really?" I ask, wide-eyed.

He nods his head in confirmation. "I don't want any distractions. I've seen the way you've been staring at that PR girl. Don't let that mess with your head. You need to keep focused."

"I'm focused, Coach," I tell him. If anything, Dani is going to push me harder, just so I can get the chance to impress her.

"Good," he says, rising out of his chair to indicate the meeting is over. "Listen, add Tank to those extra gym sessions. His name was whispered right alongside yours. Apparently, you guys are some kind of *dream team*," he scoffs with an eye roll.

I get up from the chair and smirk at Coach Harris. "You bet your ass we are."

He laughs and shakes his head in exasperation. "Go suit up. Training starts in twenty minutes."

"On it, Coach," I say with a salute. I make my way out, closing his door behind me before heading down to the locker room.

I find Tank changing into his training gear and make my way over to my locker beside his. "Where ya been?" he asks, taking a seat to tie his skates.

"Had a meeting with Coach. He wants us to step it up a bit. Add a few more gym sessions to help secure a contract."

"Shit," he groans. "This season's going to kill us."

"Yeah, but it will be worth it when you sign on that dotted line," I remind him.

"Fuck, yeah it will," he grunts.

I pull my jersey over my head and take a seat beside him. "You know, they're calling us the Dream Team?" I tell him as I grab my skates from my bag, checking the blade covers are securely attached before I put them on.

He smirks. "Really? You think with a reputation like that, we'll end up being drafted by the same team?"

"Who fucking knows," I say, as an excited grin spreads wide across my face. "But it would be pretty fucking awesome."

CHAPTER 7

DANIELLE

I sit with Sophie, sprawled out on our living room floor, as we work out the final details of our first Dragons' article. I lay out three photos, two from their training sessions and the last being my personal favorite; the locker room shot.

"Which one do you think?" I ask, studying the pictures before me.

"Well, the article is going to be a little controversial, so I think we should go with the locker room one," she tells me as she grabs a few fries, dips them in gravy, and devours them.

"How controversial are we talking?" I ask suspiciously.

She lets out a small laugh. "The title is 'Pucker Up! The Dragons are Back!' "

"You're not serious?"

"I'm dead serious. Their reputation sucks. We want to draw people in and get them to love the team again from the start, so why not have a little fun while we're at it?"

"Okay, but do it nicely. We still want to make out like they are kings on campus."

"Oh, so mentioning Jaxon's threesome with the Titty Twins wouldn't be the way to go?"

"You're such an idiot," I laugh. "Put something in there about the upcoming calendar."

"Already on it, babe."

Twenty minutes later, after putting the finishing touches on our article and emailing it off to Professor Whitaker, I hop up and make my way into the kitchen. I rifle through the fridge until my eyes land on the pretty bottle that promises me a relaxing night. I pour us both a very full, well-deserved glass of wine and make my way back into the living room.

"Oh, for me?" Sophie asks as her big blue eyes widen in excitement.

"Mmhmm," I smile, passing the glass.

"Alright, spill . . . you only give me wine when you're fishing for information," she laughs as she packs away her laptop.

"You know me so well," I laugh. "But you've got to tell me what the hell is going on between you and Tank. You've broken your one rule. No. Repeat. Performances."

"I know," she groans, draining her glass and hopping up off the ground. She heads into the kitchen and brings the whole bottle back with her, sits down, and refills her glass. She lets out a breath and focuses her attention on me. "I have no fucking idea what's going on."

I give her a wide grin. "I think you like him."

"No, it's just sex," she argues. "Really good sex. Sex so great, I couldn't help but go back for seconds," she says, lifting her glass to her lips.

"Right. So, if he were to jump in bed with someone else, it wouldn't bother you?"

"Nope, not at all," she says, avoiding eye contact. "Are you interested? Do you want to get your hands on that monster?"

"What?" I screech, spitting wine all over our cream carpets. "No, I have my hands full trying to keep Miller at bay."

"Chill out, I'm joking," she laughs as I do my best to mop up my spilled wine with the edge of my shirt. "But to answer your question, I really don't know. Maybe I like him or maybe I just like getting with him, I'm not sure." She takes another long drink and then smirks back at me. "When you said you have your hands full with Miller . . . Did you mean literally, or figuratively? I mean, your hands would be extremely full with that one."

I can't help but laugh as she raises her eyebrows in curiosity. "I saw it when he dropped his towel in the locker room and felt it pressed up against my ass at his party. And let me tell you, anybody who has their hands around that would definitely have full hands. But no, I meant figuratively, and you know it."

"Seriously? What's stopping you? He's clearly into you, and it's pretty damn obvious you like him too. Match made in heaven," she says, already going in for another refill. "Just do it already so you can come back and tell me how good it was."

"God, Sophie, put down the wine," I laugh. Only instead of putting it down, she tops off my glass. Clearly a long night is in store. "And no, you know why I can't get involved with him. He's not the relationship kind of guy, and I'm not ready to get trampled by another loser looking for a good screw."

"Come on, already. You know what they say, right?" she smirks and waits for me to give her my undivided attention. "The only way to get over a guy is to get under another."

"You know my problem isn't getting over Brett, right?"

"I know, I just really wanted to use that line," she says, all too proud of herself. "Besides, maybe Miller is the exception."

"You're such a dork," I say, doing my best to ignore her comments. But what if he *is* the exception?

Sophie falls to her hands and knees and crawls along the carpet like some kind of wildcat until she's bowling me over. "You love me," she says, then jumps to her feet, pulling me along. "Now, you've got me drunk so let's go party."

I laugh and shake my head, but the bitch has a good point. We're already drunk so we might as well have a good night.

"Jared?" I holler down the hallway.

"What do you bitches want now?"

Sophie grins wide. "You up for a night of getting fucked up?"

He's out in the living room in seconds. "Fuck, yeah."

"**A**lright guys, where's Mr. January?" I ask as I make my way into the guys' locker room to find them all topless, rubbed down in baby oil, and giving me very unimpressed glares. "Hey, don't look at me that way," I scold. "You guys are the idiots who agreed to do this shit in the first place," I laugh, taking way too much satisfaction out of this.

My gaze lands on Miller, and I take in his impressive body. His jeans ride dangerously low on his hips, making it quite obvious that he's going commando. Which reminds me, the asshole still holds my thong captive.

His broad shoulders and hard chest put on the perfect show, and my eyes lower down his body, leading me to his sculpted abs, narrow waist, and mouth-watering V. Then there are the arms, and God they look good, but they feel even better wrapped around my body.

Miller's eyes dance as he watches me take him in, knowing the effect he has on me. I push my thoughts aside and do my best to get back on track.

Bobby grumbles something inappropriate as he gets up from the bench, reminding me that he's Mr. January. I run over to his bag, grab his skates and hockey stick, then rush out of the room. Bobby dawdles behind me, and I don't miss the scowl Miller shoots in his direction.

Sophie smirks when she sees us enter our little makeshift studio and begins fiddling with the lighting.

"Alright, Bobby," I tell him. "Lose the pants."

He groans but does as he's told, making sure to keep a hand covering his junk at all times. I grab his skates and tie the laces together at the ends before slinging them over his shoulder, positioning it just right, so his skate covers his junk.

"Ah, perfect," I smile, grabbing his stick and laying it across his shoulders. He reaches up and casually loops his arms over either end of the stick and begins working his body.

"You're a pro at this," Sophie says as I get to work, clicking away on the camera. "If the whole hockey thing doesn't work out, you should go into modeling." He groans at her ongoing commentary, but there's no denying how much he loves the attention.

I move on to the next guy, then the next. All of them are equally embarrassed but secretly thrilled to be here. "Jaxon, you're up," I shout through the open door.

Two seconds later, he strolls out looking as confident as ever. "Where do you want me, babe?" he asks, flexing his pecs.

Ugh.

"Follow me," I grumble, leading him into the weight room in the ice rink. I turn away from him to adjust the setting on my camera. "Okay," I say, turning back to find him smirking at me with hooded eyes, butt naked, with a massive erection pointing right at me. "Woah, what the hell, Jax?" I screech, spinning away and holding a hand to my eyes to try and block out the image.

"Sorry, babe. I'm covered in baby oil and naked in a room with a hot chick. What did you expect?" he asks, taking a step toward me.

"Hold it right there, buddy," I demand, holding both my hands up to stop his advance. "Go and get yourself sorted out."

I hurry out of the room, not looking back to see where Jaxon goes, and head back down to the locker room, not shying away from walking straight in this time.

"Hey," Aaron calls out, spotting me launch myself through the door as he comes out of the showers. "How do I get this slimy shit off me? It won't go away."

I laugh and shrug my shoulders. "I don't know. That's a question for Sophie. Go find her," I tell him as I make my way over to Miller.

"That was fast," he comments, noticing how quickly I finished up with Jaxon.

"Yeah," I laugh. "He had a little trouble controlling himself."

Miller's face darkens, and I see the anger in his eyes. "Did he try anything on you?"

"Nah. Well, he might have, but I got out of there before he had the chance."

"Good," he mutters, though I see a darkness swelling in his eyes, and I have no doubt Miller and Jaxon will have a private word together. I just hope Jaxon comes out of it still breathing.

God, I love how he's becoming territorial over me and just that little bit possessive. Is Sophie right? Could he be the exception? It would be so good if he was. I could see myself falling so deeply in love with this guy. It's crazy.

"Hey, Tank," I call out, as I see him leaving the locker room. He turns and grunts at me. "Can you get your skates on? I've got something different for you two."

They give each other a curious glance but shrug it off and get busy lacing up their skates. "I'm not getting naked with Miller, if that's what you want," Tank warns me.

"Don't stress," I laugh. "You guys even get to keep your pants on for this."

"Damn," Miller murmurs under his breath as he finishes tying his skates.

They both stand and face me, waiting for directions. "Grab your sticks and pucks," I tell them, then instantly roll my eyes as they both grab their dicks, cackling at their own wit. God, they're idiots. "Your other sticks and pucks," I confirm, turning away and heading back up the hallway to the entrance of the ice.

I open the barrier gate and look out onto the ice, trying to work out how I'm going to get into the center without making an ass of myself. Miller comes up behind me and places his hands on my waist. "You didn't think this through, did you?" he smirks.

"Nope."

He scoops me up in his warm arms as he steps onto the ice, effortlessly gliding around. Tank hops on after us but doubles back when he sees Sophie approaching the gate. "Where do you want us?" Miller asks.

"Just drop me in the center, then you guys are going to show off a little." His eyes light up in excitement as Sophie squeals from the side. I glance back to find her hanging over Tank's shoulder as he effortlessly glides toward us.

Miller puts me down and not long after, I have Sophie standing beside me, gripping Tank's arm for balance. "Okay, drop the puck directly in front, then you guys come for it from either side with your sticks out, maybe spray up a bit of ice too," I instruct, then take a deeper look around the arena.

Miller and Tank begin to take off when an idea strikes. "Wait, wait, wait," I say. They stop immediately and turn with curious gazes. "Can we turn the arena lights off and put the spotlights on?"

"No problem," Miller says, dashing to the side, jumping the barrier, and heading into some kind of control room. The lights go out, leaving us in darkness for the shortest moment before the spotlights come on, creating big circles of light on the ice. Within seconds, Miller is back on the ice, flying toward us.

I shuffle over to adjust my position against the spotlight and get Tank to drop the puck right in the center of the ice. "Can you use your stick and pretend like you're going to hit the puck?" I ask Tank, who doesn't hesitate to get into position.

I take a few shots and pull the camera back to have a look at the screen. "Oh, yeah," I say, leaning toward Sophie. "Check this out."

She takes the camera and studies the screen as a smile takes over her face. "Fuck me, this is giving me a lady boner."

Tank and Miller skate over and take the camera from Sophie's hands, looking over the pictures. "Not bad," Tank says, and I know coming from him that's the greatest compliment I'll ever receive.

"Thanks, just do that again. I want to try it from a lower angle, getting more of the ice," I explain. They skate off as I get down on the ice and lay flat on my stomach. "Shit," I hiss through a clenched jaw as the cold seeps through my clothes. I look through the camera and let out a frosty groan. These shots are going to be awesome, I just wish I could get them without my titties freezing to the ice. But hell, no pain, no gain.

I take a few more shots of the guys then get them to mix it up. "Now, come at each other from the sides and fight for the puck," I order. They do as we ask, and we spend the next few minutes trying different things.

"I think Miller needs more oil," Sophie suggests, pulling it from her back pocket.

"Nah, he looks fine," I tell her suspiciously. When in fact, he looks more than fine.

"Nope," she smirks. "I really think you ought to help rub more oil into his skin," she says, sliding the bottle along the ice until it slams right into my chest. I roll my eyes as she calls him over. "Oh, Miller," she sings. "Dani needs to rub more oil into your skin," she teases, which we all know is bullshit because the other guys had to put it on themselves. But of course, he happily plays along.

"Sure," he says, skating over and coming to a stop right before me. He leans down, wraps his hands under my arms, and pulls me to my feet, keeping hold of me while I find my balance.

I squirt the oil into my palm and rub it between my fingers, heating it up, before placing it on his skin. I lift my hand to his strong chest and begin rubbing. He groans as the sexual tension between us intensifies. I move my hands lower, rubbing the oil into his abs and enjoying every damn second of it.

"Are you sure you don't need me to lose my pants?"

"Well, actually, I was thinking I could do the shot with you in the weight room that I was going to do with Jax," I explain, a little breathy.

"Sure, baby," he whispers, sending thrills through me at the way he calls me *baby*.

I move the oil down over his arms, then turn him so I can work on his back. "Okay," I say, giving him a push to give me space. "You're done," he goes out to the spotlight once again and turns to face me.

"How good is your aim with that puck?" I ask.

He raises a brow but doesn't respond. Instead, he simply turns toward the open barrier gate, shoots the puck, and slams it right into the side of the metal trash can. "Okay, so you're pretty good."

He stands silently with a smug, proud expression.

"So, you need to shoot the puck so it comes flying past my face, by a few inches maybe . . . but I swear to God, if you miss . . ."

"I won't miss," he promises, focusing on me. "Just tell me when you're ready."

I slide back down to my stomach, feeling my hard nipples rub against the damp material of my bra and shirt, and hope that it isn't too obvious that Miller can see. I get into position and adjust my camera. "Okay, I'm good."

Miller rears back and shoots, and just as expected, the puck sails past my face with a whoosh of air. I do my best not to flinch and take as many shots as possible before pulling the camera away, immediately bringing up the pictures.

Yep. They're awesome.

"Cool, I got it," I smile, coming up onto my knees. Thank fuck I don't have to do that again.

Miller and Tank come over to help us off the ice. "Who else have you got left to do?" Miller asks as he places me back down on the ground.

"Just you," I say.

He gives me a knowing smile then turns to Tank. "Dani's finished with the guys. Could you send them home?" he asks. Tank grunts and leads Sophie down toward the locker room, while Miller takes my hand and leads me to the weight room.

He closes the door behind him as we walk deeper into the room. He heads over to the weights then turns back to me. "What do you want?" he asks, sitting down and taking his skates off, and I realize I don't know if he's talking about the picture or our situation.

"I don't know," I tell him honestly. "Why don't you try a few things and we'll figure out what works," I say, the double meaning clear in my tone.

"Pants or no pants?" he asks, getting up and standing before me with his eyes sparkling in excitement.

"Up to you."

Miller's hand slowly reaches for the button on his jeans, and with practiced moves, he flicks it open. His eyes rest heavily on mine as I raise my camera and begin shooting. He lowers the zipper and his jeans gently fall to the ground. Revealing his perfect, naked body.

Fuck. I've never been so turned on in my life.

He turns away and leans over to pick up one of the larger dumbbells, giving me the perfect view of his toned ass. My camera gets a workout as I take shot after shot of his movements. "My ass better not end up in that calendar," he warns. "Those pictures are just for you."

He takes a seat on the bench, leaning forward just enough to cover himself, and begins to curl the weight.

Fuuuuuck.

My mouth waters, and I need to mentally slap myself to remember to lift the camera and take the shots. His impressive biceps bulge as he continues his set before switching hands. Because obviously, not working the other side would be criminal.

Miller places the weight down on the ground beside him. "Come show me that," he says, indicating the camera. I step up to him and hold out the camera.

Miller goes to grab it, but instead, he grips my arm and tugs me into him. As I fall into his arms, he takes my camera and places it on the ground beside us before adjusting me so that I straddle his lap.

I feel him grow beneath me, and I know I don't have the strength to resist him any longer.

Miller Cain: 1

Me: 0

CHAPTER 8

MILLER

"What are you doing?" Dani gasps as I bring my lips down on the sensitive skin of her neck, making my way up to her earlobe and giving it a nip, her soft needy moans spurring me on.

"What I've been needing to do since the moment I saw you."

Her hands come down on my chest, molding perfectly to my body as she grinds against me. My hands roam over her back and lower to her tight waist. I slip my hands under her shirt and slowly lift it, letting her know my intentions and giving her the chance to stop me if she really doesn't want this.

I raise her shirt up over her head and throw the thin fabric to the floor, revealing her perfect body. My eyes greedily roam over her creamy skin, over her perfect tits that sit full and perky in a red lace bra. The outlines of her nipples through the flimsy material are positively begging me to suck them into my mouth. I gaze down her waist, past her belly piercing, and over her curvy, delicious hips.

This woman is a masterpiece.

Dani watches me as I take her in before slamming her lips down on mine, giving me what I've been craving. I reach behind her and unhook her bra with the quickest flick of my wrist and let it hang open, giving her the choice if she removes it or not. She surprises me not two seconds later when she shrugs the straps off her shoulders and allows it to slide down her arms, putting those gorgeous tits on display.

I can't help myself and dive straight in. I suck one nipple into my mouth as I take the other in my hand, roaming my thumb over her hardened peak before giving it a gentle squeeze. She moans my name and arches her back, giving me more of her.

Where the hell has she been all my life?

Dani reaches down between us and takes my cock in her small hand, wrapping her fingers around my base and slowly beginning to pump her fist.

"Fuck," I groan. I've got to taste her.

Twisting my arms around her waist, I stand up from the bench, lifting her with me as she continues pumping her fist up and down my length, driving me to the edge of no return. I turn on the spot and lower her to the bench, laying her back down. I keep her nipple firmly in my mouth, my tongue flicking over the tight bud. I reach down and unclasp the button of her jeans while searching her face for approval.

"Don't stop," she moans, giving me all I need to keep going. I tug her wet jeans down her body to reveal yet another black lacy thong, and my dick twitches in her hand as she watches me. I hook my fingers in the sides of her thong, stepping just out of her reach as I remove it from her body, leaving her completely bare for me.

My cock twitches with need as I lick my lips and stare down at her naked body. I take my dick in my hand and give it a tight squeeze, willing it to hold on just a little longer.

Dani looks up at me through those thick lashes, anticipating my next move, and I lean over her as I run my fingers down her waist and across the sensitive skin of her pelvis. I run my fingers down between her folds, finding her already soaking wet and needing so much more.

Rubbing my thumb over her clit, I watch the need in her eyes as I push two fingers deep inside her. I love the way she sucks in a breath, hunger and desire pouring out of her.

"Miller," she gasps as I work her body. "More."

Not being one to disappoint, I begin to fuck her with my fingers before dropping to my knees and pushing her knees apart, admiring the way she looks with my fingers deep inside her.

The scent of her arousal hits me, and I can't wait any longer. I put my mouth on her, flicking my tongue over her clit and watching the way she squirms beneath my touch. I do it again and her back arches off the bench as she screams my name.

She's fucking intoxicating. I need it all.

I keep going, sucking, nipping, flicking, licking, giving her everything I've got. I press down on her clit, making little circles with my tongue, and send her completely over the edge as she comes hard, her tight cunt convulsing around my fingers.

I taste every last bit of her arousal until she collapses onto the bench, and I smile up at her from between her legs.

Fuck, I'm not usually one who gives without the expectation of receiving. But I would do whatever it takes to be able to live between her perfect thighs for the rest of time.

I climb up her body, resting my elbows on either side of her face. She twines her hands around the back of my neck and pulls me down to her. Dani kisses me hard and pushes her tongue into my mouth, moaning as she tastes herself on my lips.

Her hands snake down my body and grip my cock once again, and I feel her smile against my lips before she pulls back slightly. "I wasn't finished with you," she whispers and rolls us onto the floor. My arms snake around her body protectively, but it's my back that gets the brunt of it, and we land on the floor with her hand still wrapped firmly around my dick.

I think I've found an angel.

She sits up above me and scoots herself down as she continues to work my dick in her tight fist. Dani leans over me and glances up, looking at me through her thick lashes, flashing me those green eyes that are blazing with excitement.

Her tongue shoots out, lapping up the bead of moisture at the tip of my cock as her hand moves lower to cup my balls.

I groan. "Yeah, that's right baby, just like that."

Dani licks me again before opening up and slowly taking me in her mouth. She holds the base of my dick firmly in her fist while her head bobs slowly up and down, taking pleasure in every single second of my sweet torture.

She begins to move faster as my dick throbs in her mouth. She slides up and down, sucking harder and harder all while squeezing my balls. I knot my hand into her hair as she adjusts herself to take me deeper, making me groan with need.

Dani keeps up her torturous rhythm until I can't take any more. "Baby, I'm going to come in your mouth if you don't stop," I warn her, giving her the chance to pull away. She responds by humming and taking me deeper, and I fucking come harder than ever before.

She swallows me down, sucking me dry while moaning for me at the same time, and when she's done, she comes down on my body and raises her head to look at me with a proud smirk. "That was amazing," I tell her as I run my hand down her back and grab a handful of ass.

"Yeah . . . I guess it wasn't bad," she teases.

I raise my hand and bring it down on her firm ass, giving it a good spank and almost coming again when a needy groan slips from her lips.

Dani begins grinding down on me again, moaning softly. "Already?" I ask with an intrigued grin.

She leans down and kisses me gently. "No," she says regrettably, letting out a heavy sigh. "I've got a lot of work to do with the calendar. I better go."

"Fuck the calendar."

"No can do, Captain," she says with a wicked glint in her eye, getting me hard all over again.

"Go out with me?" I ask.

"We've been over this."

I smirk and rub my hand over her perfect ass, this time giving it a damn good squeeze. I roll her under me and hover over her. "I know, but one day you're going to say yes."

She smiles up at me. "Let's just hope you're still interested when that time comes."

"Don't doubt it for one second," I tell her, running my hand down her body. She shivers, and I watch in amazement as her nipples harden under my touch, and I can't help but bring my lips down on them, giving them the relief they so desperately desire.

I get home and push through the door to find Tank sprawled out on my couch, eating my food, drinking my beer, and watching my damn TV. "What the fuck, dude?" I grunt, dropping my shit onto the door.

He glances over his shoulder, gives me a nod, and turns back to the TV while he shovels a handful of potato chips into his mouth. "Where ya been?" he smirks as I flop down onto the opposite couch.

"Gym."

He scoffs as he downs another handful of chips, knowing exactly where I've been. He left me at the rink, half-naked with Dani. "Funny. I was just at the gym. Didn't see you there," he tells me, flicking through the sports channels, switching between two different games.

"You know you shouldn't be eating that shit," I tell him, indicating the packet of potato chips sitting beside him.

Tank ignores my comments and goes straight for the dig. "You like this chick more than you're letting on." He says it like it is a hard, well-known fact while turning in his seat to face me front on.

Great. The big bastard wants to talk.

I sit in silence for a second, going over my time with Dani, and I realize that this is definitely more than just trying to get in her pants. I want to get to know her, be with her, and wake up with her warm body curled around mine. Hell, I even want to be the guy she comes running to when her day has gone to shit and be the sorry dickhead who gets sent to the store when she runs out of tampons.

Fuck me.

"Yeah, man," I admit, looking him in the eye. "I do."

He nods his head and gives me a smile that clearly says *I told you so.* "What are you waiting for then? Ask her out."

"I fucking have," I groan, throwing my hands up in frustration. "Twice already. She keeps shooting me down."

Tank lets out a booming laugh. "Shit, I never thought I'd see the day the great Miller Cain gets rejected."

"Shut up," I tell him, reaching for the potato chips. "It's not like that."

"What's it like then?"

"I don't know, man. It's obvious she's into me, but she was burned by her ex and isn't ready to start anything," I explain. "And she's pretty damn certain that I'm going to break her heart."

"Are you?" he questions. "You've only known this chick for two weeks. Are you sure it's not just something physical?"

"Trust me, if I do, it wouldn't be intentional," I tell him. "She draws me in. I thought it was just about sex, but it's more than that. Hell, I crave her attention. She's the first girl in a long time who's left me needing more."

"I know the feeling, man," he tells me with a smirk, referring to Sophie. "Give her the time she needs. If she's as serious about this as you are, she'll come around when she's ready."

"Since when did you start getting all soft?" I joke.

He scoffs but answers anyway. "Since I've realized that I'm leaving this place at the end of the season, and I'll do whatever it takes to have that girl come with me."

"Fuck," I say, shocked at his admission. "You're in deeper than I thought."

"Yeah, I know, man," he says. "At least Dani is the relationship kind of girl. Sophie is hard as ice when it comes to getting her to admit anything."

"Don't stress man," I say, getting up and clapping him on the back. "You've got all season to convince her."

"Nah, I've got to lock her down before she gets bored and moves on," he laughs. "Now, what do you say we actually head to the gym and then to Micky's for a beer?"

"Sounds like the best fucking plan you've had all day."

CHAPTER 9

DANIELLE

"Check this one out," I laugh as I flick through the photos from the shoot. Sophie and Jared squish in to get the perfect view of the man-meat on the screen.

Jared leans over my shoulder to get closer, stealing the mouse, and zooming in on Shorty's crotch. "Is that his dick, or his thumb?"

Sophie snorts her wine all over the screen but leans in for a closer look, her brows furrowed with intense concentration. "I'd say it's his dick," she laughs. "No wonder they call him Shorty."

"Alright, you idiots, back up," I demand, wiping the spattered wine off the screen. "I'm not going to be able to look at the kid again after seeing that," I say, hitting delete on the image.

I had promised Coach Harris that all photos will be respectable, and any slip-ups would be permanently deleted so his skaters won't land in hot water. However, I didn't promise that I wouldn't have a viewing party in my room while I worked on it.

We spend a good portion of our afternoon flicking through the images, fixing up the lighting and contrast in Photoshop as we go. We make sure to delete anything that shows a little too much skin, no matter how attractive that skin may be, ensuring the calendar remains PG.

I continue working on the images with Sophie and Jared oohing and ahhing beside me. I've already got a good selection of images that would work perfectly when I get to the shots of Tank and Miller shirtless on the ice. I must say, these are easily going to be my favorites. The boys look amazing under the spotlight. Amazingly drool-worthy.

After touching up a few of the photos and emailing a shot of Tank to Sophie, who insisted the image is required for her spank bank, I add my favorites to the growing pile of images in the maybe pile. My heart breaks knowing I'm going to have to narrow it down.

I click next and come to the image of Miller in the weight room, popping the button on his jeans, and my stomach clenches, the memory of what happened in there fresh in my mind. "Wowza," Sophie says, getting close and personal with the screen. "Holy hell. This photo is definitely making it in the calendar."

"Look at his eyes," Jared says, more than impressed. "He wasn't posing for the camera here. This was all for you, Dani girl."

My cheeks flush, and I refuse to comment, making a show of getting back to editing the images. But unfortunately for me, Sophie knows me all too well. "Yeah, something definitely went down in that room," she says with a wide grin, pride in her eyes as she gives Jared a high five behind me.

I flick to the next image, only to see Miller's perfect ass looking back at me. "Fuck me," Sophie blanches, eyes wide. "Email me that."

"Where are you all?" Ashton calls from the kitchen.

"Dani's room," Jared yells.

Not a moment later, Ashton makes his appearance in my doorway and his gaze immediately falls to the screen. "Sweet, baby Jesus. Is that Miller Cain's ass?" he asks, his jaw dropping.

"Indeed it is," I say, physically unable to remove my eyes from the screen. I go about saving his ass images to another folder before Sophie takes over and saves her favorite as the desktop background.

"Yeah, that's exactly where that belongs," she comments. Who am I to disagree?

We go about editing the rest of Miller's images, making sure to save a few more in my Miller folder along the way. By dinner time, we've narrowed the selection down to the final twelve images and formatted the rest of the calendar.

We sit back on the couch and bid farewell to Jared and Ashton, who head out for their weekly Wednesday date night, while we order in. Sophie and I get cozy in our pajamas, which consist of tight tank tops and black panties, and turn on a movie.

We're busy ogling Christian Grey's ass when there's a knock at the door. I get up to grab our dinner, giving the guy a show. After quickly paying, I head back into the living room, detouring by the kitchen for cutlery and wine.

Putting our dinner on the coffee table, I hand Sophie a fork as she slides off the couch, down to the carpet beside me, and we begin inhaling our dinner straight from the takeout containers.

"Spill the beans," she demands when we finish with dinner.

"What beans are you talking about?" I ask, getting up off the floor, flopping back onto the couch, and swinging my feet up over the armrest.

Sophie gives me a blank stare. "Don't play dumb with me, babe," she says. "Something happened in that weight room, and you need to give me details."

I watch her for a moment. Realizing she's not about to back down, I let out a heavy sigh. "Okay, fine."

Sophie squeals in excitement and makes a show of getting ready for story time. As I begin giving her the steamy details of my morning, a knock sounds at the door.

Our conversation quickly falls away and we look at each other in confusion. "Are you expecting anyone?" she asks me, her brows furrowed.

Trying to peer around the living room window, I search the front of the cottage but don't see a damn thing. "No. You?" I question.

Sophie shakes her head and I get up, hating the idea of not knowing who stands at our door. I'm not one for surprises and this whole adult concept of having a home where people are able to come and knock on the door has never really sat well with me. If you want to drop in, that's fine, but text me first so I'm not caught in my fucking underwear. "Come on," I say, holding my hand out to Sophie. "If it's a murderer, then we're going down together."

She lets out a sigh and reaches for my hand. "Fair point," she nods, letting me yank her up off the ground before walking with me to the door. My fingers curl around the handle as I slowly inch the door open, finding not one, but two morons staring back at us. They both seem more than pleased to have found us both in nothing but our tight tanks and panties.

"Well, well," Sophie says, focusing her gaze on Miller, a wide grin stretching across her delicate face. "I heard you eat pussy like a pro."

Fuck.

My cheeks flame as Tank bursts into laughter beside him. I knew spilling the beans to Sophie would come back and bite me on the ass. I just didn't realize it would happen so quickly.

Miller's dark gaze meets mine, and a cheesy as fuck grin stretches across his face. "Like a pro, hey?" he questions, knowing damn well how mortified I am.

Trying to brush it off, I shrug a shoulder. "Oh, you know, you were okay."

"Really?" he smirks, his eyes glistening with silent laughter and pride. "It didn't sound just *okay* when you were screaming for more. Maybe I need to jog your memory."

Oh, dear God. Yes, please.

Before I get a chance to respond, Sophie's purring tone cuts through the room. "Eyes are up here, Big Guy," she says, her attention focused solely on Tank, who's studying her body like he might die without it. His gaze slowly travels back up, and by the time he reaches her eyes, the sexual tension between them is nearly knocking me over.

Needing to look away, I glance back at Miller, hating how shy I feel around him despite knowing exactly where his mouth has been. "Dare I ask why you two are hovering in our doorway?"

"We were heading to Micky's for dinner and a few drinks and thought you might like to come," he explains.

Sophie grins, unable to break her stare with Tank. "I always like to come."

I ignore her and get back to Miller, leaning against the drywall and crossing my arms over my chest, loving this playfulness between us. "You wouldn't be trying to trick me into a date, would you?" I muse.

Miller laughs at my suggestion, but the spark in his eyes gives him away. "Not at all," he lies.

"We just ate," Sophie informs them. "But we were going to have a movie night if you guys wanted to join?"

"I'm in," Tank says, marching forward, not even bothering to ask what movie we're watching. He grabs Sophie and lifts her in the same instance. She giggles as her legs wrap around his waist, then without a glance in our direction, he begins walking her down the hallway.

A moment later, we hear a door slam followed by a loud moan.

Miller laughs at their display but looks back at me, a little unsure. "Sorry, if I'd known they were that bad, I would never have brought him here."

"It's okay," I say, realizing Sophie is most likely going to be occupied for the rest of the night. "So, are you serious about hanging out?"

"You better fucking believe I am."

Stepping back out of the doorway, I wave him in and he doesn't hesitate, rubbing past my body on the way. He moves into the living room and takes a seat in my favorite spot. "Do you want something to eat?" I say, moving past the living room and into the kitchen.

He gets up and follows me into the kitchen. "I could eat," he says as I go about pulling food out of the fridge and grabbing him a drink. Miller looks around our small kitchen and comes to a stop in front of my laptop that sits on the counter.

"Is that my ass?"

Ahh, shit. Might as well own it.

"Yep," I confirm, pulling my laptop across the counter. "Sophie decided it was an ass worthy of my background."

"Good to know," he says, not embarrassed in the slightest.

A dull moan comes from down the hallway, and I cringe as I pull up the pictures of him and Tank, flipping it around to show him. "Check these out."

He looks over the images and raises an impressed eyebrow. "Holy shit, you really know what you're doing behind that camera," he says. "Can you send me these?"

"Sure," I say, pulling my laptop back around and bringing up my email. "Which ones do you want?"

He gets up and joins me on my side of the bench while he skims over the images again. Miller points out the ones he likes, before putting in his email address and hitting send.

"I finished the calendar," I tell him, a little too proud of myself. "I just need Coach Harris and the Dean to sign off before we can get it printed. Then we can start selling them during your games."

"Really? Already?" he questions. I pull up the calendar and hand over the laptop for him to scroll through. "Fuck, it's off-putting seeing Bobby like this."

"I know, but trust me, the girls will love it, and there are probably some guys who will, too," I say, as Sophie screams out for Tank to take her harder.

Miller continues scrolling, as though hearing a girl screaming to be railed is nothing he isn't used to hearing on the regular, and stops when he gets to the image of himself in the weights room. A wicked grin stretches across his lips and as he raises his gaze to meet mine, my cheeks begin to flush. "Why August?"

I can't help but grin right back at him, a little embarrassed to be caught out like this. "My birthday is in August."

Miller steps right into me, his dark gaze holding me captive. My heart starts to race as he takes my waist and pulls me in hard against his body. "I wouldn't have it any other way," he murmurs, before lowering his face to mine. His lips hover so close that I feel his soft breath against my skin. Just as I go to push up on my tippy-toes, he's gone again, stepping back around to the opposite side of the counter, a wicked smirk on his face.

That fucker.

"That's not fair," I tell him.

He looks back at me, innocence in his eyes. "What's not fair?" he questions, reaching for the laptop and dragging it across the table again as though he didn't just get me all worked up.

"Don't you go acting all coy with me, Miller Cain. You know exactly what you were doing getting me all hot and bothered and then just walking away."

"Who? Me?" he questions, the innocent act quickly morphing into devilish charm. "I would never."

I go to roll my eyes and suddenly he's right there, gripping my waist, pulling me in close to him as he glances back at the laptop. "You're really good at this," he says.

"Thanks," I say, his food completely forgotten. "I love photography."

"So, why aren't you studying photography?"

"I am, but it's more like a hobby, rather than what I want for a career," I explain. "PR is just so much more exciting."

"How so?" he questions, letting me lead him back through to the living room and getting comfortable on the couch.

I lean over and grab my phone off the coffee table and bring up my Facebook app. "Take this for instance," I say, logging into the Dragons' Facebook page I created earlier in the week. "I created this page for you idiots a few days ago and shared it a few times because, for some insane reason, you haven't already done this. I got fifteen hundred followers straight off the bat. I added a sneak peek of the calendar about two hours ago, and now you're up to two thousand followers," I explain. "I guess I like working on something positive and physically being able to see the results."

"Holy shit," he says, taking the phone from my hand and looking closer at the page. "We really have two thousand followers already? Are there even that many people in the school?"

"Yeah," I laugh. "Imagine what that number might be when the season actually starts, let alone when you win the championship."

"You're too good for us," he tells me.

I give him a devilish grin. "Yeah, I know," I laugh, taking the phone back and giving it another look, updating the screen as I go to find another twenty-five followers. "I'll probably do some promos and giveaways on here, but it would be cool if a few of you guys post every now and then."

Miller nods, more than eager to do his part. "Consider it done."

"Oh, and I'm going to convince Coach Harris to let me take over the website. It needs some serious work and a few updates. Maybe I'll put up a merchandise page, then fans from everywhere can buy your calendar," I smile. "Sophie and I are going to kill this assignment."

His eyes soften as he watches me. "You really do love this stuff, don't you?"

I nod my head enthusiastically. "Yeah. I'm practically living a dream this year," I tell him.

"Me too," he murmurs, slipping his hand around my neck and bringing me down on top of him. The tension builds in the room, and as he captures my stare, he slowly pulls me in closer, until his lips are finally pressing against mine. I melt into him, my heart racing a million miles an hour as he kisses me gently at first, then really begins to move, deepening our kiss.

I adjust myself on his lap until I'm straddling him and can feel that delicious cock hardening beneath me. His hands slide up the back of my top, roaming over my skin as he explores my body, sending a thrill shooting through me. He works his way down my torso, crossing to my waist and going lower until his fingers are pushing inside my panties. My body aches for him and then finally, I feel him there, his fingers gently skimming over my sensitive clit.

I suck in a breath, and he does it again, this time adding more pressure and circling over the tight bud. I groan into his mouth and he pushes his fingers deep inside me.

In. Out. In. Out.

"Oh, God," I groan, getting closer and closer to the edge, having to break our kiss and tip my head back. I feel his eyes on me, watching as I ride his fingers, and I've never felt so fucking beautiful in my life.

Miller continues his sensual assault on me until it's too much for me to bear. "Come for me," he demands. His words throw me right over the edge, and my world explodes around him. My pussy convulses, spasming around his fingers, but he doesn't dare stop. He keeps moving, keeps massaging deep inside of me as I ride out my high.

My fingers dig into his shoulder as my orgasm rocks through me, and then finally, I collapse against his strong body and close my eyes as I come down from the high. Miller's arm snakes around my waist, his lips moving against my neck. "You're so fucking gorgeous when you come for me."

His words have me ready to go all over again when we hear Sophie and Tank exiting her room from down the hallway. Miller grins and reluctantly pulls his fingers out of me as I climb off his lap. "Good timing," he murmurs with a wink that drives me wild with need.

I'm just getting to my feet and straightening my clothes when Sophie and Tank appear around the corner and join us in the living room. "So, how about that movie?" Sophie says awkwardly, taking a seat on the opposite side of the room from Tank. The two of them are barely able to look at one another for some reason.

Hmmm, trouble in paradise? Either that or someone accidentally put something in the wrong hole.

"I'm thinking Micky's," I say.

CHAPTER 10

MILLER

I t's game night. The first match of the season, and my guys are pumped. It's a home game so the stadium is packed, and I'm pretty sure that has something to do with all of Dani's promotions. Before she and Sophie started this assignment, we were despised around here. Don't get me wrong, we have the loyal, die-hard fans we love, but the rest . . . they like to go with the flow.

Tonight is not only the first game of the season, but tonight we release our calendar. Dani said she's had quite a bit of interest so far and has stuck a few freshmen at a table, putting them in charge of making sales so she can watch the game. I have to be honest, knowing she'll be watching me tonight has me more than ready to absolutely dominate the opposition.

I stand with my team as Coach gives us his first pep talk of the season. "Alright boys, you need to get out there and show those guys who owns this ice," he starts, his face turning red as he pumps us up. "This is our season, our house, and nobody comes between us and victory. We'll wipe the floor clean with them. Show them how to play like men." His tone gets louder with every word, the determination radiating out of him as he stares each of us in the eye. "We have a reputation to win back. We know we deserve it, but they don't. So, go out there and take what's ours!"

We all holler and chant as we hear our team called over the speakers, my cue to lead my boys out of the locker room and into our stadium. The crowd cheers as we make our appearance, and I don't miss the booing peppered throughout the stands, but I do my best to ignore it. It won't be long until we prove to them who the true Kings of Denver are.

We skate out onto the ice, and I look up at the grandstand, searching for a face that I know is hiding among the rest. There's no way she would miss this. It takes only a second before I find that familiar wave of thick golden hair. Dani catches my stare and blows me a kiss, and being the dork that I am, I pretend to catch it and laugh as she rolls her eyes in embarrassment.

We get started with a quick warm-up, flying around the ice and taking a few practice shots before heading back to the side to let our opponents do the same.

Ten minutes later, we're called to the ice. The referee takes his position, and at the sound of the buzzer, the game begins.

I speed off like a bat out of hell and so do my boys. Each of us knows exactly where we need to be. Not two minutes in, I claim the first point of the season. Our fans cheer, and I look up to find Dani standing with her camera plastered to her face, capturing the moment with a wide grin across her full lips. For some reason I can't explain, seeing her happiness is a million times better than the rush of watching the puck slam into the back of the net.

"Good job, Cain," Coach hollers from the barrier, bringing me back to the here and now as Tank claps me on the back.

We don't waste a moment and the game continues, growing more intense with every passing minute. We do what we can to keep the upper hand and our opponents grow frustrated as the game goes on, which is when the real action starts—the reason I fell in love with the game in the first place.

Their right defense attempts to body slam Tank into the barriers, but he's too quick. Tank sidesteps and takes the puck out from under him, throwing the opponent off balance and sending him sprawling to his knees, giving Tank a clear shot at the goal. He rears back, and like magic, the puck slides across the ice and straight into the back of the net.

The crowd gets to their feet, roaring for their team, but we keep our heads in the game. It's not long until the buzzer sounds through the arena, signaling the end of our first period.

We barrel off the ice and Coach Harris gets straight into his spiel, giving us guidance and pointing out the weaknesses he was able to catch from the other team. I take a drink, and before I know it, we're back on the ice, dominating the rink once again.

The game continues with intense ferocity, neither team wanting to be the ones to have to claim a loss for the first game of the season. But I fully intend to wrap up this season as the undefeated champions.

The countdown is on, and before I know it, we're down to the last few minutes of the game. We're exhausted, but we're in better shape than our opposition. The scoreboard reads 4-2 our way, and that's exactly how I intend for it to stay. Though, I'm certainly not going to argue if my boys want to kick it up a notch.

The last few minutes fly by, and as the buzzer sounds through the arena, my body stalls in shock. The mighty Dragons have officially been declared the winners of tonight's game. Coach roars and throws his clipboard high into the sky, which barely avoids Bobby's face as it comes back down, and we step off the ice. I know damn well nothing will stop us now.

Twenty minutes later, we're showered, dressed, and ready for a night of celebrations. "Where to, boys?" Aaron asks as he grabs his skate bag off the bench, his face still red from the intense workout that game just put us through.

"Tradition," Shorty says. "Home game, so it's Micky's bar."

Everyone grunts their approval as we make our way out of the locker room and into the throng of loyal fans who wait for us at the other end of the hallway. They take us in greedily, clapping us on the back and celebrating along with us, while some go the extra distance and shove pens and notepads in our faces, asking for autographs. It takes a few minutes to get through the crowd and we're just about there when I spot Dani a few feet away, the merchandise table keeping her insanely busy. I call out her name and watch as her head snaps up and begins searching me out.

Dani's eyes land on mine and she gives me one hell of a gorgeous smile. "Meet us at Micky's?" I shout, hoping she can lip-read as the roar of the crowd gets louder when they begin to chant the Dragons' war cry.

She nods and turns back to the lady in front of her, handing over at least five copies of the calendar. My eyes practically bulge out of my head. Shit, it must be selling well.

Making our way out the front of the stadium, we pour into the parking lot. A few of the boys climb into my SUV and dump their bags in the back. Two minutes later, we pull up at Micky's and get the party started.

The bar is packed with college students, and we're welcomed in like celebrities. A table is cleared and the boys settle in, ready for a great night. Waitresses deliver beer and the music is cranked up.

Our table is swarmed with every available girl in the bar looking for a good time, and I bat away a few needy chicks, keeping my eyes glued to the door. The anticipation builds as I wait for that one particular girl who's going to turn this already fantastic night into an incredible one.

"Here's to being undefeated," Jaxon hollers like the moron he is as he raises his glass.

I can't wipe the smile off my face as the whole bar cheers right along with him, raising their drinks and chanting to the mighty Dragons. Does winning one game even count as being undefeated?

A familiar wave of golden hair steals my attention, and my back straightens, locking my stare onto her sexy little body. I get up from the table and make my way across the bar, in case for some reason she can't quite find the loudest table in the place. "Sorry, I took so long," Dani says as I step into her, taking her waist and pulling her in. "Apparently, you guys are the sexiest man-meat on campus and every girl within a hundred-mile radius needed a calendar for her spank bank."

"What did you expect?" I tease, indicating my body as if it's God's gift to womankind.

"You're an idiot," she laughs, swatting at my chest. "But you did great tonight."

I give her a cheesy smile and wink. "Let's get you a drink."

Taking her hand, I lead her back to the table where the boys jump up, offering their seats. Dani laughs them off and goes to sit beside me, but I give her a tug, making her fall into my lap. My hand rests against her thigh as she hooks her arm around my neck, right where she belongs.

"Where's Sophie?" Tank asks from across the table, raising his voice to be heard over the crowd and stealing my girl's attention away from me.

"Don't know," she says thoughtfully, shrugging her shoulders. "She said something about meeting up with a friend."

Tank nods and sits back in his chair as he thinks it over, his eyes dropping to the table. Something pulls in my chest as I recognize the look on his face. Something is definitely up with those two. I'm just not sure what.

The night flies by way too fast and suddenly it's one in the morning and Dani has me by the balls, dancing in the middle of Micky's. She drags me across the dancefloor, toward the bar, and I go willingly, watching in adoration as she orders a round of shots for the boys and throws one back like a fucking goddess. She smirks up at me and finds a stool, however instead of sitting on it like I expect her to do, she begins to climb up onto the bar.

Ahh, fuck no.

She's absolutely plastered.

Dani starts dancing and shaking her glorious ass in my face as the men in the bar begin to crowd around. One even goes as far as thrusting a twenty-dollar bill in her face, which she gingerly plucks out of his hands. As she goes to grab another, I shake my head. I'm all for women doing whatever the fuck they want that makes them happy, but this girl right here belongs to me. If she wants to shake her ass, then she can do that while grinding it up against my rock-hard cock.

I grab her by the hand and tug her down off the bar, throw her over my shoulder, and make my way back to the table while she giggles and squeezes my ass. "Can you watch her?" I ask Tank. "I'm going to take a quick piss then get her home." He barely glances my way before nodding and getting back to nursing his beer.

I head off to the bathroom and after taking care of business, I stand at the basin, washing my hands when a drunk surfer dude crashes through the door. He can barely hold himself up. He throws his hand against the wall to steady himself and then looks around the small bathroom, stopping when his gaze falls on me.

A wicked smirk crosses his face as he looks me up and down, and I let out a sigh, realizing he must be one of the many disappointed fans from last year. This shit never gets old. "The big shot hockey guy," he slurs, taking a step toward me. "She's too good for you."

The fuck? Maybe this isn't what I thought it was.

"Who's too good for me?" I question, already regretting entertaining his bullshit.

He gets right in my face, and I smell the rum on his breath. "Dani. That fucking bitch is mine. You'll see. She'll come running back."

My back straightens at the mention of her name. Is this the ex? "Tell me then, how come she's spent the night on my lap and not yours? Why's she not with you now?"

His face drops in anger as he raises a hand to poke me in the chest. "That's none of your fucking business," he snaps.

"You see, that's where you're wrong," I say, grabbing his hand from my chest and twisting it away, my blood boiling through my veins. "Everything to do with Dani is my business."

Knowing this isn't going to end well if I hang around, I push him away and walk out of the bathroom before I beat the shit out of him and ruin my career before it's even begun.

I head back to the table to find Bobby half sprawled across it, leaning in toward Dani in order to hear her over the music. "How many calendars did you sell?" he asks.

"Ah . . . like two hundred maybe," she says, still as giddy as ever, practically bouncing on her chair.

"Shit," Bobby says as Tank raises his eyebrows in surprise. "So, you must have made, what? Like four hundred dollars?" he asks looking down at his fingers, trying to do the math.

"No," she giggles. "More like four thousand dollars."

"Fuck," Tank says, beating me to the punchline.

She smiles up at him. "Yep, and tonight's only your first game. You guys are going to be giving women lady boners all over the state by the end of the season."

"Okay," I say, cutting in. "Let's get you home."

"What?" she groans. "But I'm having so much fun."

I laugh at her pouty face, loving the way her eyes get so big when she's trying to get her way. "Don't stress, we can do it all again when we win next week," I say, getting cheers from all the boys at the table.

"Deal," she says, getting up from her chair. I put my hand out to steady her as she continues to wobble and she laces her fingers through mine, smiling up at me with such adoration in her eyes it nearly knocks me right off my fucking feet. My heart aches knowing she isn't really mine. If she hadn't been drinking, she probably would have told me to fuck off by now, needing just that bit of space between us.

I walk her fifteen minutes to her place and stop at her door when she turns to face me. "You're being unusually quiet," she challenges, almost daring me to tell her what's on my mind.

"Yeah, sorry," I say, still not sure if I should bring this up. "I was debating whether or not to ask you something."

"Sure," she smiles. "Hit me with it."

Arching a brow, I try not to grin at the cockiness stretched wide across her face. "You may not like it," I warn.

Dani leans up against the closed door, props her foot against it, and crosses her arms over her chest trying to look hard. "Try me."

I take a deep breath, hoping I'm not going to upset her. "Your ex cornered me at Micky's tonight," I explain, watching the way her back stiffens and the spark in her green eyes begins to fade. "So, I guess that leaves me wondering what the story is."

Her body goes rigid, and I instantly hate myself for bringing it up. "Shit," she sighs, before taking a moment. I watch her, waiting to see how she wants to play this before she waves toward the outdoor seating on the porch. "Wait here."

My brows furrow as she bolts inside and returns a minute later with a blanket. She takes my hand and drags me to the small sitting area, pulls me down, and curls up beside me. "You're not going to like this story but promise me you won't try to fix anything."

"I can't do that," I tell her.

"Then I can't tell you what happened."

"Fine," I sigh, not liking this one bit. "I promise."

"Okay," she starts, looking out into the street to avoid my eyes, her tone shaky and hesitant. "Wow. This is harder than I thought. Apart from Sophie, I haven't told anybody this."

I put my arm around her shoulders and pull her in tight, giving her all my support and comfort. "It's okay, take your time. But remember, you don't need to tell me anything you're not ready for. If it's too much, we can stop right now."

She takes a deep breath and shakes her head, her determination to get the words out stronger than I could have ever known. "I started dating Brett two years ago after we met at some bullshit party the swim team put on. He swept me off my feet, right from the get-go. You could say it was love at first sight." She scoffs and rolls her eyes. "I was crazy about him, and we were inseparable. A few months in, he was begging me to move in with him, but I loved living in the dorms with Sophie, and call me old-fashioned, but I didn't want to move in with a man who my parents hadn't met and approved of yet. So, we waited out the year, and over Christmas break, he came home with me and charmed the pants off my parents. Even went as far as asking my father for his blessing to marry me. Which of course, my dad happily gave."

She pauses and takes a deep breath, and I can tell this is where it gets hard for her. "So, when we got back, I moved in, and it was magical. Well, the first few months were. He started failing his business degree and would come home stressed out and angry and would snap at me about little things. I always did my best to make sure the washing was done and dinner was cooked so he could focus on his studies. Looking back now, it makes me sound pathetic, but I loved him, and I wanted everything to be perfect."

She gives me a tight smile and looks out toward the road, watching as the cars silently drive by. "I had gone out with Sophie and Jared to this bar for her birthday, and even though it was pretty trashy, we were having a great time," she smiles. "Right up until Brett showed up to find me dancing with Jared. He stormed in, grabbed me under the arm, and hauled ass out of there. He called me every name under the sun, even though I'd told him a million times that Jared was gay. Apparently, that didn't change the fact that I was still a whore. I didn't realize until the next morning that my arm was covered in bruises."

My body tenses under her, knowing that dickhead put his hands on my girl, and feeling the movement, she turns in my arms and gives me a dazzling smile that breaks my heart. "Calm down," she murmurs, almost teasing. "I haven't even got to the best part yet."

"Please tell me it doesn't get worse than that?" I beg of her.

Dani squeezes my hand, and suddenly she's the one giving me support. "Oh, it got plenty worse," she says with a scoff. "It started with the name-calling and not letting me go out. He got super possessive, and one night he left his phone out on the bench when a text came through. I saw a girl's name and I couldn't help myself. I unlocked the phone and opened the text to find she was confirming the hotel they were going to meet in and if he wanted her to dress in black or red lingerie."

"Fuck, babe. You don't need to tell me the rest," I say, knowing where this is leading. I don't want her to have to relive it again.

"No, I need to tell you," Dani insists, squeezing my hand. "I want you to understand me and to know why I have such a hard time letting you get close."

I give her a nod and pull her against me once again.

"Okay," Dani breathes, tears welling in her green eyes. "So, I asked him about the girl and he lost his shit, saying he fucks her because I'm a whore and that it's my fault I wasn't woman enough for him. He had been drinking and we got into this huge fight. I said I was going to leave. I'd had enough of his bullshit, so I went to start packing . . ." she pauses, taking a breath. "He grabbed me by the hair and yanked me back to him, saying I was his and wasn't leaving until he was through with me."

Dani wipes at her eyes and continues. "I broke free of his hold and started packing anyway. There was no way I was staying there with him. He must have thought I was just cooling off in our room, and when he walked in to find me ready to leave, he lost it. He didn't even give me a chance to defend myself, just reared back and let his fist do the talking. He stopped immediately, realizing what he'd done, and began apologizing, but there was no going back for me. He'd already put me through hell, and I wasn't sticking around for more. So I left and moved in here with Sophie."

She sits in silence beside me, and I grab her around the waist to pull her up onto my lap. "You're more than woman enough for me," I promise her. "You're fucking everything."

Dani wraps her arms around me and nuzzles her face into my neck, and I feel her smile against my skin. I can't help but hold her tight, content to sit here outside her home for the rest of my life.

We sit in silence for a short while before I realize she's fallen asleep, and a soft smile spreads across my lips. Scooping her up in my arms, I make my way inside and down to her room before slipping her under her blankets. I watch her a moment before realizing I'm being a fucking creeper and turn to leave when her soft whisper fills the room. "Stay with me."

Her words are like music to my ears, but I shake my head. "God, babe. Don't tempt me," I beg her. "You have no idea how badly I want to spend the night with you, but I know you'll regret that decision in the morning."

"I know," she admits. "But stay anyway."

I walk over to her bed and lean down over her. "Goodnight, sweet girl," I say, pressing my lips to hers.

Dani grabs me and moans against my lips, melting into my kiss as she tries to pull me down to her. "Please, I need you," she says, gripping the fabric of my shirt and trying to pull it up my body.

"Not tonight, babe," I smirk, hating myself for being such a fucking moron. "Try me again tomorrow when you haven't drunk the whole bar."

"Fine," she grumbles, gripping her blankets and pulling them up to her shoulders. I press my lips to hers once more and get the softest kiss in return before making my way back to her door. And just as the door is about to close between us, I hear a devilish purr coming from her room behind me. "I guess I'll have to take care of it myself."

My dick hardens painfully in my pants, the worst kind of punishment for leaving her high and dry. Though from the sound of it, my girl is soaking wet.

Closing the door behind me, I mentally scold myself while I walk out of her home, and as I hear her muffled moans and the sound of my name on her lips, I know without a doubt that I will never walk away from this girl.

CHAPTER 11

DANIELLE

"Shit, babe, you've got to wake up," Sophie laughs as she launches herself onto my bed.

"Go away," I groan, attempting to push her off.

"Hell no, you've got to see this," she says, still in a fit of laughter as she thrusts her phone toward my face.

I squint up at the morning light as a killer hangover makes itself known. A collection of horrendous memories come crashing through my mind, and I start to feel the uneasy ache in my stomach needing to eject last night's mistakes.

Sitting up in bed, I rub my hands down my face and grab her phone, trying to figure out what's got her all worked up at such an ungodly hour. Focusing on what she's so desperate to show me, I find the Dragons' Facebook page staring back at me with a photo of myself dancing on the bar in nothing but a Dragon's jersey, the name *CAIN* written across the back. My stomach drops, and I glance down at the caption; 'Cain's number one girl'.

"Ahhh, fuck," I groan. "Who the hell posted that?" I click on the photo and bring up the details to see that it's now been viewed over four thousand times and shared another three hundred.

My heart begins to race as humiliation fills my veins. How the hell did this happen?

Sophie continues laughing as she takes her phone back, and I grab my own to find it overflowing with notifications. I bring up the admin stats for the Dragons' page and go to remove the post. "There's no point deleting it," Sophie says, rushing in before I can complete my task. "It's been shared too many times. It's only going to cause more speculation when people think Miller has something to hide."

"Damn it," I groan. "Do you know who posted it?"

"Nope. All the guys have the login details. Any one of them could have put it up. Hell, it could have been Coach Harris for all we know," she laughs. "Besides, you were all wasted, so I'm not sure even the culprit knows he did it."

I flop back against my bed, wishing I could press rewind on this morning and start over. "How do you know we were wasted?" I question, my tone groggy from sleep. "Weren't you busy meeting with your *friend?*"

"I ran into a very satisfied Miller coming out of your bedroom last night," she says, her brows bouncing with interest. "Did you finally give him the goodies?"

"Huh? Miller was in my room?" I think back over the night, trying to put the pieces together when it all comes rushing back, one mistake after the next. Embarrassment washes through me. I threw myself at him after telling him about my relationship with Brett, and now he probably thinks I'm damaged goods.

"He sure as hell was," she tells me. "So give it up. Did you let him rock your world?"

"No," I groan, covering my face, remembering exactly how I tried to pull him down on me. "I tried to, but he tucked me in bed. Apparently, screwing me while I was drunk out of my mind isn't his thing. But it doesn't matter anyway. I told him about Brett, so he probably thinks I'm a desperate loser."

"Don't be ridiculous. That guy is head over heels for you," she tells me. "Nothing you tell him could make him think less of you. I'm sure he probably spent the night trying to hunt Brett down."

"Would this be before or after Brett cornered him at Micky's?"

"Shit, you really did have an interesting night," she laughs.

"Sure did," I mutter, willing my stomach to ease. "How'd your night go? You're usually in bed until midday on a Saturday."

Sophie lets out a confused huff and makes herself comfortable in my bed, pulling at the blankets so much my feet peek out the other end. "I sort of had a date," she admits, almost sounding sheepish.

"Yeah, I figured. But don't you mean booty call?"

"What makes you think it was a booty call?" she asks, narrowing her blue eyes at me.

I curl up into her side, closing my eyes as I start my explanation. "Babe, you've been my best friend for three years. When you come to me at ten o'clock on a Friday night saying you're meeting up with a friend, I know it's for some kind of fucked-up wild orgy. Besides, apart from me, you have no girlfriends because they're all whiny bitches, which only leaves guy friends, who you only allow to be your friend if they come with dick piercings."

"Damn. You know me too well."

"Sure do," I tell her. "So, who was the lucky guy you faked an orgasm for?"

"It was Robbie," she says with a disappointed sigh. "And I didn't need to fake anything."

"What? Did Robbie finally figure out what to do?"

She laughs. "No, I couldn't fake it because I didn't go through with it."

My eyes bug out of my head. "What?" I screech. "What do you mean? You've never turned down a good screw in all the years I've known you."

"I know," she whines. "It's Tank. He's ruined me. It's like my pussy has made a home out of his big ass dick and won't accept anything else."

I laugh, all too amused by her situation. "Shit, babe. You're falling for him."

"No, tell me I'm not," she begs, looking at me with real fear in her wide eyes. "I don't fall for guys. I love 'em and leave 'em."

"Sorry, hun," I tell her, hating to be the bearer of bad news. "Your pussy has spoken."

"Damn it," she groans. "So, what do we do now? I think we're both screwed."

"No, no. You're screwed. I'm perfectly fine staying right here and avoiding Miller as much as possible while you go out and find Tank to put the poor guy out of his misery."

"That sounds like an awful idea," she moans, burrowing her face deeper into my pillow. "I say we fake our deaths, move to Australia, and never talk to them again. We can spend the rest of our lives living it up on the beach and getting naked with hot surfer dudes."

"I heard that," Jared says as he walks past my room.

"Shit, we're going to have to take him out," I laugh.

"I'll do it," Sophie declares. "You're too soft."

Jared laughs from the kitchen and calls out again. "Just make sure you cremate my body and scatter my ashes at sea so I can forever live on with the sailors."

I laugh and roll my eyes. "You've got yourself a deal."

"Sophie, Danielle," Professor Whitaker says as the bell sounds through her auditorium. "Can I see you both for a moment?"

We give each other a brief look and shrug as the class begins to clear out. We make our way down the stairs and wait by her desk as she finishes collecting her notes.

She makes her way over to us and puts her things down. "I just wanted to commend you both for the work you've done on the assignment so far. The article you submitted for the Dragons was fresh and intriguing. It worked in favor of drawing a new crowd while simultaneously keeping the regular fans appropriately updated."

"Thank you," we say in unison.

"I heard some good things from Coach Harris," she says, almost sounding impressed that anyone was able to gain a compliment out of the guy. "He's quite pleased, and apparently, your efforts have created a positive effect on restoring their reputation. I believe he's quite taken with you both."

"Really?" Sophie scoffs. "He certainly didn't give us that impression."

"Oh?" she laughs. "You know how these athletic types are. Coach Harris is certainly no exception to that." She comes around the side of her desk while looking at the two of us. "Did you have success with your calendar?"

"Oh, yes," I say, pulling my phone out and showing her a few of the promotional images I have.

"Wow, you seem to be taking this assignment quite seriously. Do you mind if I ask which venues you're using to promote this?" she asks, quickly flicking through the images, not lingering on any of them and keeping it professional.

"We created a Facebook page and other social media accounts which have managed to get quite a following, so we've posted about it there and on their website. Then we set up a stall at their game, which was a hit," Sophie explains.

Professor Whitaker hands my phone back to me. "Excellent work," she encourages. "What do you plan to do with the proceeds?"

"We aren't too sure yet, but we believe Coach Harris would like to donate it to the Denver Youth Hockey Program. We'll probably award it to them at one of the later games of the season."

"I think that would be a wise idea. Perhaps you could invite some of the children to come and skate with the Dragons," she suggests, leaning against her desk. I see the excitement in her eyes and realize she loves this just as much as I do.

Sophie and I get into a lengthy conversation with her as we bring forward all our ideas and plans for the next few months, and she goes through all the pros and cons, making sure we're all on the same page. I eat up every word of her advice.

"I won't keep you any longer," she says, glancing at the time on her phone and realizing we've been here almost twenty minutes. "I've got a heap of work to get through."

"Sure thing. Thank you," Sophie says, as I give Professor Whitaker a grateful smile.

"I look forward to your next article," she tells us, taking her seat at her desk as we exit the room.

We make our way out into the hallway while giving each other smug expressions, knowing damn well we're killing this assignment. "So, what do you say we do for the afternoon?" Sophie questions, handing me her bag as she pulls her hair up into a bun high on her head. "Head to the gym? Lounge out watching a movie? Or perv on the guys?"

Excitement thrums through my veins. "Do you even have to ask?" I smirk as she breaks into laughter. We head over to the ice rink and sneak in through the side entrance, before quietly making our way up the grandstand. We take our seats, and I glance down to the ice, smiling as my eyes land on Miller. I take in the way he dominates the ice, his moves mesmerizing me.

Tingles spread over my body the same way they do every time I watch him skate. He's amazing, there's simply no other way to put it. He glides across the ice like he was born to lead this team. He rushes forward with his hockey stick and effortlessly steals the puck off another player before shooting it forward. My eyes follow the puck as it sails through the air, past the goalie, and slams into the netting behind him.

The need to jump up and cheer for him crashes through me, but I do my best to rein it in. As if sensing my gaze on him, Miller turns and looks up into the grandstand, his eyes instantly finding mine. He gives me a smug, wicked grin before getting on with his training.

I haven't seen him since I drunkenly attempted to seduce him on Friday night, and in all honesty, I was sure he was avoiding me. But there's no way that's the case after the look he just gave me. God, just thinking about it does all sorts of things to me.

"They're so sexy when they're training," Sophie sighs beside me.

"I know," I reply, equally as dazed by the scene unfolding before me. He's like a god on the ice, as fast as lightning and so lethal, you wouldn't want to get in his way. He draws the attention of the room, whether it's on the ice or at a party, and damn him, I am no exception to that. I'm the moth and he's the flame.

Sophie giggles beside me, and I follow her gaze down to Tank who's got Jaxon by his ankle, dragging him across the slick ice with a childish grin plastered across his face. Coach Harris roars his disapproval as the rest of the team works together to bring Tank down.

"You sure about this whole Tank thing? I mean, it's not too late to back out," I joke. "We could hijack the funds from the calendar and make our great escape. We could be sipping cocktails at Bondi by tomorrow afternoon."

"Fuck, that sounds good," she muses then smirks. "But so does stripping him naked and seeing just how deep I can take him down my throat."

Oh geez. She's got it bad.

Forty minutes later, Coach wraps up the training session and sends the boys to the locker room. "Let's get out of here before they want to talk about their feelings," Sophie says.

"Done," I laugh as we hastily make it out of the arena before we're doomed to face reality.

We walk home, only stopping to grab a coffee when a bouquet of flowers greets us at the front door. "Please be for me," Sophie says, reaching down to pluck the card from the top. Her face falls before handing me the card. "Here," she grumbles.

"What? They're for me?" I ask, taking the card and flipping it over to find it completely blank.

"Who's it from?" Sophie asks as she picks up the flowers and heads inside.

I follow behind. "Don't know. There's nothing on the card, but I have a pretty good idea," I tell her, knowing there's only one man in my life right now.

We head into the kitchen, and I get busy arranging the flowers in a vase, knowing damn well these will end up in Sophie's room by the end of the day. I take a quick photo and open a new text to Miller.

Dani - Thanks . . . ?

Miller - For what? Where did you disappear to? You're not avoiding me, are you?

Dani - The flowers? And no, I'm not avoiding you at all ;)

Miller - Go out with me?

Dani - . . .

Miller - I'm not going to hurt you, Dani.

Dani - I'm starting to see that.

Miller - Good.

Miller - By the way, I'm going to kick the guy's ass that's sending my girl flowers.

CHAPTER 12

DANIELLE

It's three weeks into the season and we're killing it. The Dragons are undefeated and kicking ass. Coach Harris is doing an amazing job busting our balls every training session, and it's clearly paying off. The championship is going to be ours.

I turn off the shower and wrap a towel around my waist as I head back into the locker room after another brutal training session when I hear Dani's voice coming from outside the door. "Are you all decent in there?" she calls from just outside.

The boys all murmur a noncommittal "Yeah," even though the majority of them are as undressed as I am. She pops her head into the locker room and rolls her eyes at the state of my men and groans. Sophie, however, doesn't give one single fuck. She strolls right past

Dani and makes herself comfortable on a bench.

Dani follows behind and catches my eye, immediately looking away from my wet body. I smirk as I watch her clench her thighs together to relieve the ache between her legs that she knows only I can fix. It's been weeks since I tasted her, and fuck, I would do anything to get between those perfect legs again.

This woman is driving me crazy. The need I have for her grows more intense every day, and I know without a doubt that I'm beginning to fall for her. If only she would come to her damn senses and let me in. She's mine. Hell, even the boys know it, and I'm pretty damn sure she knows it too. She's just too damn stubborn to admit it.

"To what do we owe this pleasure?" I ask, forcing that green gaze back to me.

Dani smirks when she realizes I've noticed her clenching thighs and her obvious need for me. "I, ahh, there's something I wanted to pitch to you guys," she explains with a small cringe that puts a few of the guys on edge.

"Go on," Tank says cautiously. After all, her last idea ended up with us all naked in a calendar—a calendar I'm pretty sure Tank's mom ordered.

"Well, with the calendar doing so well, we want to use that momentum to keep the interest going. I briefly brought this up at the start of the season, but how many of you guys are single?" she asks.

Every single one of them raises their hands apart from me and Tank, something Dani doesn't miss. Her eyes narrow suspiciously, clearly trying to figure out why the hell my hand isn't raised. I give her yet another smirk, but when hurt flashes behind her eyes and she looks away, my brows furrow in confusion.

Quickly shaking it off, her soft gaze moves to Sophie's and they grin at each other, the wheels in their heads spinning with whatever ridiculous idea they're about to hit us with.

"Let's hear it," I say.

"We're going to auction you off," Sophie grins as the guys start cheering around us.

"Care to clarify?" Tank asks, narrowing his gaze at the woman who's been running aimlessly through his head.

"Well," Dani says slowly, stepping forward to make sure they can all hear. "For those of you who are single," she starts, giving me and Tank a hard stare. "And as long you're comfortable with it, we're going to hold an auction where the highest bidder can win a date with you," she explains. "All proceeds will be added to the funds donated to The Denver Youth Hockey Program."

The boys cheer once again, and Jaxon asks about the kind of date he's going to have to take this girl on.

"I don't care what you do on your date as long as you show them a good time," she says. "And for the record, you can't sleep with them, or have any sort of sexual relations while on the date."

"What?" they all protest.

"Your dates would have paid for your time. If you flop your dicks out or perform any sexual favors, you could get charged with prostitution. If you're that interested, take your date home and ask her out for the following night. Take her on a proper date," Dani says, making sure all her bases are covered.

"So, what kind of women are going to be at this auction?" Shorty asks.

Sophie grins and meets him right in the eye. "Who said it would be just women invited to bid?" she says with an evil smirk.

"What are you trying to say?" he asks.

"The auction is open to all students on campus. We wouldn't want to discriminate against anybody by closing it off to women only," she tells us, enjoying breaking the news to the boys.

They all groan, but nonetheless agree to be auctioned off, knowing it's for a good cause and for our own reputation. And hell, who knows, this auction might just strike up the best bromance we ever did see. It could be one for the ages.

The girls go to leave, and I follow them out in my towel, gently taking Dani's elbow and turning her to face me. "What are you doing?" she gasps. "You're practically naked."

I roll my eyes at her nervous worry. "It's fine. The ice rink is closed for the next few hours. Nobody but you and the boys will get the pleasure of seeing my naked ass."

"And me," Sophie calls from up ahead.

Dani tries her hardest not to smile as her cheeks flush, and unable to stop myself, I reach up and run my fingers across her soft skin. Her face melts into my palm as I pull her closer, leaning in and inhaling her addictive scent. "Go out with me?" I whisper.

She leans back out of my hold and watches me curiously. "But you just admitted in there that you're not single," she reminds me.

"I know," I smirk, reaching out for her once again. "Because I'm not. I've got a girl, she just won't admit it."

Dani glances away, but I catch the faint smile on her lips. Wrapping my fingers around her jaw, I bring her gaze back to mine. "Go out with me," I say once again, letting her see the raw honesty and need I have for her.

She takes a deep breath and searches my face, indecision and nervousness flashing in her eyes. A silent moment passes between us before a sigh slips through her lips. "Okay, you can take me to dinner. But it's *not* a date," she insists.

My chest swells with joy, and I grin back at her, relieved she's finally letting me in and giving me a chance to break down her walls. I drop my hands to her waist, pull her body hard against mine, and press my lips against hers, kissing her deeply.

Dani groans and melts into me, kissing me eagerly as her arms entwine around my neck, the two of us fitting together so perfectly.

I pull away, leaving her wanting more, and she does what she can to steady herself. Her heated eyes lock on mine as I hold onto her tightly. I step away, moving toward the locker room while walking backward to keep my stare on her. "There's no way you're changing my mind, babe. It's definitely a date," I tell her, watching the way her jaw slackens, preparing to argue. Before she gets the chance, I slip back into the locker room, a wide grin stretched across my face.

I find Tank as soon as I walk in, dressed and ready to go. "Where the fuck did you go?" he questions, eyeing me still in my towel.

"Just got myself a date," I smirk.

His face lights up in understanding. "Damn right you did," he cheers, reaching up and giving me a high five as I pass by. I get myself dressed and pack up my shit, my mind already consumed with all the ways I could make this date the best night of her life.

"C ain," Coach says as he makes his way into the locker room. "Great game."

"Thanks, Coach," I say with a nod as the boys cheer and chant around me. We've added yet another victory to our belts.

"As for the rest of you, it was sloppy. We barely got by. I saw far too many suicide passes. It's no wonder Jaxon got body checked. I expect more. I'm scheduling an extra training session this week, so be prepared and keep checking the notice board for session times." The boys groan, but after a sharp look from Coach, they snap right back into their celebrations. "Get out of here," Coach orders.

The crowd waiting for us on the other side of the door seems to have doubled over the last few weeks, and I know that's solely because of Dani and Sophie making us look like the gods we pretend to be. I push my way through the crowd in search of the one face that I desperately need to see, getting slaps of approval on the back as I go.

My eyes land on her almost instantly as if she called for me, and I make my way over to her, finding her with Jared. "Hey," she grins.

"Hey, yourself," I say, leaning in and kissing her on the cheek.

"Where's Sophie tonight?"

"Oh, you know," she says. "She said something about jumping Tank in the locker room."

"And you didn't feel that way inclined?" I laugh.

She gives me an innocent smile which I see through perfectly. "I guess I could go and join them. I'm sure Tank wouldn't mind, but Sophie's been a little territorial lately."

"I'm sure he wouldn't," I laugh, knowing damn well I walked straight into that one. "But you know that's not what I meant."

She smiles up at me, her beautiful eyes sparkling, blowing me the fuck away and making my chest ache with raw emotion. "I'm not sure I follow," she says sweetly.

"You're such a smartass," I grin. "Are you going home or do you feel like coming out with the boys?"

"We might come out for a bit," she says, glancing toward Jared to gauge his thoughts.

"Don't look at me. I don't give a shit what we do as long as there's beer," he shrugs.

I grab her by the hand and lace my fingers through hers, but she stiffens and looks up at me suspiciously. She's still so nervous, but it won't be long until she realizes I'm not going to hurt her. I squeeze her hand and watch as her gaze softens and she starts to relax.

I lead her outside as we wait for the rest of the boys to crowd around. Tank and Sophie never show, but I'm not surprised. He's probably ten inches deep right now. We figure out our plans, and I send him a quick text knowing he'll show up eventually.

Fifteen minutes later, we pull up outside Jaxon's place, which he rents from the college with Shorty and Aaron. The door stands wide open, the music blaring, and the mass texts sent out have the place crammed with bodies.

Jared and Dani stick around me, but the moment Jared's boyfriend appears in the doorway, he takes off, leaving me alone with my girl.

After refilling both our drinks, I lead her outside for some fresh air and take her over to a quiet space where we can have some privacy. Finding a chair, I sit down and pull her into my lap, rubbing my hand up and down her leg while my other hand stays firmly laced through hers. Dani twists on my lap and faces me, those green eyes still unsure but also so full of confidence as she brings her lips down to mine.

Finally, it's her making the move.

She kisses me with everything she's got, and the sweetest taste of strawberry vodka on her lips is enough to drive me crazy. I deepen the kiss and she moans into me before biting my bottom lip. Dani slides her hand up my shirt and spreads her fingers over my chest while she grinds herself onto my dick.

When we finally pull apart, I can't help but stare up at her, completely in awe of this beautiful woman. "I will never get enough of you," I tell her.

She looks down at me, the softest smile resting on her lips. "I know what you mean."

We sit together for a while until Sophie and Tank barge through the back door. Sophie grabs Dani and yanks her off my lap, demanding she takes her dancing. I watch as she takes off to the makeshift dance floor, shaking her ass just perfectly and making me want to sink my teeth into her creamy skin.

The boys begin to gather around, dragging chairs over and plonking down as we celebrate our win together. I look over to watch my girl dance when a petite body drops into my lap. I go to push the girl off but can't when her arms lock around my neck. She holds me tight, and I do what I can to get a look at who the hell is sitting on my lap. That spot is reserved for someone else.

"Stop pushing me away you big jerk and give me a hug," her little voice laughs.

What the hell? It couldn't be. I focus harder on the person before me, taking in her dark hair and dark eyes that look so much like mine, even though they have a little too much makeup on for my liking.

"Holy fucking shit. Mia?" I beam, relaxing and pulling her in hard against me, not realizing just how much I missed the brat until this very moment. "What the hell are you doing here?"

"I wanted to surprise you, so I came for your game," she tells me.

"What? How long have you been here? You should have told me. I could have reserved seats," I tell her.

"Please," she scoffs, swatting my shoulder. "You know I don't like all that special attention. I just wanted to see you play. You've gotten pretty good since the last time I saw you, Captain," she smirks.

"Who's this nice piece of ass, *Captain?*" Jaxon asks, mimicking Mia's tone.

Both our heads instantly whip in his direction as Tank murmurs an "Oh fuck," from beside me.

"The fuck did you say?" I ask, fixing him with a hard glare.

He flinches at my tone but carries on. "You're already keeping Dani to yourself," he laughs, then looks at Mia. "Why not share?"

I stand up and hand Mia off to Tank, then I take one big step forward and grab Jaxon by his shirt, yanking him to his feet. "Watch your fucking mouth," I snap.

"What's your problem, man?" he questions.

"My problem, Jaxon, is that's my baby sister you're talking about," I snarl.

His eyes widen and flash to Mia for a brief moment before snapping back to mine, clearly taking in our similarities. "Ahh, fuck, man. Shit, I'm sorry," he says, raising both his hands in surrender. "If I knew I never would—"

"Why don't you go and get Mia a chick drink like the little bitch you are," I tell him.

His lips tighten, but he gives a sharp nod as I release my hold on his shirt and he scurries away. I sit back down and Mia makes herself comfortable at my side as she introduces herself to the rest of the boys.

"Fuck, I've missed you," I tell her, pulling her hard against me and squeezing the life out of her. "How're things back home?"

"Ugh," she says, pushing me away. "Get off me, you grot," she laughs, then dives into a recap of life at home, giving me all the details about Mom's latest boyfriend, who apparently looks like he might actually stick around. As Mia chatters away about school, friends, and the latest fashion trends from her favorite magazine, it has me really missing home.

"Wait, while you're here," I start. "I want you to meet someone."

Her face brightens as she realizes that there's finally someone in my life that's worth the introduction. I've had casual girlfriends before, but no one I've actually wanted to take home. Hell, Dani makes me want to take her home and keep her there.

I get up and drag Mia inside as I search for Dani on the dancefloor, but she's not there. I move along to the kitchen, then the living room, and even knock on the bathroom door. After finding no trace of her, Sophie or Jared, I get the hint that they aren't here.

"Sorry, Kid. It looks like she's gone," I explain. "When are you heading home? Do you have time tomorrow?"

"I've got to leave first thing in the morning. I have time for breakfast if you're paying." She smiles and bats her eyelashes at me, knowing that I can't refuse my baby sister.

"Yeah, okay," I say, caving to her will yet again. "Let me drive you back to my place. You can stay there tonight."

"No, that's okay. I've got my car here," she tells me.

"Don't be ridiculous, you've been drinking. Tank can drop your car off in the morning."

"What? I don't want that big bastard driving my car, he'll burst all four tires just getting in," she mutters, before seeing the look on my face and reaching into her bag to pull out her keys. She reluctantly hands them over, and I have to pry them from her fingers. "He'll be careful, right? I worked too many hours to pay for that car."

"Your car will be fine" I laugh.

I say goodnight to the guys and give Tank specific instructions about Mia's car before handing him the keys. He raises his eyebrows at Mia and shakes her keys in front of his face, making a show of throwing them in the air and pretending to lose them to get the perfect rise out of her. It's obvious he has little sisters of his own. I knock him in the arm and head out, but I can't stop the smile from gracing my face.

I make it home in record time, debating whether or not it would be okay to stop by Dani's place to make sure she's alright. On second thought, that might be a little stalkerish.

I show Mia to the spare room and double check that I remembered to change the sheets after Jaxon's threesome the other week. She gives me a hug goodnight and then proceeds to take over my bathroom.

After leaving her be, I drop down on my bed, unable to get Dani off my mind.

Miller - You keep disappearing on me. Hope you're okay.

CHAPTER 13

DANIELLE

I dance the night away with Sophie and Jared, drinking, partying, and having the time of my life. Things between me and Miller seem to be moving forward, and I can finally feel myself lowering my walls to let him in. After all, he's been nothing but amazing. Or *amaze-balls*, as Sophie would put it.

"I'll get us another drink," Sophie calls over the music.

I give her a nod because there's no point trying to project my voice over this sound. I shimmy up against Jared as we dance to Tay Tay, shaking our asses with our hands high in the air. Sophie returns with a bottle of vodka, and we begin taking shots, making our night that much more exciting.

"Get the boys," Jared smirks, momentarily forgetting that his boyfriend is around here somewhere. "I want to dance up against Tank and Miller like a Dragon sandwich."

Sophie laughs. "Oh, hell yeah. I want to be a part of that sandwich too."

"Me too," I slur, feeling the room start to spin. "I want a Miller sandwich."

Together, we head for the back door, giggling as the three of us attempt to get through the door frame at the same time and fail miserably. I know without a doubt my shoulder is going to be bruised in the morning, but right now, the only thing that matters to me is getting Miller back in my arms and maybe in my bed.

"Shit," Jared mutters as he looks out toward the backyard, his body stiffening as his tone drops.

When Sophie gasps, I look up to see what has their attention. "God, I'm going to kick his ass," she snaps.

My eyes land on Miller and more importantly, the beautiful girl snuggled in on his lap. His hand is curled around her waist as he looks at her with such adoration that it makes me feel like I'm intruding. The way they are with each other, it's clear they've meant something to each other for a long time. Which makes me nothing but a fool.

Fuck me.

My heart sinks. I knew it was too good to be true. It was all a game to him. A game that he has clearly grown bored of.

Sophie grabs me by the hand and pulls me back into the house with Jared following behind. Without a backward glance, we head straight for the front door and leave the Dragons behind. "You okay, babe?" Sophie asks, slipping her hand into mine and holding me close as I feel my world starting to crumble.

"No," I tell her, feeling empty inside. "I really liked that one."

"I know," she sighs, her heart breaking right along with mine.

"I'd kick his ass if it wasn't so likely he'd snap me like a twig," Jared says as he pulls me against him.

Words escape me as we make our way home, dragging my feet like the pathetic fool I am. "Well, doing the rest of the assignment is going to be a tad awkward now," Sophie murmurs as we push our way through the door.

Crap. I didn't even think about that. I groan as I stumble down the hallway and into my room. I find my pajamas then head into the bathroom and strip out of my clothes for a hot shower. Sophie makes her way into the bathroom and begins brushing her teeth as I step into the hot water. "What are you going to do about your date tomorrow night?" she asks.

"I think his ego could stand getting knocked down a few steps. Maybe he'll even get stood up for the first time in his life," I say, getting an odd satisfaction out of the thought, although it doesn't take long for that satisfaction to disappear as the hurt takes over once again.

I finish up in the shower and head back to my room. After snuggling into my bed, I pull the blankets right up, and as I go to plug my phone into the charger, I notice a text message from the douchebag himself.

Miller - You keep disappearing on me. Hope you're okay.

My chest aches at his words, and I consider replying, despite knowing I should just forget about him.

Dani - Wasn't feeling well. Jared and Sophie took me home. Not sure tomorrow night is such a great idea.

Delete.

Damn it, the fucker can just work it out himself.

And with that, I turn my phone off and crash back onto my pillow, tears in my eyes and a heart aching to be loved.

It's barely six in the morning when I wake from the shittiest sleep known to man, and desperately needing to clear my head, I take myself for a run. After pulling on my shorts and training crop, I throw my hair up and head out the door.

A new day, a new me. No more Miller Cain weighing me down.

I head out into the early morning breeze and run until my lungs give out. Not even realizing I've made my way down his street, my eyes bug out of my head when I find myself right in front of his house as the front door opens. Panic tears through me, and I search for somewhere to hide, but when a person who clearly isn't Miller appears in the doorway, relief pounds through my veins.

That relief quickly morphs into devastation as I realize it's the girl from last night. That prick took her home. Just perfect. I bet she was an easy fuck. She probably spread her legs in seconds for the King of the Dragons.

"Hurry up, Mills," she calls, not realizing that the runner out on the street is falling to pieces. "You promised me a breakfast date."

Just great. This chick has a nickname for him already. I'm sure she's been up half the night planning their wedding. She seems a little young for him, but hey, who am I to judge? It's not like we were actually together. It's not like I was starting to see the rest of our lives starting to play out.

"Alright, chill. I'm coming," I hear him grunt from inside. What a jerk. Plans a date with this chick for the morning and one with me for the same night.

Wonderful.

Realizing the time for escape is quickly diminishing, I break into a run and sprint past his place. The fear that he'll come out and discover me gawking at his new girlfriend like the loser I am is what spurs me on. And to think I actually told him about Brett. What an idiot.

I make it home and instantly slide myself right back into bed. There's just no point in anything today.

It's well after midday when I drag my ass out of bed and grab my phone before heading into the kitchen. I sit up on a stool as Jared cooks bacon and eggs and I turn my phone back on to find a slew of texts.

Four new messages. One from Mom and three from Miller.

Mom - Hi honey, just checking in. We miss you.

Miller - Morning. What happened to you last night? I wanted you to meet someone.

Miller - You still alive? I'll pick you up at seven for our non-date.

Miller - ??

Fuck, I can't have him coming around here.

Dani - Don't worry about me, I'm fine. Tonight isn't such a great idea.

My phone rings immediately, his name flashing up on my screen. I hit ignore and get to work on downing my bacon and egg roll as Jared watches me curiously through narrowed eyes. Miller attempts to call a few more times before finally giving up and leaving me to celebrate my pity party for one.

Once I'm finished eating, Jared and I curl up on the couch to watch *The Legend of Tarzan,* because who doesn't want to watch Alexander Skarsgård's extremely ripped body getting around half-naked? We *ooh* and *ahh* at the screen and pause at all the right places while I wait for Jared to wipe the drool off his face.

Jared hops up and heads into the kitchen, bringing a grin to my face when I hear the familiar sound of popcorn in the microwave, followed by that heavenly, buttery smell. He returns a few minutes later with two overflowing bowls and hands me one. Before his ass even hits the couch beside me, I'm scooping a massive handful right into my mouth.

A knock sounds at the door and Jared immediately looks at me with big puppy dog eyes, pleading for me to answer it. "Nope, no way,"

I tell him. "Today is my wallow day. And besides, you're the closest."

Knowing there's no way he's about to win this round, he lets out a huff and gets back to his feet. "Fine," he grumbles, placing his bowl down on the coffee table and making sure I hit pause on the perfection that is Tarzan.

I listen as he makes his way to the door, wondering who the hell it could be since neither of us have plans. He pulls the door open, and I feel the tension all the way from the living room. "What are you doing here?" he demands in a tone that makes my back stiffen.

"I just need to see her," I hear Miller respond in a pained voice.

Ahh, fuck.

"I think you should go," Jared tells him, more than ready to hold him back. "You've done enough."

"The fuck? What is it that you think I've done? Please, clue me in," Miller snaps.

Jared sighs and the sound breaks my heart. "I had high hopes for you, man."

"Good, because I'm not going anywhere. I promised my girl a date, and I intend to keep that promise," Miller says with confidence.

"Come on, man. Cut your losses and run. You're not seeing her today.".

"Dude, don't keep me from her. If I have to knock you out, I will."

Shit.

I groan and flick my blanket off before setting my popcorn beside Jared's. I get up and storm my way to the front door, hating how fucking delicious he looks in the doorway. "Miller, it's not going to happen," I say, pushing past Jared, who harrumphs and leaves.

"Fuck that, baby. I've waited long enough for you, and I'm not letting you give up now," he tells me, with an urgency in his eyes that has me dying on the inside. "When will you see that we're perfect together?"

"I did see that and I wanted it," I tell him as a lone tear escapes my eye. "I wanted it so bad it hurt."

He steps toward me and reaches up, making me flinch at his touch, but I don't pull away as he wipes the teardrop with his thumb. There's confusion in his eyes, but he's not ready to back down just yet. "Then what the hell happened?"

"What happened?" I scoff in disbelief. "As if you don't know. That chick was curled around you so tight you couldn't peel her off if you tried. You made me look like an idiot and then adding salt to the wound, you go and take her home."

Miller gapes at me a moment before a wide grin stretches across his face, his eyes dancing with silent laughter. Without warning, he rushes me, pressing me up against the wall and taking me by the waist. "You were jealous," he smirks.

"Get off me, you big jerk," I snap, trying to push him away.

"How many times do I need to tell you that I'm not going anywhere?" he insists, tightening his grip on my waist.

I shake my head, the tears still falling. "You're delusional if you think I'm going to let you play me."

"You know I'm crazy about you, which means you're delusional for thinking I would ever try to hurt you. I haven't even looked at another girl since I met you," he says with such sincerity that it has my heart breaking all over again.

"You're a moron. I saw it with my own eyes," I snap.

He pushes me harder against the wall and presses his body up against mine. "Fuck, I love it when you're angry," he whispers.

Need pulses through my traitorous bitch of a body as I feel his erection pressing up against my belly. "Miller, you need to go," I say, my voice breaking.

He takes a deep breath and leans back so he can look me in the eye. "Mia, the girl from last night. She's my little sister. She came to surprise me at the game, and I let her crash at my place," he explains.

Fuck. Sister?

"I told you, I want to be with you. I haven't felt like this about anyone before, and fuck, I'm not going to screw this up," he says.

"Sister?" I confirm.

He nods. "Little sister."

My heart races as I take his face in both my hands and look him in the eyes, the tears only getting worse as the emotional rollercoaster exhausts me. "I'm sorry," I tell him with every bit of honesty I possess. "I fucked up."

"Yeah, you did," he agrees, leaning forward and pressing his lips to mine in the open doorway.

Sophie steps through at that exact moment. "Fuck, you two give me whiplash," she comments as she passes us, Tank trailing behind her.

A giggle escapes me as Miller pulls back. "Can I take you on that date now?" he asks with a satisfied grin.

"No," I say and smirk as his face falls. "I said you could take me out for dinner. I've just had lunch and I'm in my pajamas."

"What are we going to do until dinner time?" he asks, suggestively.

"Oh, I have a few ideas," I tell him, leaning forward and pressing my lips to the sensitive skin on his neck.

He lets out a moan and presses himself into me so I can feel the hard, thick outline of his erection grinding against me. His hands wind down my body and grab my ass before effortlessly lifting me into his arms. Locking my legs around his waist, he kicks the door closed behind him and sails down the hallway, his lips fused to mine.

CHAPTER 14

MILLER

We crash down onto Dani's bed, her legs still locked around my waist as she grips my shirt and pulls it over my head. Her nails dig into my back with urgency, and with every little touch, she drives me wild with desire.

"God, I need you," she pants between kisses.

My hands find the fabric of her shirt, and I shimmy it up between our bodies before pulling it over her head. I drop it to the ground and make quick work of her bra, needing to feel her skin beneath my fingers, needing to take those perfect nipples into my mouth. Tossing her bra aside, I pull back to take in her stunning body, only the desire is too much, and I lean down and suck her nipple into my mouth. She moans my name as she grinds against me, searching for relief, which

I'm more than happy to give her.

Making my way down her body, I hook my fingers into the waistband of her pajama shorts and pull them down her toned legs, panties, and all, exposing her sweet cunt. Hunger fires through me, and I trail my fingers down her body and over her clit, watching the way her body jolts with anticipation. I keep going until I'm at her entrance and don't hesitate as I plunge two fingers deep inside her, smirking as her body arches off the bed with my name on her lips.

I work her body, moving my fingers in and out of her, massaging her walls and using my thumb to press down on her clit, rubbing small circles as she squirms beneath me. I can't wait any longer. I have to taste her.

Moving down her bed, I watch her suck in a breath, seeing the intention in my eyes, and as she moans, I dive right in, giving her exactly what she needs. My tongue flicks over her sensitive clit, once, twice, three times, and she reaches down, knotting her hands into my hair. "Oh, fuck. Miller," she groans.

I give her exactly what she wants, nipping, sucking, licking as my fingers continue working her cunt. Her body arches off the bed, unable to keep still. She's so fucking responsive. "Shit, I'm going to come," she tells me, her grip tightening in my hair.

I grin against her but don't dare stop. I need to taste her as she comes. Need to feel that sweet pussy spasming around my fingers.

Keeping her going, I watch as she throws her head back and comes hard for me, her legs locking around my head as her pussy convulses and spasms. I keep going, eating her sweet cunt until her high rocks through her body and she's finally able to relax.

"Holy shit," she pants as I make my way back up to her face, stopping to take her nipple into my mouth. I press my lips to hers, letting her taste herself, and she moans into my mouth as her hands slip between our bodies and begin undoing my belt.

Dani rids me of my pants in record time and frees my heavy cock, her fingers greedily curling around me and tightening at my base. She starts working her way up and down, her thumb roaming over my tip and making my body jolt with undeniable pleasure.

"Fuck, babe," I groan as she presses her lips to the base of my neck, her tongue roaming over my skin and working its way up.

Her hand is like my fucking kryptonite. Scrap that, Dani is my kryptonite. As she works me, I reach down between us, slowly rubbing her clit before pushing my fingers back inside her. She groans and rocks her hips, asking for more, and damn it, I'm going to give it to her.

Needing to be inside her, I reach for my jeans and grab a condom. "No," she says, and I raise my brow in question. "I want to feel you inside me. I'm on the pill," she tells me, wrapping her legs around my waist to draw me back to her.

"You sure?" I ask.

"Yeah . . . I mean, as long as you're comfortable with it and you're not going to, you know, give me anything?" she cringes.

I smirk down at her, having no idea how I landed myself such an amazing woman. "Yeah, baby, I'm good. I've never done this without one of these little guys," I tell her as I toss the condom on her bedside table.

"Well," she smirks. "What are you waiting for, Captain?"

Fuck me.

I don't need any more encouragement than that. I position myself at her entrance, watching her face as I slowly push into her. Dani sucks in a breath as I let out a soft groan at the way her pussy envelopes me, squeezing tight until I'm as deep as her body will allow. Her nails dig into my shoulders as she moans my name once again. It's a sound I will never tire of.

Pulling back, I start to move, and we both gasp at the agonizingly slow rhythm.

She's fucking perfect.

Picking up my pace, I roam my hands over her body then slam deep inside her. "Yes," she gasps, and I do it again, fucking her hard. I grab her ass and raise her ever so slightly, taking her deeper than before.

Dani's walls start to clench around my cock, and she groans my name, but I'm not nearly finished with her yet. Pressing down on her clit, I rub tight, fast circles and she sucks in a gasp. "Holy shit, Miller," she pants. "Yes."

She pulls me down closer to her, and I kiss her eagerly, my balls tightening, desperate for a release. She presses her body up against mine, and I scoop my arm around her waist, holding her to me. "I'm gonna come," she pants.

"Fucking give it to me, Dani," I growl in her ear. "I need to feel you squeezing my cock."

"Oh, God," she moans, tipping her head back.

I don't stop moving, fucking her just the way she needs. As I thrust back into her tight cunt, she comes undone, her walls convulsing around me, squeezing me tight as her orgasm claims her. I come with her, shooting my load deep inside her, but I don't stop moving until she comes down from her high.

"Fuck, that was amazing," I tell her, looking down at her flushed face, gasping for air.

She smiles up at me, melting my heart. Yep, I'm a goner. I'm definitely falling in love with this girl.

"Good," she tells me. "Because I need to shower, and I'm not nearly done with you yet."

She clambers off the bed, grabbing my hand and pulling me along with her, and I do what I can to cover my junk as we break out into the hallway. She drags me toward the bathroom, and there's no doubt by the smirk on Jared's face, he got one hell of an eyeful of my still-very-hard dick.

An hour later, the water runs cold, and I wrap a towel around Dani after having taken her twice more. Her hair drips all over the bathroom floor, and she laughs as we scurry back to her room. We chill for a while, and after leaving her to get dressed for our non-date, I sit with Tank out in the living room watching the game.

Dani emerges twenty minutes later in a little black dress with the sexiest fuck-me-heels I've ever seen. She does a slow turn, revealing just how backless the little number is, and I suddenly don't know if I want to take her out to show her off or keep her locked up so I can have her all over again.

Tank lets out an appreciative low whistle that has me wanting to rip his throat out, but what can I do? Every guy we see tonight is going to do the same thing. It's inevitable.

She flicks her golden hair over her shoulder and struts toward me, looking like the absolute goddess she is. "So, where are we going?" she asks.

I shake my head. "You'll have to wait and see," I tell her as she grabs hold of me and pulls me over the back of the couch. I have to scramble to help her, but damn, I fucking love this playful side of her.

"You're seriously not going to tell me?" she laughs.

"Nope. I've had a very long time to plan this out. I'm not about to ruin the surprise now."

She smiles up at me as Sophie appears in the hallway wearing nothing but a bra and undies, and as hot as she is, for the first time in my life I find myself looking away.

"I thought you were getting dressed?" Tank complains.

She gives him a sultry look. "I was, but I decided I wanted to do something else tonight," she says, reaching behind her to unclasp her bra before dropping it to the ground. "Whoops," she smirks.

Tank growls low in his throat as he charges for Sophie and grabs her by the ass, lifting her over his shoulder and disappearing back down the hallway. The sharp slap of his hand on her ass echoes through the small cottage.

Dani laughs, shaking her head at their display. "Those two are perfect for each other."

I bring her attention back to me. "Just like another couple I know."

"Couple?" she asks, raising her eyebrows at me.

"Yeah. I told you, I'm done waiting," I tell her, hoping she truly hears me this time. "You're mine. I know it. You know it. Hell, the whole fucking campus knows it. So it's about time you accept it and embrace the goodness that is us."

She looks at me with curiosity and is silent for a while. "So, if I'm yours, does that make you all mine to do and have as I please?"

"Abso-fucking-lutely."

She grins up at me and launches herself into my arms, crushing her soft lips to mine. I feel her smile against me, and I know she's just overcome something massive. She's finally ready to leave the past behind and focus on her future. To move past all the hurt and betrayal her ex caused and let herself trust again. She can look forward to a future with me where she won't always be looking over her shoulder or worrying about where I am at night because, no matter what, I'll always be coming home to her. She'll never have to fear that she'll be hurt again, whether it's physically, mentally, or emotionally.

Dani pulls back from me with a new air about her, and I realize a huge weight has been lifted off her shoulders. "Come on," I tell her, lacing my fingers through hers and escorting her out to my Escalade. "Let me take you out for the night of your life."

We drive for half an hour, and I pull up by an outdoor restaurant that overlooks the lake.

"Wow, this is beautiful," Dani says as she takes in the lake and open-air restaurant. "I had no idea this was here."

"Neither did I until Tank clued me in."

I lead her down into the restaurant and find our table. "So, tell me more about your sister," she asks as we sit down. "I feel kind of bad for leaving before I could meet her."

"Don't worry, she can meet you another time," I tell her, then smile at the fond memories of my little sister, trying to figure out a way to sum up the million amazing things about her. "Mia is . . . I don't know how to put it. She's a bit of everything. She's frustrating and charming at the same time and easily the best little sister a guy could ask for," I smile.

"It's nice she came to watch you skate. I kind of wish I had a sibling like that," she says.

"Yeah, to tell the truth, I'm kind of pissed she drove all the way here. She hasn't been driving for that long."

"Really? How old is she? I could have sworn she looked around nineteen or twenty."

"Nah," I laugh. "She wishes. She's only seventeen. She'll be finishing high school this year and will hopefully be here next year. She wants to be a doctor."

"Wow, that's huge," she smiles.

"Yeah, it is. She's the kind of girl who will work her ass off to get what she wants. She's a bit like you."

Her face flushes, but our conversation falls short when the waiter arrives with menus and water for the table. "Okay," she says, looking back up at me, "Tell me about last season. I've been dying to know. What was that big fight about?"

"What is this? Twenty-one questions?" I laugh.

"It can be," she smiles and fixes me with an innocent look as if to say *I'm waiting*.

"Fine," I smirk, knowing damn well I would give in to anything this woman asked of me. "So, we were up against the team from L.A., and Danny, our captain, had a bit of trouble with a few of the guys on the other team. All because of some girl. I think someone slept with someone else's sister or something like that. So, come game night, it got rough. It was penalty after penalty. A fucking bloodbath. The further in we got, the uglier the game became. There were taunts and comments thrown around everywhere. We were just minutes out from the end and only two points down when it turned into a fucking blood bath. We lost the championship and our reputation, all because Danny couldn't keep his dick in his pants."

"Woah. I wasn't expecting that," she says, trying to hide her amused smirk. "I mean there are heaps of stories going around about what happened, but nothing quite like that."

"Yeah . . . Coach didn't want that one getting out."

"Shit," she laughs. "What happened to Danny?"

"He was supposed to get signed to the NHL, but he lost his contract. Ruined his career before it even began," I explain.

"Well, it's a good thing the Dragons have a good captain this season."

"You bet your ass they do," I laugh.

We spend the next hour lost in conversation as we dig deeper into each other's lives. I find myself lost in her eyes, watching the way she comes alive with animation as she speaks of her parents and life. When the conversation seems to reach a natural stopping point, I settle the bill and drive her back home, stopping by the ice creamery on the way.

"You want to do something really stupid?" I ask, pulling up to the curb outside her house.

"Do something stupid with Miller Cain? Um . . . of course," she laughs.

I pull out of her street and drive the two minutes up the road to the campus parking lot. "What are we doing here?" she asks, her brows furrowed as she glances around.

"You'll see," I smirk, hopping out of my truck and meeting her around the back. Taking her hand, I lead her through the college and sneak through the back entrance of the athletic building. She follows along nervously as I make my way up and down what feels like a million hallways.

"Where the hell are you taking me?" she whisper-yells beside me.

I smirk down at her. "Wait and see."

Pushing through yet another door, it opens into a huge open room with an Olympic-size swimming pool. I turn and watch her face as she registers where she is. Her eyes widen and her mouth pops open as she takes in the massive pool before her. "Fancy a swim?" I taunt, taking a step toward her and shrugging out of my shirt.

She instantly begins shaking her head. "No. No way," she says, stepping back as her eyes hungrily travel down my torso. "Don't you dare."

"You better lose the dress real fast," I order.

Her eyes snap to mine. "I'm not going in," she says with an attitude that gets me hard.

"Lose it now, or you'll have nothing dry to put on afterward," I warn, taking another step toward her and popping the button on my jeans.

Dani subtly slips out of her fuck-me-heels while giving me a seductive look. My jeans fall to the floor and I step out of them, watching her as she watches me. She bites down on her lower lip and studies me with hooded eyes, but I'm no fool. This chick is getting ready to bolt, and just as expected, she takes off at a million miles an hour.

I race after her, easily catching her and throwing her over my shoulder. "No," she screeches, batting at my back as she desperately tries to get out of my hold.

"Last chance to lose the dress," I laugh.

"No, no, no, no . . . It's going to be cold."

"Damn straight it is." I let out one last laugh as I pull her off my shoulder and carry her in my arms. I can't help but smile as she squeezes her eyes shut in preparation for the water.

Dani squeals as I leap forward and plunge us deep into the freezing water. We swim up to the surface and gasp for air. "Shit, it's cold," she laughs then narrows her green eyes on me. "I can't believe you just did that."

"Believe it, baby," I tell her. I make my way over to her and wrap her in my arms. "I really wish you'd lost the dress."

"I bet you do," she smirks before pulling her dress up over her head and flinging it to the side, making a wet slapping sound as it lands against the tiles. "This better?" she asks, her tone dropping low as her eyes become hooded.

"Definitely." I move into her, and her legs come up around me as she brings her soft lips to mine. "You are nothing short of perfection," I tell her, our lips moving together.

We spend a good half hour in the pool before her lips begin turning blue, and I help her out, giving her my shirt to wear. I can't help but be both thankful and disappointed that it comes halfway down her thighs. I lead her back out the maze of hallways and back to the car, and before I know it, we're pulling to a stop in front of her home.

"Thanks for tonight," she tells me as I walk her to her door. "It was honestly the best date I've ever been on. You know, for a non-date," she adds, her eyes sparkling with silent laughter.

"That was definitely not a non-date," I tell her. "But I'm glad you had a good time. It was the best date I've ever been on too. Actually, come to think of it, it's the only date I've ever been on."

Dani's eyes grow round, and she gapes at me as though I have two heads. "What?" she screeches. "How is that possible? You're like the biggest man-whore around here."

I shrug as if it's no big deal. "*Was* the biggest man-whore," I correct. "There has never been a girl worth taking out. Not until you."

"But you've had girlfriends, right?" she asks, a little confused.

"Yeah," I laugh. "I've had plenty, but never thought they were worth dating. I just kept them around for the easy ass."

"Oh, God," she laughs, swatting at my chest. "That's so wrong."

"Hey, I was a different guy back then," I defend, catching her hands and pulling her into my chest.

She laughs, then looks up at me with a nervous glint in her eye. "Did you want to stay the night?"

"Baby, you know I do. But you better be sure because I'm not going to be able to say no," I tell her honestly.

"I'm sure," she smiles, then takes me by the hand and leads me inside to her bedroom, where I show her all over again just how much she means to me.

CHAPTER 15

DANIELLE

I never thought waking up next to a man could be so amazing. I mean, sure, I'd woken up beside Brett countless times, but with Miller, it's different. It's right.

I snuggle into his warm body and his arms tighten around me. "Good morning," he croons, his voice thick with sleep.

"Morning." I roll in his arms and place a feather-soft kiss on his lips before sitting up in bed and trying to scoot to the edge.

"Where do you think you're going?" he questions as he grabs my waist and pulls me back down to the bed, pinning my body with his. He hovers above me, his dark gaze fixed on mine.

"I have to pee," I laugh as I try to escape from under him.

"Just five more minutes," he begs, adjusting his body harder into mine so I can feel his arousal.

I separate my legs and hook them around his hips so I can feel his length pressing against my core. "Damn it," I laugh as I wrap my arms around his neck and pull him down to me.

Miller groans and brings his lips down to my neck, forcing a moan out of me, and I grind myself up against him, his hand disappearing down between my legs. His fingers circle my clit then slide down to my entrance to find me ready and waiting.

My hands move down his toned body, and I hook my thumbs into the waistband of his underwear, before pushing them down just enough to free his thick cock.

The need for him is too great, and I bypass the foreplay and curl my fingers around his length before guiding him inside me. We both groan as he thrusts into me, seating himself deep inside. He takes control and pushes me over the edge not two minutes later.

We come together, panting against each other's skin. "I could get used to waking up like that," he murmurs, his gaze so soft and sincere.

"Me too," I whisper, running my nails up and down his strong, muscled back.

"Alright," he says a moment later, sitting up and pulling me with him. "Get your ass dressed so I can take you out for breakfast."

A wide grin stretches across my face, and I quickly rush through a shower, rinsing the chlorine from my hair, before darting back into my room and getting dressed. I hear Miller out in the kitchen chatting away to Tank, Jared, and Ashton, and I can't help but smile. I love the way our two groups are coming together.

After pulling on a yellow summer dress, I throw my hair up into a messy bun and finish off the look with a little mascara and lip gloss. I stand in front of the mirror and am pleased to find the old me. The me who was confident and happy. The me who found herself sexy and bold, not the jumpy, uneasy girl Brett turned me into. I have Miller to thank for that.

Miller Cain has saved me from myself.

Grabbing my handbag, I pull my phone from the charger on my bedside table to find a text from an unknown number. I quickly scan over it on my way out of my room.

Unknown - Baby, I miss you. Did you get my flowers? Come back to me.

Anxiety pulses through my body and I find myself pausing in the hallway. It couldn't be Brett, could it? Has he found my new number already? And why, after all this time?

Dani - Who is this?
Unknown - It's Brett. I wasn't lying when I said you were mine. I want you back, Dani. You know we're perfect together.

Holy crap. The flowers were from him. God, now I'm glad Sophie stole them off the dining table and put them in her room.

Fear trickles through me, but I know it's stupid. I'm with Miller now, and there's not a damn thing Brett can do about it. He's stupid if he thinks I'll ever go back to him after the hell he put me through.

Dani - Delete my number, Brett. I've moved on.
Brett - The hockey guy? Come on, baby, stop being ridiculous and come home.

Deciding not to respond, I throw my phone in my handbag and take a deep breath to calm my nerves. I'm not going to let that douchebag ruin this for me. I quickly double back to my room and glance in the mirror one more time before finding my way to the kitchen in search of the man I am quickly falling in love with.

Miller's eyes find me the second I step into the kitchen. His eyes roam up and down my body with an appreciative smile, then come to a stop on my face. His brows pull together and he steps into me, wrapping his arms around my body. "You okay?" he murmurs, his voice filled with concern.

"Yeah," I smile up at him, shaking it off. "I am now."

"I'd like to thank you all for coming out to our 'One Night With' auction today, to help support the Dragons as we raise funds for the Denver Youth Hockey Program," I say into the microphone. I stand up on my makeshift stage in front of what must be at least one thousand men and women, who quieten down at hearing my voice through the speakers from all their chanting and cheering for my boys.

It has been such a crazy day. Although I spent the last few weeks promoting the shit out of the auction, far more people have shown up than I ever could have imagined.

We had originally set up in one of the lecture halls, but after the massive turnout, we had to move it to the ice rink, where I currently stand in the middle of the ice on a little stage, looking up into the grandstand with a thousand faces staring back at me. The eyes on me do nothing for my nerves, but there's no way in hell Sophie was going to stand up here, so this gig is all mine.

"Alright, let's meet our boys," I sing. "Please put your hands together for the undefeated Kings of Denver, the mighty Denver Dragons!"

The crowd roars as Miller leads the boys onto the ice. They all show off as they skate around the rink, motioning for the crowd to get as loud as possible. For an arena that can hold eight thousand people, this crowd is certainly doing a great job of filling it with noise.

Miller makes a hand gesture to the boys, and they make a quick, final lap before coming and taking their seats in the row of chairs lined up on the ice, facing the crowd.

"Okay. Before we get started, let's cover a few things," I say, getting a collective groan from the crowd and the boys. "As many of you would be aware, the majority of the team are single and have generously volunteered themselves to be auctioned off tonight." I receive a scoff from every single one of my boys. "Okay, so maybe I may have slightly twisted their arms, but what the hell. They still showed up and that's all that counts."

The crowd cheers and whoops for the boys, and I laugh before continuing. "We are playing by standard auction rules. If you would like to make a bid on one of these fine young men, just raise your hand."

I spare the boys a quick glance before turning back to the stands. "Alright, let's get this party started," I holler through the microphone, sending the crowd into another round of cheers. "Calm down, calm down. I'm sure you would all like to get this over with as quickly as possible to get the most out of your time with these boys."

I spin to face the boys and smirk at them. Every last one of them narrows their eyes at me, trying to work out what secret I hold. My gaze roams over the team before sailing across to the barriers and coming to a stop on Coach Harris who watches at the sidelines. "Coach," I start, "please step forward and show these fine people what you're made of."

The boys grin at me as Coach Harris' mouth pops open in shock. Yeah, we definitely didn't discuss this.

"No," he says, shaking his head. "This wasn't part of the deal."

The crowd boos and I turn my gaze on them. "Can I hear from all the lovely women and men out there who would love the chance to win 'One Night With' the strapping Coach Harris?" The crowd roars, causing his face to turn beet red.

"You've got to lead by example," Tank laughs before cutting across the ice and waving Coach into the center.

Coach groans, but eventually obliges and stands in the center, playing along as he flexes his muscles for his eager fans, which naturally, sends them wild. Coach Harris definitely keeps in shape, so I'm not surprised.

I start the auction off at a hundred dollars, and I must say, we're all shocked when we sell him off for five hundred and sixty dollars to none other than Professor Whitaker. We're going to rake it in tonight. Coach struts back to his position at the end of the row of Dragons, looking extremely pleased with himself.

I turn my attention back to the boys. "Alright, which one of you misfits is up next?"

A man from the crowd shoots up and hollers, "I wouldn't mind winning you for the night, Dani."

The audience breaks into laughter, but Miller's not having it. He shoots to his feet. "She's not for sale," he snaps, staring the man down with unfiltered venom.

The man in the crowd backs off as the women sigh dreamily at Miller's protective-boyfriend side. The moment he could, Miller made it a well-known fact that we're together. In fact, after the last four weeks of accepting the inevitable, we have apparently now become the new "it couple" on campus.

FML.

"Cut it out," I warn playfully. "I don't know about you, but I'd like to see what kind of dough these boys bring in," I say, getting right back on point. "Bobby," I say, looking at the man in question. "Why don't you lead the team off tonight?" I gesture to the center of the ice. In true Bobby fashion, he groans and makes his way over, though there's no mistaking the excited sparkle deep within his eyes. In fact, I see it in all of their eyes.

Bobby goes for eight hundred and forty-five dollars and the

audience gives a round of applause. The auction moves on steadily with the prices rising higher and higher as I get closer to the seniors.

The boys snicker and giggle to themselves when Jaxon is sold for one thousand, three hundred dollars to Jared. I realize that the team must have put Jared up to it because I know for a fact that he's crazy in love with his boyfriend and would never bid on Jaxon. I bet the team paid him to do it. My suspicion is confirmed the second I lock eyes with Jared, who gives me the wickedest grin I've ever seen.

I roll my eyes and get on with it, excited to see how far we can take this.

As each boy gets auctioned off, I'm left with the Dream Team, Tank and Miller, the two team members who are currently not single. "Okay, ladies and gentlemen, that completes our single volunteers for our 'One Night With' auction," I explain as the audience boos, each and every one of them wanting to get their hands on the two major prizes in the team. "But . . . I have personally spoken to the girlfriends of these two fine specimens, and they have agreed to put their men up for auction," I tell them, getting cheers and hollers from the crowd while Tank and Miller get out of their chairs to protest. "As long as you horn dogs promise to keep your hands to yourselves," I warn, causing the crowd to laugh as one.

The boys skate over, and Miller takes the microphone from my hands and flicks the off switch. "No," he says immediately. "I'm a one-woman man."

"I second that," Tank says.

"Quit it," I say. "Don't think of it as a date. Just imagine it as spending time with a fan for a good cause. Do it for your team."

"Fuck the team," Miller says. "I don't want to take someone else out."

I roll my tongue over my bottom lip. "Do this for your team, and I'll let you claim my ass."

Miller's brow arches. "Really?"

"Uh-huh."

"Fine," he growls unhappily as Tank groans right along with him. Joke's on him, though. I would have let him claim my ass anyway.

Miller makes his way back to his seat while Tank stands front and center. The bidding starts straight away, starting at one thousand and getting higher by the second. Fans all around raise their hands over and over, trying their luck at getting their "One Night With" Tank.

Sophie stands by the side, watching with raised brows and her mouth hanging open, much like the rest of us. The figure keeps rising higher and higher, finally coming to a close at three thousand, four hundred and fifty-eight dollars. To think, Sophie gets to take that home for free.

Tank takes his seat, looking extremely impressed with himself, as Miller stands and skates to the center. He glances over at me with regret in his eyes, and I know this is killing him, but I can't say no. He's the captain and needs to do this for his team. I blow him a kiss, which seems to brighten his mood.

The Miller Show immediately turns on as he puts on a front for the crowd, showing himself off with the cocky attitude that the crowd truly believes he possesses. They eat it up like he's their last meal.

The bidding quickly takes off. Just like Tank, it starts at one thousand. It goes higher and higher as bidder after bidder raises their hands.

The bidding flies easily past three thousand and jumps to three and a half when he releases one of those damn sexy half-smirks that only a man can do.

He glances at me with mischief in his eyes, and no matter how much he hates taking another woman out, he truly does love the attention. He slowly shrugs out of his shirt, showing off his perfect body and sending the crowd wild. Particularly the women, but I'd be lying if I didn't say I saw a few men getting a good look at my man too.

The bidding rises to four thousand and then to five and comes to a screeching halt when one very familiar woman stands up, raises her hand, and calls out, "Ten thousand dollars."

Miller's head whips around to the voice with confusion, probably wondering why some strange cougar is dropping so much money on him.

I hear a chorus of "Fuck," murmured through the surprised crowd. "Mom?" I ask, stunned.

The crowd hushes as they try to figure out what's happening with eyes flicking between me and my crazy mother. "Sorry, hon. I couldn't let you auction off your man," she shouts over the distance.

I see Miller visibly relax from the corner of my eye, and I can't help but smile for my own relief. "Well, there you have it, guys," I say into the microphone. "Thank you so much for making it out tonight. Please make sure that all of our successful bidders make their way down to sort payment and find your man," I explain. "And boys," I say, fixing them all with a hard stare. "Remember what we discussed in the locker room," I remind them, referring to the rule about no sexual favors. They all groan and smirk as they nod along.

"Alright, get out of here," I laugh.

The crowd quickly shuffles out of the ice rink as the boys make their way over to me.

"That was surprising," Coach Harris says, extremely stunned.

"Do you have any idea how much money we raised?" Aaron asks.

"Not sure," I tell them. "But my guess would be somewhere upwards of twenty-five grand. I won't know until I can sit down with a calculator, but that, including the thirty we've already made from the calendars, is pretty damn impressive."

The boys laugh as we celebrate our huge win for the night. "Go get your skates off. You've all got a woman to impress," I say, then glance over to Jaxon. "Except you. Jared loves Chinese food, by the way."

"Shut up," he groans as they all break away and head for the locker room.

Miller stays behind and helps me down off the little stage before carrying me to the side where I can stand without making a fool of myself. "Looks like I've got a date with your mom," he comments.

"Looks like it," I laugh.

"Any tips?" he asks nervously.

"No, she's super easy," I tell him. "Just be your normal, charming self. But if that fails, lose your shirt."

CHAPTER 16

MILLER

"Hey man, have you seen this?" Tank asks as he kicks his way through my front door.

I hit pause on my game as I glance up at him. "Seen what?"

He throws his phone down into my lap as he passes me and heads for the kitchen, opening the fridge and pulling out a beer. "The girls' latest article was just posted."

"Ahh," I say, picking up his phone to find the article. I quickly read through it and find a huge grin on my face by the time I get to the end. "Fuck, they make us sound so much better than we are," I laugh as I scroll through the pictures Dani attached to the article. I get to the end to find it's already been viewed over two thousand times.

Tank comes and joins me on the couch, picking up my discarded controller and hitting play. "I know," he says. "They're killing this assignment." He grins proudly, and I must say, it's a nice change to see this guy finally with a woman he loves.

"Yeah," I smile. "So, what's up?"

"Nothing. Wanted to chill."

"Bullshit. I saw you two hours ago. You never want to chill after a gym session."

He places the controller down on the coffee table next to his beer and takes a deep breath. "I'm thinking about asking Sophie to move in with me," he says just as I lift my drink to my lips and tip its contents down my throat.

I do my best not to spray it all over my living room as I take him in. "What?" I ask, completely shocked. Tank prides himself on living alone and hates company. Hell, the dickhead didn't even want to move in with me. "That's pretty serious. It's a huge step for you."

"I know, man," he says. "But I can't imagine not living with her. We're practically together every night anyway."

"True. How do you think she's going to take it?" I ask with a smirk, knowing just how hard Tank has had to fight to get any sort of commitment out of that girl.

"Fuck man, you know what she's like," he laughs. "It won't be good. She'll have my balls for even asking, but she'll give in eventually."

"Yeah, she will," I agree.

"How are things going with Dani?" he asks, picking up the controller once again.

I smile, thinking about my sweet girl. "Great," I tell him honestly. "She's amazing, but I feel like she's hiding something."

"Hiding something?" he asks with curiosity. "What? Like she's cheating?"

"Nah, nothing like that," I tell him. "I don't know, it's like something has her running scared. She puts on a brave face and acts like nothing's wrong, but I can see it. Something's bothering her."

"Did you ask her about it?"

"Nah," I comment with sarcasm then give him a stupid look. "Of course I asked her, you fucking idiot. What kind of shitty boyfriend do you think I am?"

"Sorry, man, it was just a question. No need to bust my balls."

I smirk at him and shake my head in exasperation. "I've asked her a few times and she just shrugs it off, but I'll get to the bottom of it. Even if I've got to beat a few heads together to do it."

He nods, and I know he's thinking that he would do the same thing for Sophie. "Alright, man. Let me know if you need my help with anything."

"Sure."

We sit for another thirty minutes, going back and forth between the Xbox controllers when I finally decide to get up, grab in the second one, and switch to an NHL game so I can beat his ass on the screen as well as the ice.

A soft knock at the door startles me, and I put my controller on the table before heading to see who it is. I open the door to find Dani and Sophie standing before me with bags upon bags of groceries. "Well, well, to what do I owe this pleasure?" I ask, getting pushed aside by the girls who rush in toward the kitchen and put the groceries down on the counter, only to glance down at their reddening hands with groans of pain.

"We're making you two dinner," Dani declares as she strides up and presses a kiss to my lips.

"Oh really?" I ask, catching her around the waist before she has a chance to escape me. I deepen the kiss and moan as her tongue slips into my mouth.

Dani raises her hands to my chest and gently pushes me back. "Get out of here. We have work to do." She ushers me out of the kitchen, and I'm pushed back into the living room, unable to help the grin that takes over my face as I flop back onto the couch beside Tank.

"Who was that?" he asks, taking in my face.

"The girls. They're in the kitchen. They want to cook us dinner."

Tank's face falls. "Shit. What are we going to do?"

I laugh at his response, knowing there's nothing worse than Sophie and Dani's cooking from past experience. There's a reason they live with Jared and let him rule the kitchen. "What we always do, man. Suffer through the pain with a smile."

"Damn it," he sighs. "There's nothing I wouldn't do for that girl."

I groan at the early morning sunshine streaming through my window as my alarm goes off beside me. I reach over, turn it off, and uncurl myself from Dani's naked body. She groans in her sleep as I climb out from around her and pull the blankets back up to tuck her in.

Heading into the bathroom, I do my best to piss with my morning wood and quickly get ready for training, not wanting to disturb Dani's sleep. I go about the house making sure I've got everything I need, feeling good that today is going to be yet another great day.

Once I've downed a protein shake, I head back up to my room and kiss Dani goodbye. She stirs under my touch. "Where are you going?" she mumbles into her pillow with her eyes closed as her fingers lace through mine.

"Practice," I remind her as I run my finger along the side of her face, tucking a lock of golden hair behind her ear so it doesn't tickle her face. "Go back to sleep."

"Mmmkay."

I smile down at her and give her another kiss. "I'll see you later," I whisper as she falls back asleep, her hand coming loose from mine.

I pull the blanket back up again and get up off the bed. "Mmmm, love you," she moans in her sleep as she burrows her face into the pillow.

What? Did she just say *love you?*

"Baby?" I whisper into the darkness to no reply. Damn, she's asleep. I could have sworn she said she loves me. I knew today was going to be a great fucking day. I leave her be and make my way out the door, feeling pretty damn good about myself.

I get to the rink right on time and meet the boys in the locker room. "Look alive, boys," I holler across the room to the bunch of nitwits who all look half asleep.

"What's with all the energy?" Jaxon groans as he takes a seat to lace up his skates.

"You'd be like this too if you had the hottest chick on campus in your bed," I say, making sure to nail him in the back of the head as I pass.

I take my spot next to Tank and get to work on my training gear. "Seriously though," Tank starts, "what's with the good mood?"

I grin over at him like a five-year-old boy. "Dani said she loves me this morning."

"Shit, man. That's what I'm talking about," he grins as he holds his hand up for a fist bump.

"Well . . . she kind of said it."

"Huh?" he grunts, looking at me in confusion, letting his fist fall away before I get the chance to bump it, leaving me hanging.

I can't help the grin on my face, knowing exactly how he's going to react to this. "She was kind of asleep when she said it."

"Fuck, man," he booms in laughter, falling to the chair and holding his stomach as the boys watch with curious stares. "That shit doesn't count."

"Fucking does," I argue, ready to go down on this hill.

"Maybe to you," he scoffs at my expense. "But not to her."

Fuck. I hate it when he's right. I slouch down into my chair and get started on my skates when Coach Harris walks in. "Alright, ladies. On your feet."

We quickly finish up in the locker room and file out onto the ice to get started with our usual sprints and practice shots. Each and every one of us pulls it together and gives one hundred percent during training, and by the end of our two-hour session, we practically fall back into the locker room, dripping with sweat.

"Good work, boys," Coach praises as we start stripping off our sweaty gear. "Now, we're two-thirds of the way through the season and it's getting close to crunch time. We've been spotting a few scouts at the games, and I don't need to remind you what that means for all of your futures," he says as his gaze specifically lands on me and Tank. We both give him an understanding nod. "Good," he murmurs with a slight grin. I must remember to thank Dani. Coach has apparently continued dating Professor Whitaker after the auction and seems a shitload happier since.

"Now, game night, tomorrow night. You're up against the team from New York. Last year, these guys almost cleaned the ice with your asses. You had the speed and strength, but they possessed agility and footwork. So keep your heads in the game. No doubt they'll be playing dirty, so get in the attack zone and get that damn biscuit in the basket."

We nod, more than ready for tomorrow's game as he begins to wrap it up. "Okay, get yourselves cleaned up. I expect you all to put in at least an hour of gym time today, preferably focusing on your speed and agility." He gives us all a hard stare and disappears out the door.

We all leave together as the Zamboni finishes up on the ice and the

Figure Fairies get started on their session. Jaxon, Bobby, and Aaron all hang back to get the girls' attention, hoping they might want to drop their panties for them the same way the Puck Bunnies do, but these Figure Fairies are not the kind of chicks you want to mess with.

Tank and I keep walking, making our way out front and getting into our trucks after making plans to meet at the gym at 5 p.m. I get my ass back home to find Dani strutting around my place in a tight little tank and tiny sleep shorts. Did I mention she's not wearing a bra?

I dump my gear at the front door and collapse on the closest couch. Dani makes her way over and straddles my lap, and my hands instantly take possession of her waist. She bends down and places a kiss on my lips. "I missed waking up with you this morning."

"I missed it, too," I tell her, pulling her down harder against me. "But I've got to say, I loved hearing your sleepy monologue as I was leaving."

"Oh, shit," she gasps, sitting up a little straighter and looking at me with wide eyes. "What did I say?" She thinks hard, trying to remember what she might have slipped up with, and with each passing second, she only looks more concerned.

"Nothing, babe," I say, kissing her while grabbing her ass. I stand and lift her with me, the movement prompting her to wrap her legs around my waist. Heading to the stairs, I walk us up to my bedroom. "But, just so you know," I tell her, looking her right in the eyes so I have her full attention. "I love you too."

Her body tightens in my arms as she looks at me in shock. "You do?" she asks as her eyes grow watery.

"So fucking much," I declare.

She leans forward and kisses me with everything she's got. "You don't know how amazing it is to hear that," she says between kisses.

"I bet it feels a little something like when I heard you say it this morning."

"God, you're such a smartass," she laughs as I dump her on the edge of my bed and drop to my knees while I rip her shorts off her body.

Dani puts a foot up on my chest, halting my progression, and I take hold of her foot and wait to hear what she needs from me. She pulls her foot from my grasp and sits up on the edge of the bed, placing me right between her thighs and at eye level. She looks at me nervously and bites her lip.

I reach up and free her lip from her teeth. "What is it, Dani?" I ask.

She looks deep into my eyes and scoots herself forward so she falls into my lap. I catch her effortlessly and look down at her. "I love you," she tells me from the absolute bottom of her heart, the emotion loud and clear in both her voice and eyes.

My chest aches for her as I desperately catch her lips in mine and hold her against me. I raise us off the floor and gently lay her on the bed, taking the utmost care as I worship her body and make love to her. Knowing for the first time in my life, that not only do I love this beautiful woman with everything I am, but she will be my wife. The mother of my children. The only woman that I will ever give myself to for the rest of my life.

CHAPTER 17

DANIELLE

Sophie and I sit in the grandstand watching our men annihilate the team from New York. They've put in one of the best games of the season, and I know there was a scout here somewhere who wanted to check out the Dream Team in action.

They're down to the last few minutes of the game. Coach Harris is red in the face, screaming from the barrier. We already know we've won this one, but he wants them to finish it strong. Who can blame him?

Miller looks up at me and gives me the cheekiest grin before stealing the puck from the New York forward with absolute ease. He adds a little fancy ass footwork before powering on with amazing speed, as Tank and Bobby do an incredible job of keeping his line clear.

I watch as he stares down the opposition's goalie and shoots for everything he's worth. The puck enters the goal and, not two seconds later, the buzzer sounds, signaling the end of yet another brilliant game. Once again, my boys are left undefeated.

We cheer with pride as the boys line up through the center of the ice, shaking the hands of the opposing team. They leave the ice as proud men and disappear into the locker room. The spectators slowly clear out, leaving the die-hard fans gathered around, waiting to congratulate the boys and find out where the party is going to be tonight.

I make my way down to the merchandise stand to find out how our sales are going. After adding the boy's jerseys to our collection, I'm not surprised to find that they've been selling like hotcakes, especially the ones that say *CAIN* across the back. Though I must admit, I might have bought one of those myself then surprised Miller in the bedroom when he got home the other night.

"How are you doing, girls?" I ask when I finally make it through the crowd that's trying to get to my boys.

"Yeah, good," the freshman says. "We've been getting smashed. I think we're going to need a third person to help us out."

"Okay, sure. I'll get it cleared with Coach Harris. I'm sure it'll be fine," I tell them as they hastily continue making sales. I check the stock and get busy helping them out when a familiar set of hands circle my waist.

"Fuck, you're sexy with my name on your back," Miller says in my ear because, obviously, I couldn't resist wearing his jersey tonight.

I turn in his arms and give him a congratulatory kiss. "And you're sexy when you're dominating that ice."

Miller grins wide. "Are you girls up for Micky's tonight?"

"You bet," I smile.

The boys usher him away, and I promise that Sophie and I will meet them at the bar once we've helped the freshman girls finish up here.

An hour later, Sophie and I push our way through the door to Micky's to find the place absolutely pumping. There are bodies everywhere, and it's no secret why they're here when they begin chanting the Dragons' war cry. We push our way through the crowd, which is made a lot easier when Jaxon calls out for the crowd to part for Dragon royalty. Hell, Miller and I are now known as the Dragons' King and Queen.

I find Miller among the bodies and sit down on his lap, feeling right at home. The night erupts around us as the boys continue drinking and celebrating. Miller only has a few and, after the many disastrous nights I've had in this particular bar, I decide only a few sounds like a pretty good idea.

I spend my night splitting my time between dancing with Sophie, laughing with the boys, and making out with Miller as his hands slip into my underwear beneath the table.

A few hours later, Coach Harris pushes his way through the door with a man dressed in a very expensive suit, looking as important as ever. "Fuck," Miller says in shock as he eyes the man, recognizing him instantly. Tank looks up at Miller's tone and immediately imitates his shocked gaze.

Coach Harris leads the man over to our table and Miller and Tank stand, causing the rest of the boys to follow suit. "Well, if it isn't the Dream Team," the man grins, reaching out to shake hands with Miller and then Tank.

"Who's that?" I ask Jaxon, leaning over to whisper.

"Looks like a scout or maybe an executive from one of the NHL teams, but I have no idea where he's from. This is huge though. They never come out to meet the players like this," he says in awe, watching the scene unfold before him as if looking into his own future.

The boys talk with Coach Harris and the man for a while when I realize that Sophie is absolutely smashed. I let Jaxon and Bobby know that I'm taking her home so I don't interrupt the boys during their meeting of a lifetime.

I buy a bottle of water and practically force it down Sophie's throat as she gives me the latest update on her and Tank's sexcapades, which as usual, involves far too many details. We stop by the local burger place and grab some fries to munch on for the rest of the walk home.

Somehow, a fifteen-minute walk turns into a forty-five-minute stroll, and when we finally make it home, I tuck Sophie into bed after she begs me to help her pee.

My phone rings and I fish it out of my pocket to find Miller's name on the screen. "Why hello, superstar," I say with a wide grin as I answer the phone.

"Hey babe, just checking you got home okay?" he asks.

"Barely," I laugh. "It took us a while, but we got here eventually."

I hear the muffled noise of the bar in the background and realize he must be standing out front "So, was that a scout?" I ask, hoping it was all good news.

"Not quite," he says with pride loud and clear in his voice. "He owns the Chicago Raiders, one of the best teams in the league. They seem pretty interested in signing both me and Tank, but he won't make any promises until the end of the season. Apparently, there are a few other teams looking at us."

"Holy shit," I gasp. "That's amazing."

"Can I come to your place to celebrate?" he asks seductively.

"Of course you can," I laugh. "Stay and celebrate with the team though. I'll wait up for you."

His response is cut off when there's a knock at the door. "Are you at my door already?" I laugh excitedly as I make my way through the kitchen and living room.

"I wish," he groans, sending shivers all over my body.

"Hold on a minute," I say as I answer the door with the phone still pressed against my ear.

I pull the door open to find a very drunken Brett standing before me. "Fuck," I gasp as he smirks down at me, looking my body up and down with hunger in his eyes.

"What is it?" Miller asks in alarm.

I ignore his question as I stare my past in the face. "You need to leave," I demand with a snarl as my heart begins to beat rapidly in my chest.

"I'm not going anywhere, baby," Brett slurs. "I told you. I want what's mine."

I gasp and step back from the doorway, dropping the phone as I attempt to slam the door. He jams his foot in the frame and forces it back open between us. "Come on, Dani," he says, stepping up to me and pressing me into the wall. The stench of rum wafting off him makes me sick. "Don't be such a fucking prude. I know you want it, you dirty little slut."

"Brett, I asked you to leave," I snap, turning my face away from him as he tries to lean into me and begins untucking his shirt from his pants . . . the shirt that I bought for him.

He grabs my jaw and forces my face back to his, and I look up into his dark eyes. "You're. Fucking. Mine." he growls.

"Get out," I cry, hoping Sophie can hear me, but I know it's no use because she would be well and truly passed out by now. Trying my hardest to get out of his grasp, I squirm against him, but I'm too small and he's far too strong. He must have spent the last year working out.

He laughs at my attempts and runs a hand down the side of my body, grasping my breast with force. I cry out in pain, knowing it will leave a bruise. "Yeah, I knew you would like that. You're such a fucking whore."

A whimper escapes me as I realize what's about to happen. He leans down and kisses the side of my face, working his way to my neck and leaving a nasty trail of saliva behind as his hand reaches down to release his belt buckle. His free hand slips into my shirt and grasps my tit, pinching down hard on my nipple, causing me to flinch in pain.

A tear slides down my face as I continue trying to push him away.

With his dirty cock free, he presses his erection up against my stomach while his other hand cups me between my legs.

"Please, just leave," I beg. "I'm with someone else now."

He leans back from me and slaps me hard across the face. "No. You're mine, not his," Brett snarls, rage blooming in his stare.

His hands find the waistband of my shorts and begin making their way inside. I feel his fingers roughly graze past my clit and force their way into my entrance. He pumps hard once, then twice when he's ripped away from my body and thrown into the opposite wall, falling to the floor with a thump.

Miller stands between us, shaking in rage with a cold, haunted look in his dark eyes. He grabs Brett off the ground and forces him to his feet by the collar of his shirt, holding him in place while he lunges out with a right hook and knocks Brett to the ground again. He jumps straight at him and proceeds to lay into him until he's out cold.

Miller makes a quick call as my body slumps to the floor with relief. A loud sob escapes me, and I'm suddenly wrapped in the safety of his arms. "Shhh," he soothes as I cry into his chest. He runs his fingers through my hair and studies the red mark on my face.

We sit there for the next ten minutes until a cop car pulls up, followed by Tank's truck.

Tank immediately takes in the scene before him and a snarl comes ripping up his throat. He looks me over, studying every inch of my body. "Are you okay?" he asks, concerned.

I give him a small nod as Miller promises to explain everything in the morning. Tank makes his way into the house and heads toward the kitchen, letting us know he'll stay up if we need him.

The two officers get out of the car and come to inspect the situation. "Good evening," the first officer says. "I'm Officer Wilson, and this is my partner Officer Samuels," he says, conducting introductions.

Miller helps to pick me up off the floor as the officers begin their questioning. They call for an ambulance and I'm thankful that Brett is finally taken away. The officers come inside and take a seat in the living room as Miller goes over his version of the night. They give each other a look when Miller gets to the part where he knocked Brett out, and I hope it has no impact on his future.

"Thank you," Office Samuels says, then turns her green eyes on me. "Miss . . .?"

"Danielle," I answer.

"Danielle, do you mind going over what happened here tonight?"

I give a slight nod and decide the full story will be best. I ask Miller to grab my phone from the doorway as I begin telling the officers about my history with Brett. Once Miller returns, I show them the messages I've been getting from him over the past few months. Miller's back stiffens as message after message is shown, and I know he's going to want to have a serious chat about this.

I give them every detail of the night with tears spilling from my eyes.

"Now, Danielle, we suggest you come down to the station and press charges. I'd also suggest a restraining order," Officer Samuels says.

I look over to Miller who gives me a firm nod. He's in total agreement with the officers. "Okay," I say. "Does it need to be now or can I come down in the morning?"

"The morning is fine," she smiles.

The two officers get up and Miller escorts them out. He returns a moment later and instantly scoops me into his arms. "Are you okay?" he asks as I stare off into the distance.

"Yeah, I'll be fine," I tell him. "I just want to shower and get him off me."

"Okay," he nods, getting up and leading me down the hallway. "I'll wait for you out here."

"No," I say urgently, grabbing onto him in a panic. "Don't leave me. I don't want to be alone."

"Are you sure?" he asks. "I figured you wouldn't want me touching you right now."

"You're the only person who could possibly help me forget everything that just happened. I need you."

"Okay," he nods, leading me into the bathroom. He helps me undress, and I watch myself in the mirror as he exposes my skin. There is a shallow bruise appearing on my face and red marks around my right breast. Miller kisses me on the forehead as he takes in my body, and I realize seeing me like this is just as hard for him as it is for me.

I turn around and pull off his shirt, then move onto his jeans, letting them fall to the floor. We step into the hot water, and he washes my body clean of any reminder of Brett. Miller holds me tight as the hot water rushes over us and eventually turns cold.

We silently make our way into the bedroom. I do my best at towel-drying my hair and slide into bed beside him.

"I'm sorry," I tell him as he turns the side lamp off.

"Sorry about what?" he asks, coming up behind me and holding me close to the pillow.

"For not telling you about the messages," I say. "I just didn't want you to worry. I never expected him to do something like this."

"It's okay, babe. I understand," he soothes. "Just don't hold back anything like this again. I want to know. I need to know so I can protect you from things like this. I don't want to see you get hurt."

"I promise," I tell him as I nuzzle into his body.

"I love you so much," he reminds me.

"I know. I love you, too." I say, rolling in his arms and planting a kiss on his chest as the world falls to darkness around me.

CHAPTER 18

MILLER

I have never been so scared in my life, being on that call with Dani and hearing her being sexually assaulted by a violent man. A man who just happens to be her ex. Fuck, my body shakes with anger every time I think about it. Which happens to be all the fucking time.

What the hell would have happened if I hadn't called Dani? Or if I hadn't gotten there in time? Fuck, I know exactly what would have happened. That bastard would have raped my girl, would have taken away her innocence, her light. He would have taken away everything she has fought to get back, which he stole from her in the first place.

And all I did was knock him out. Shit, I should have put him down like the animal he is.

I stayed with Dani all night after the cops left. She fell asleep in my arms, and I can't even explain how happy I was that she still allowed my touch after everything she went through. What cut me to pieces though was *how* she slept in my arms—waking up every thirty minutes, jumping in her sleep as her unconscious mind replayed it over and over again. If I didn't have my girl in my arms, I would have been down at the hospital waiting for that dickhead to wake up just so I could knock him out again.

She woke this morning looking like she hadn't slept a wink, which she really hadn't. She sat down with Sophie and had a coffee while they both sobbed. They got dressed and headed down to the station together to press formal charges and get the paperwork sorted for the restraining order while Tank and I headed out for training.

I skate along the ice with my mind clearly not in the game as I miss shot after shot with Tank clapping me on the back each time, urging me to continue on. I grow more frustrated with myself as the session goes on. I drop Jaxon twice after shooting sloppy passes and lose my shit at a few of the boys.

Coach sends me off the ice for ten minutes to calm down and asks to see me at the end of the session.

We're about twenty minutes from the end of training when the two cops from last night make their presence known. Coach calls for us to stop, and I make my way over, my gut already knowing exactly why they're here.

"Officer Wilson, Officer Samuels," I say by way of greeting.

They each give me a tight smile. "Mr. Cain," Office Wilson says with a nod. "We need to take you down to the station. You're being charged with assault," he adds regretfully. He clearly doesn't want to be doing this.

I nod in understanding and make my way off the ice, with Officer Wilson following me into the locker room.

We come out moments later to find Coach, red in the face, drilling Officer Samuels on what the hell is going on. "Sir, you need to stand down," she warns.

"Coach," I say interrupting. "It's okay. I'll come by when I'm done with this and explain what's going on."

His lips tighten as he studies me, trying to work out what kind of trouble I've gotten myself into before glancing at Tank, who has his mouth zipped shut. Coach should know better than that. There's no way Tank is going to talk. "This needs to stay quiet," he demands, glancing from the officers to all the players.

"I'll be back, Coach," I promise as I follow the officers out the door. They discreetly usher me into their vehicle, knowing the kind of bad press something like this could do, and I mildly wonder how Dani would approach this from a PR angle. Although whatever it is, I know she would do it excellently.

They drive me to the station, and I'm surprised to find Dani still here. She's in the middle of picking up her things to leave when she sees me being ushered in, and her brows pinch together. "What's going on?" she asks, her eyes wide.

"It's okay, babe. Brett is pressing assault charges," I explain.

Her face drops instantly. "What? Are you serious? After everything he's done?"

"Don't worry," I calm her. "It won't stick, and if it does, we can fight it."

She nods in understanding, but the worry doesn't leave her face as she clutches her things to her chest and takes a seat once again. "Don't wait around, babe. This could take a while and you've been here all day," I say. "I'll call you when I'm done."

"Okay," she says with a frown, allowing Sophie to drag her out the door.

"You two seem to be getting dealt a shitty hand at the moment," Office Samuels says discreetly.

"Tell me about it," I agree.

She takes me to the back room to explain the charges against me. However, between the charges pressed against Brett, the restraining order, and both mine and Dani's statements, it's more than likely the charges against me will be dropped.

After signing a few papers, I'm out of there an hour later and making my way back to the ice rink. I find Coach Harris anxiously waiting for me in his office, and I sit down in the chair opposite his desk.

He looks up at me, and for the first time since I've met the man, there's a mix of emotions swimming in his eyes. "Out of all the guys, you're not the one I'd expect to be having trouble with the law," he comments.

"I know, Coach," I tell him, regretfully. "I'm being charged with assault."

"What?" he snarls. "How stupid can you be? An assault charge is enough to throw away your whole future. The NHL won't even consider someone with a criminal record," he growls, pushing out of his chair and pacing his office. "You have two minutes to explain how the fuck you got in this situation."

I do exactly that, giving him the full rundown of what happened last night and a brief history of Dani's past where Brett is involved.

"Fuck," he whispers, his face falling as hears more of the story, making it clear how much he has come to care for the girls. "How's she doing?"

"Alright," I tell him. "She's putting on a brave face, but I know she's hurting."

He nods in understanding and moves around the front of his desk to take a seat directly in front of me. "Look, I can't condone violence," he says, leaning forward and placing a hand on my shoulder. "But had I been in your position, I would have done the same thing. Possibly worse. I think you handled yourself remarkably well," he commends.

"Thanks, Coach," I say, feeling uncomfortable accepting any sort of praise in this situation.

"Now, what have you been told about the charges?" he asks, getting back on track.

I explain everything the cops told me and let him know the likelihood of the charges being dropped. He seems wary but still accepts that this is the best possible outcome in such a shitty situation.

Coach sends me on my way, and I stop by the locker room to collect all my gear before making my way out to the parking lot. The second I'm settled in my SUV, I pull out my phone and bring up Dani's number.

"Hey," her beautiful, worried voice says. She answers on the first ring as though she's been waiting with her phone in hand. "How did it go?"

I relax at the sound of her voice, hating that she's worried. "Okay," I tell her. "Are you home? I'll come by and explain."

"Yeah, I'm home," she says.

"Alright, I'll be there in five," I assure her before hanging up and sliding my phone into my pocket. I hit the gas and make my way to her place, counting down the minutes until I can feel her safe in my arms once again.

I pull up to find Dani and Sophie sprawled on the ground in front of their open doorway, a hammer and screwdriver in Sophie's hands while Dani clutches onto some type of security camera while scanning over the installation instructions.

"You need a little help with that?" I ask, pleased they're proactively looking out for their safety.

Dani looks up at me from the floor. "No," she says, getting a groan out of Sophie. "We can manage."

"Okay, sure. I'll just sit over here and wait till you're done," I say, indicating the outdoor couch by the door. It gives me the perfect view of Dani's ass as she tries to work out the lock.

"Excellent," she smiles sarcastically, giving me a bit of her usual sass, and I realize the restraining order must give her a feeling of security, and I couldn't be happier.

I sit by the door for at least thirty minutes, more than amused as

I watch her fumble around the door. "Need some help?" I ask again with a smirk.

"No, I don't need help," she tells me with a huff. "I can definitely do it myself. But if you're offering to do it, I'm not going to say no."

I laugh as I get up off the chair and make my way over to the door, leaning down and pressing a kiss to her lips before picking her up. I dump her on the couch then make myself comfortable in front of the door as Sophie takes advantage of the opportunity and scurries away. I undo everything the girls' have attempted to do and have the camera installed two minutes later before showing Dani how to access the feed through an app on her phone.

Dani huffs as she watches me in frustration. "Whatever," she grumbles to herself, an amused smile playing on her lips as I join her on the couch. "Okay, tell me all about it."

I give her the rundown, the same way I'd done with Coach Harris. "So, what does this mean for hockey?" she questions.

I let out a deep breath and curl my arms around her. "If the charges go through, I can kiss my hockey career goodbye," I tell her honestly.

"Shit," she gasps. "I'm so sorry. This is all my fault."

"Like hell it is," I tell her, grabbing her waist and turning her to face me. "Not one bit of this is on you. You've done nothing wrong except for being the sexiest damn woman I've ever met." She gives me a soft smile that doesn't reach her eyes. "It's going to be okay and if it's not, we'll fight like hell until it is."

"You're too amazing for me," she says.

"Yeah, I'm pretty damn great."

Dani relaxes against me as she breaks into laughter. "Come on," she says. "It's been a long day. Let me cook you dinner so I can get you to bed."

"No," I say a little too quickly. "I'll cook. You go relax."

There's no better feeling than being on the ice and looking up into the grandstand to see the woman of your dreams staring down at you, wearing your name on her back, and cheering for you as you score in some of the most important games of your life.

I push forward, flying past the referee and a few of the opposing skaters. I narrowly miss getting shoulder charged and have to add a bit of footwork to keep control of the puck. I flick the puck over to Tank to avoid losing it to the opposition.

Tank easily keeps up with me and sends it straight back moments before he's slammed into the boards. I catch the puck against my stick and push forward, flying toward the goal. I rear back and slam the puck forward. It sails across the ice, slides straight past the goalkeeper, and rocks into the back of the net.

The crowd gets to their feet and cheers, breaking into their fourth chorus of the Dragon's war cry. I skate around the back of the net as my boys crowd around, clapping me on the back and cheering my name. I push past them and quickly check on Tank, who seems to be fine.

"Nice one, bro," he says, pulling me toward him and clapping me on the back.

"Couldn't have done it without you," I smirk.

"Yeah, that one and the four before it," he laughs.

"Good point."

I glance up to the crowd to find my girl on her feet, arms in the air, screaming my name like an absolute lunatic. The biggest grin sails across my face as I take in her little performance. I could definitely get used to this.

The boys and I make our way over to Coach, who does his best to keep a straight face, but it's pretty damn obvious that he's ecstatic right now. "Okay, boys. We've got three minutes left. You've already won the game, but let's keep it strong. Show them who owns this town," he smirks.

We break and head back to the center of the ice to do just that.

Three minutes later and another point to our name, the buzzer sounds, declaring us yet again the undefeated Kings of Denver.

CHAPTER 19

DANIELLE

"Come on," I encourage as we both dip down into another weighted squat, "Just two more sets."

"I can't do anymore," Sophie whines as her legs begin to shake.

"Don't you dare give up," I warn. She keeps on going but doesn't make it to the end without calling me a skanky whore first.

"Ohmigod," we hear squealed from the entrance of the gym. "It's them."

Two blonde girls, who can't be more than eighteen, come sprinting up to us wearing nothing but tiny little shorts and matching crops. "Ohmigod, ohmigod," the first one says.

"Can we help you?" Sophie asks, raising an irritated brow, knowing exactly what they want.

"Oh, wow. We just wanted to say hi," blonde number two says, looking Sophie up and down. "You guys are like, totally famous."

"Okay," I say, looking around, trying to work out the easiest escape.

"Holy crap," the first one shrieks as she frantically begins looking around. "Are Miller and Tank here too? Can you like, introduce us?"

"No," Sophie says with a nasty tone, clearly annoyed with bimbo one and two.

"Goodbye ladies," I cut in before Sophie brings out her true colors.

"Oh, um . . . bye," they say, making room for us to squeeze past them.

We grab our things, take a quick drink, and make our escape out the front door. "That shit is getting really annoying," Sophie groans as we set ourselves at a slow jog to finish our workout.

"I know," I agree. "It seems to be getting worse, but the Dragons' popularity is our fault. You know, apart from the fact they're undefeated and incredibly talented."

She lets out another groan. "It's just frustrating. I never know if they just want to say hi or if they're looking for an introduction to try and steal him away. God, they're all little skanks," she seethes.

"Tell me about it. I had this girl last week tell me I couldn't possibly give my man what he needs and that he won't be satisfied until he has a real woman like her," I explain.

"Now I know that's bullshit because I've heard you guys going at it, that man is definitely satisfied," Sophie so kindly offers.

I can't help but laugh as we continue jogging down the pathway to our house. "So, what's the plan for tonight?" I ask when I finally catch my breath.

"Well, the boys will be training all night, so I'm thinking girls' night," she suggests.

"Love it."

We get home ten minutes later and fight to the death over who gets the first shower. Which means I'm currently sitting in my bedroom waiting for my turn.

I hear my phone ringing from out in the kitchen, and I jump up and sprint down the hallway. I turn the corner into the kitchen and grin as I see Miller's name come up on the caller ID. I grab my phone and quickly hit the answer button before it's too late. "Hey. Aren't you supposed to be on the ice?" I ask.

"Yeah, we're just about to get on," he tells me. "But I had to tell you something first."

"Okay," I say. "Spill it."

"I just got a call from Officer Samuels. The assault charges have been dropped."

A weight immediately lifts off my shoulders. I can't even begin to describe how happy and relieved it makes me knowing Miller's future isn't going to be thrown away because of my stupidity. "Wow," I tell him. "That's amazing."

"Yeah. She said he barely had a leg to stand on, especially after the judge saw your statement. She also said the restraining order was officially served today and that he'll be in and out of court for the next few months."

I nod, despite him not being able to see me. "I guess that's the best we can ask for."

"Yeah, well, he deserves to be behind bars," he grunts.

"Can't argue that," I scoff.

"What are you doing tonight?"

"Soph and I are heading out for a girl's night. Well, assuming she ever gets out of the shower."

"Alright babe, be safe. Coach is calling us to get started. I'll come by after training," he tells me.

"Alright, see you later," I say. Miller ends the call, leaving me standing in the kitchen with a ridiculous, goofy grin spreading right across my face. God, I don't think I'll ever get used to the way he makes me feel.

I hear Sophie finish in the shower, and I make my way to the bathroom, pushing my way through the door just in time for Sophie to grab a towel and wrap it around her body. "Good timing," she laughs. "You nearly got an eyeful of my sexy ass."

"Right, because that's something I've never seen before," I laugh, seeing as though we are both known to run around the house butt naked.

"Point well made," she tells me as I begin stripping for my shower.

I reach in and turn the taps on as Sophie finally leaves the bathroom. As she pulls the door shut behind her, I step through the shower door into the hot stream of water. It runs straight down my back, and I tilt my head to let the spray coat my face.

I do my best to have a quick shower, but I'm pretty sure after washing and conditioning my hair, shaving my legs, and singing a few songs, I've been in here for at least half an hour.

I wrap my towel around me and waltz down to my room, running into Jared on the way. "Where are you two going?" he asks as Sophie comes out of her room in her underwear and joins me.

"Girls' night," Sophie sings.

"Oh. Can I come?" he asks, excitedly. "We haven't gone out together in ages."

"Well, yeah," I tell him. "It's a girls' night. Of course you're coming."

"Woohoo," he sings as he slings into my room. I drop my towel and pull on a skimpy little thong and matching bra, one that I know Miller just happens to love. "Fuck, that's sexy," Jared tells me as he checks me out.

"I know," I grin. I turn my attention to my closet and begin rifling through it until I find one of the many little black dresses in my collection and pull it out. Yep, perfect for a girls' night. I pull the dress on and begin searching for my hairbrush.

"What do you think?" Sophie asks, pulling a bright red halter dress from my closet and holding it up against her body.

"Definitely," I tell her. She unzips it and begins squeezing into the little red number. She does a turn for us, and even though I've seen her in this dress a million times, she never fails to blow me away.

Jared disappears into his room to change as Sophie and I take over the bathroom, spreading out our hairdryers, straighteners, curling irons, and makeup.

Jared selects only the best playlist and soon enough, the bass pounds through the whole house. He appears a few minutes later with a few glasses of wine and makes himself comfortable between us before getting to work on perfecting his hair.

I smile at my friends through the mirror, receiving the same smile back, and I realize just how perfect this moment is. Nothing on earth could possibly be better than how life is at the moment. I have amazing friends and a boyfriend who I love and who just happens to love me in return.

An hour later, we're finally ready. We make our way to the front door and head out. With our stomachs rumbling, we make our way to the closest restaurant, order something quick and easy, and leave as soon as we can.

We finally arrive at the club and after waiting in line for what seems like forever, we get carded at the door and make our grand entrance. We beeline straight to the bar and each order a pink pussy shot. We down them as one, grab glasses of champagne, and then head out to the dance floor.

We spend the night in a blissful state, dancing and moving to the music. Jared does his best to appear as either of our boyfriends when we are approached by other men in the club. Even though their interest is flattering, I'm a one-man kinda girl.

I pull my phone out, making sure to send Miller a drunken text to let him know just how much I love him, causing Sophie and Jared to do the same. We giggle at each other as we sail right past the tipsy stage and into being well and truly drunk.

We dance for another hour before we make our way home. I get a text from Miller saying he shouldn't be too much longer, and I grin as I plan out my sexual attack on him. I gasp and slam my hand over my mouth when I realize I've been planning my exploits out loud then I fall into another fit of giggles.

We push our way through the door, and I make my way to my room, kicking my heels off as I go. I look down at my phone and work out that Miller should be back soon. I strip off my dress and get myself nicely positioned on my bed to give him the full effect the moment he walks in.

"**G**ET UP!" Miller shouts with an urgency that terrifies me.

I'm startled out of my sleep as I feel his arms dig violently under me and yank me up against his body. I look around frantically, completely confused as to what the fuck is going on. I take in a deep breath and regret it as my lungs fill with smoke.

What the hell? I squint into the dark room and notice the flames licking up the side of the wall.

Shit.

The house is on fire.

Miller holds me tightly as he rushes from my room. He heads up the hallway and kicks in Jared's door. "Get up," he yells. "There's a fire. Get Sophie out."

Jared jumps into motion, rushing out of his door and down the other end of the hallway to Sophie's room. Miller sprints down the hallway where I can see a red and orange glow surrounded by the hazy smoke. He comes out into the living room, and I gasp in shock as I'm struck with the overwhelming view of the fire taking over our house.

The flames take up every inch of the living room, completely engulfing it, and destroying everything in its path. As Miller rushes toward the front door, I glance back over his shoulder to see the flames steadily overtaking the kitchen while preparing to take down the dining room too.

I'm hit with the realization of just how close I came to death. My bedroom is on the opposite wall to the dining room, and with how quickly these flames are traveling, I wouldn't have had much time.

Clinging tighter to Miller's neck, I take everything in. He bursts through the open doorway and out into the cold night, dropping down into the grass.

I glance back at the door, anxious to see Jared and Sophie as my head spins, the alcohol still pumping through my veins. Not a moment later, my nerves calm as Jared spills through the door, holding Sophie's hand tightly. They collapse into the dewy grass next to Miller and me.

"Are you all okay?" Miller asks us urgently, keeping his focus trained hard on me.

"Yeah, I think so," I tell him, realizing my throat is a bit hoarse. I must have breathed in a bit of smoke before he got there. I hear both Sophie and Jared give their own responses and am relieved when they say they're fine.

The front window shatters as the flames begin to take over more of the house. I hear the distant sound of sirens a few streets away and rip my stunned gaze away from the house and over to the pacing Miller. "Did you call emergency services?"

"Yeah," he says, looking over at me, pulling his eyebrows together as he takes me in. "I called as I was pulling up. I saw the smoke from a few streets away. I just didn't realize it was your place," he tells me.

He turns and walks to his truck, and I'm about to call out for him not to leave when he reaches into the back and pulls out his jersey. He walks back and bends down to me on the ground. "You know I love you in your lingerie, but I don't think the whole world needs to see what's mine," he murmurs as he hands over the jersey.

I look down at my body and realize I am indeed in nothing but a very stringy thong and bra. I smirk up at him. "I was trying to surprise you," I explain. "But I must have fallen asleep."

"Consider me extremely surprised," he tells me, taking the jersey back from my shaking hands and pulling it over my head as the fire engine pulls up. I push my arms through the oversized sleeves and watch in amazement as the fire department takes control of the situation. Miller pulls me to my feet and the jersey falls past my waist, covering my very exposed ass before falling past my knees.

One fireman ushers us further away from our house as they all work together, unloading the hoses and working hard to extinguish the flames.

The police arrive just moments later and get straight into it. They put police tape up, sectioning off all the nosey neighbors, and usher us toward the ambulance that I didn't notice before.

Sophie, Jared, and I are all checked out while Miller talks to the cops. The police then take all of our statements, which isn't much since we were all asleep. Tank shows up moments later to check on Sophie, while Ashton arrives only a few seconds after him.

What feels like hours later, the flames are finally out. Miller and Jared talk to the firefighter in charge, who explains that it's best if we leave. There aren't many possessions left in our home and we won't be allowed access until tomorrow. I overhear them telling Miller that they'll still be here for a while longer to determine the cause of the fire.

Miller helps me up into his SUV after making sure Sophie and Jared have places to go. He gets in and starts the engine, reaching over and taking my hand in his. "Are you really okay?" he questions, now that the shock has started to wear off.

"Yeah," I tell him with a tight smile, feeling my chest aching for my lost home. "I'll be alright. Just a bit shaken."

"Okay," he says, then quietly hits the gas.

We drive in silence for a little while when I look over at him. "What's the matter?" I ask, taking in the frown on his handsome face.

He takes a deep breath and looks over at me. "That was fucked up, babe," he tells me, squeezing my hand. "The second I saw your house and all the smoke, I thought I'd lost you."

"It's okay. I'm okay," I reassure him.

"I know, babe. It's just too many close calls with you lately," he sighs.

"Yeah, I know," I whisper, dropping my gaze to my thighs. "You can wrap me in bubble wrap from now on."

He smirks over at me. "I might just do that."

We arrive at his place and take a quick shower together, washing the smell of smoke from our bodies. "Thank you," I tell him as his arms wrap around me. "That's twice you've saved me now."

He looks down at me with such adoration and presses his lips to mine. "There's not a thing I wouldn't do for you, Dani."

"I know," I tell him. "I love you so much."

"I love you, too," he tells me, pressing another kiss to my lips. "Now, let me take you to bed. I'm exhausted, and I bet you're right there with me."

I nod up at him and he gives me a smile that melts my heart. After pulling me out from under the warm spray of water and wrapping a towel around me, he leads me over to his dresser and takes out a shirt for me, but I shake my head and opt to put his jersey back on.

We climb into bed and he wraps me in his arms. I fall into a deep sleep, knowing that no matter how screwed up a situation may be, I will always be okay as long as I have this man by my side.

I realize that without a doubt, Miller Cain is going to be part of my life for the rest of time, and I know with one hundred percent certainty that I will walk down the aisle to him and he will be my husband. He will be signed to the NHL, and I will be right there with him, supporting him with everything I have. He will be the first one to hold our child, and the one that child will call Daddy with complete adoration. He's the one who will hold my heart, and every piece of me, until the end of eternity.

CHAPTER 20

MILLER

Visions of my beautiful Dani, sleeping soundlessly in her bedroom as flames engulf the walls haunt my mind, and I get up and make my way into the bathroom. Leaning over the sink, I turn on the tap, cupping my hands together under the water. I wait until the water is flowing over the edges and bring it up to splash my face as I try to erase the images from my head.

I can't help the feeling that the fire wasn't an accident. After all, Tank had told me just last week that Sophie's family was in a house fire when she was a teenager, and ever since, she has been pedantic about turning off the power points and making sure the house is as fireproof as possible. Hell, she even attached a fire blanket to the wall between the stove and microwave.

I sneak out of the bathroom and head downstairs, not wanting to wake up Dani. I head into the garage that I converted into a home gym and push myself through a grueling workout. It's not the best version of a home gym, but it's perfect for times like this when the idea of leaving my home, leaving my girl alone makes me want to hurl. An hour and a half later, I have used up every last ounce of my energy and head back upstairs to wash away the stench of sweat.

After getting out of the shower and pulling on a pair of sweats, I find myself in the kitchen cooking breakfast for my girl. Not knowing what she might want, I decide on bacon and eggs with a side of pancakes and coffee.

I'm standing by the stove flipping the eggs when I hear her making her way into the kitchen. I turn around to find her leaning against the counter, her eyes roaming up and down my body as she greedily checks me out. She bites down on her bottom lip, not aware that she's been caught.

She looks sexy as fuck in nothing but my jersey, which is falling off her shoulder. I feel myself harden in my sweats, and judging by the look in her eyes, she notices. I turn the stove off and stalk toward her. "See something you like, babe?" I ask.

Her eyes are filled with hunger as they slide back up my body and meet my eyes. I finally get my hands on her, grabbing her around the waist and lifting her onto the counter as her palms come down on my chest. I lay her back on the cold countertop and grab her legs, opening them wide and revealing her to me.

I hook my fingers into the waistband of her thong and tear it from her body, desperately needing to taste her. I find her more than ready for me, a deliciously sweet treat just begging to be tasted.

My mouth closes over her sweet cunt, flicking my tongue over her clit and watching as she squirms beneath my touch. "Miller," Dani screams, needing more. "Yes."

I give her exactly what she wants, relentlessly nipping, sucking, and licking until she comes apart beneath me.

Not nearly done with her, I climb up onto the counter and hover above her. She pulls me down and catches my lips in hers as her hands roam over my body and make their way down to my pants. She pushes my sweats down over my ass, frees my cock, and instantly wraps her fingers around me. "Fuck," I groan, feeling her hand pump up and down my length.

"I need you inside me," she breathes between kisses, adjusting beneath me and wrapping her legs around my waist. I don't need to be told twice. I position my cock at her entrance and slam myself deep inside her. We both groan in pleasure as I pull back, only to thrust myself back in.

In. Out. In. Out.

The pleasure is overwhelming as her tight cunt squeezes around me. I repeat the process as her nails dig into my back. Her pussy tightens around me, telling me she's close, and I bring my hand down between us, rubbing tight circles over her clit. Dani screams out as she clenches around my cock. I feel my release creeping up on me. "Come with me, baby," I tell her, adding more pressure on her clit.

"Fuck," she cries as she explodes around me, clenching down

harder as I come with her, both of us falling victim to the other's body.

I drop my forehead to hers as we both gasp for air. "Good morning," I murmur, nuzzling my face into her neck and roaming my lips over her sensitive skin.

Dani smiles up at me, trying to push me away as my kiss tickles her neck. "Good morning to you, too," she giggles, hooking her arms under mine and simply holding me. She sighs deeply and closes her eyes, looking so completely at peace. My heart swells just watching her.

"Fuck, I love you," I tell her.

Her beautiful green eyes open and she beams up at me from under her long lashes. "I'll never get tired of hearing that," she breathes, the sincerity in her tone making me wish I could fall in love with her all over again.

"Good, because I'll never get tired of telling you."

Dani smiles up at me and lifts her head, just enough to capture my lips in a gentle kiss. "You know, a girl could get used to waking up like this. I must have hit the jackpot."

I look deep into her eyes so she understands I'm serious. "Would you like to get used to it?"

Dani watches me for a moment, her brows furrowed as she stares back at me. "Are you asking me to marry you or to move in with you?" she asks, slightly alarmed.

My eyes widen as I understand where she got confused. "Fuck, babe. Move in. Definitely move in."

Her beautiful eyes fill with relief, and as if only just now realizing what I'm asking, they begin welling up with tears. I hope they're tears of joy. "Are you sure?" she asks as a small smile begins to creep across her face.

"I've never been so sure in my life. You're it for me, Dani, and I know with one hundred percent certainty, I want to be with you. I've known it for a while, but last night just confirmed it all for me. I don't know what I would have done if anything had happened to you."

Her tears begin to spill over as she looks up at me with complete joy and happiness. "Okay," she finally says. "I'll move in."

"Yeah?" I ask, a little shocked she didn't put up more of a fight. Especially considering the shit she went through after moving in with Brett.

"Yeah," she laughs, pulling me down to her to kiss me once again. Her legs tighten around me as I harden between her thighs. With just a few words, she's made me the happiest motherfucker on earth. And so I do the one thing I know will prove to her just how fucking ready I am to share my life with her—I slide back inside her and fuck her again, right here on the kitchen counter.

I pull up behind Tank's truck in front of the police station, hop out of my SUV, and head around to Dani's side to help her out. We walk hand in hand, and I smirk over at Dani who pulls and wiggles around in her borrowed clothes. I hold the door open for her to slip in before me, and we find Sophie, Tank, Jared, and Ashton already seated in the waiting area.

Sophie launches herself out of her chair the moment she sees Dani. The two collide in the middle of the station, holding onto each other with everything they've got, tearing up and sniffling as they check each other over.

"I'm so glad you're okay," Sophie cries as Dani pulls her harder against her chest.

I make my way past the girls and take a seat next to Tank while giving Jared and Ashton a nod. I glance at Tank to see him watching Sophie, looking as relaxed as ever.

"You convinced her to move in with you."

He turns to me with a grin. "Fuck off. Like you didn't do the same thing."

I grin back at him. "Fuck, yeah," I laugh, looking over at the girls to see them both suddenly squeal and start jumping up and down. I guess they've just told each other. I catch Dani's eyes and she gives me a brilliant smile. I know without a doubt that I would do everything in my power to see that smile every moment of every day.

Officer Samuels pushes through a door into the waiting area and immediately gets all of our attention. "Thank you all for coming down this morning," she says, then steps back and gestures to the door. "Please, come on through."

She turns on her heel and leads us all down the hallway and into a small meeting room. There are only four chairs, so the girls, Jared, and Ashton take seats while Tank and I stand behind our girls.

Officer Samuels takes a quick drink of water and takes a seat on the opposite side of the table, facing us all. "Thanks again for coming down," she starts. "First of all, I know you all gave your statements last night, but sometimes a good night's rest can add clarity to a situation. So I just want to double check if there was anything you remembered or wanted to add?" she asks, looking around. We all shake our heads and she gets on with it. "Okay, great."

"Now, unfortunately, due to the fire, your home is not livable and will most likely be demolished shortly," she says, giving the girls a regretful look. "The fire chief has completed his inspection and has come to the conclusion that this was arson, which makes your home a crime scene. So, this morning we will be heading over there to commence our investigation. Once we have been through, we will escort you into the home to collect what's left of your possessions," she explains.

"With that in mind," she continues, looking toward Dani. "With the restraining order being served yesterday, we believe we might already have a suspect. We will be bringing Brett in for questioning and, with any luck, our search warrant will come through today."

Her gaze turns toward Sophie and Jared. "Do either of you have any reason to be suspicious of anyone else or have anyone in your lives who wants to cause you harm?"

Jared scoffs then speaks up. "Well, where do I start?" he says. "I'm gay and these two are currently dating the two hottest campus celebrities. It could have been anyone. A hate crime against me or a sick way to get the girls out of the picture to eliminate the competition for Tank and Miller's affections."

Officer Samuels glances toward me and Tank with a questioning brow. "We have a bit of a fan base at the moment," Tank explains. "But I haven't noticed anything to be alarmed about," he continues, glancing at me.

"I agree. I don't think it's a Dragon's fan."

"Never thought it was," Sophie mumbles under her breath.

"What was that, babe?" Tank asks, placing his hands on her shoulders in support.

"I said, I never thought it was. We all know it was Brett, especially after serving the restraining order yesterday. We just need to prove it," she says, then turns to Dani and takes her hand. "Sorry, babe, but your crazy, psycho ex tried to kill you and nearly succeeded," she says, causing a shiver to sail down my spine.

Dani looks up at Officer Samuels. "What's going to happen if it is him?"

"Ultimately, it's up to the judge. However, we are pushing for attempted rape and with arson charges on top of that, he will most likely be looking at ten to fifteen years behind bars."

"Good," she nods.

Officer Samuels gets us all to sign some paperwork and asks us to meet them at the girls' place in a few hours to go through their possessions.

We head out together and have lunch down at Micky's. I ply Dani with a few drinks to help prepare her for what we're about to see.

As instructed, we arrive at the girls' place a few hours later to inspect the damage.

Dani climbs out of my SUV and stands firmly in the grass before the house, looking up at it in horror. I reluctantly rip my eyes from hers to the house and find it barely a skeleton of the home that was here just yesterday. The structure is black and smoky with the whole front burnt to a crisp. I can't imagine what the inside looks like, let alone what the girls and Jared must be feeling right now.

Sophie hops out of Tank's truck and walks over to Dani, reaching out to take her hand. They both stand in silence as they take in what's left of their home. I glance over to Jared to see him making his way over to the girls. He wraps his arms around them both and pulls them into his chest. The girls cry into him, and he does his best to soothe them. I desperately want to go to Dani and tell her everything is going to be okay, but she needs this moment with her friends.

Officer Samuels comes out of the house wearing a grim expression, followed by a few others, all sporting bright yellow hard hats. Her eyes land on our group and she makes her way over. She reaches out to Sophie and places a gentle hand on her shoulder.

Sophie turns around as Jared drops his arms, and the three of them concentrate on whatever Officer Samuels is saying. A few moments later, Dani turns around and walks over to us. "We're going in," she says, looking down at the ground. "We'll need hard hats."

"Okay," I say, taking her hand and leading her over to the truck that holds all the equipment. I grab a few hats and help her to put one on. I knock her on the head and smirk when she finally smiles up at me, a silent message letting me know she's as alright as she can be. I put on my hat and lead her over to the others before handing out the rest of the hard hats.

Once we're all ready, we follow Officer Samuels into the house.

Dani gasps as we bypass the living room, tightening her hold on my hand as she takes in the charred remains of her home. I pull her closer and hold her to me as we make our way deeper into what used to be their home.

The kitchen is the same as the living room; absolutely gone, and unable to wait a moment longer, Sophie takes off and heads down the hallway toward her room with Tank following. Jared and Ashton do the same, and I lead Dani toward her room and stop her halfway down the hallway. I turn her in my arms and look down at her. "Are you sure you're ready to see this?" I ask as I study her reaction.

Her eyes begin to water. "No. But it's now or never, right?"

I rub my hands up and down Dani's arms as she takes a deep breath. She turns back around and continues down the blackened hall. She stops by her door, takes another deep breath, and steps over the threshold.

CHAPTER 21

DANIELLE

I step into what used to be my bedroom and sink to my knees onto the sooty carpet as a loud sob rips through my chest. I'm distantly aware of Miller behind me, holding onto my shoulders as I cry into my hands.

This place had been my home since the day I left Brett. It had been my salvation from a bad life, the place where I became whole again.

I glance around my room to find absolutely nothing. The room is barely a frame. My bed, my camera, my laptop, my clothes, all of my possessions. Just gone.

Miller grabs me under my arms and hauls me to my feet so he can hold me tight to his chest as I cry into his shirt. I feel his hand rubbing circles on my back as he tries to soothe me. "They're just things. Things can be replaced," he tells me. "It will be okay."

I nod into his chest. I know he's right, but it doesn't change the fact that it still hurts like a bitch. I don't know what I would do without him today. He has been my rock, keeping me going when all I've wanted to do is crumble into a ball and give up. I pull myself out of his arms and make my way around the room, making note of everything before coming to my closet, hoping to God that something might have survived inside.

I swing the door open and jump back out of the way as the door comes off the hinges, falling toward me. Miller jumps in, throwing his arm up and preventing the door from falling on my head. He finds somewhere safe to place his hands on the charred wood and picks it up, placing it at the other end of the room.

Letting out a breath, I peek into the wardrobe and sigh as every last bit of hope escapes me. Just as I expected, there's absolutely nothing left.

I hear a gasp behind me and realize that Sophie has made her way into the room. "Shit, Dani," she says, looking around the room, clearly stuck for words.

"I know," I tell her. "It's all gone."

"It's okay," she tells me. "It just gives us an excuse to go shopping."

I give her a small smile, appreciating her fake enthusiasm. It's solely for my benefit, trying to make out like this isn't a big deal and that it's all going to be okay.

"Come on," Sophie says a moment later, taking my hand and leading me out of the room. "I've got a few things we can share until we can get new stuff."

I leave my room and promise myself that I will never look back. I'm starting new with Miller. A new perspective to go with my new home. If my friends are safe, I'll be okay, and as long as I have Miller by my side, nothing can hurt me.

I make my way down the hall and into Sophie's room, pleased to see she still has a few things worth saving. I help her pack up what's left while Miller heads down to Jared's room and gives him a hand.

Two hours later, we've finished packing everything we can, and with tears in our eyes, we say goodbye to our home.

I hop into Miller's SUV, and we head to the store so I can get a few of the necessities I'll need until Sophie and I get a real chance to replace what we've lost once our renter's insurance claim goes through. Walking around the store with Miller is a whole new experience, one that surprisingly cheers me up.

His first stop is the underwear section, and he does his best to fill the basket with the smallest pieces he can find. I try to explain to him that we're just getting the necessities and don't need this stuff, but he ensures me that this is definitely a necessity.

Our whole shopping trip goes pretty much like this, with Miller and I arguing over what counts as a necessity. A thirty-minute shopping trip turns into a good two hours before we finally make it to the checkout and then he takes me to our home.

I'm sitting in Miller's truck, chatting away with Mom and filling her in on everything that has happened over the past few days as Miller drives us to the ice rink for tonight's game. Which just happens to be one of the most important games of the season. It's the game that will determine if my boys make it to The Frozen Four, the semi-finals.

I pull my feet up under me as I skim over the details of the fire and attempted rape as I don't want to worry Mom. But also because I see Miller's knuckles turning white as he grasps the steering wheel harder with each new sentence I utter.

I want Miller to be in the right frame of mind for tonight's game. I would hate for my issues to mess with his head and screw up his chances at winning tonight, even though I know he's a god on that ice and nothing can stop him. Hell, his anger from my issues would most likely spur him to skate faster and hit harder, but I'm not taking any chances.

I get to the good part of the conversation, letting Mom know all about my new living arrangements, and smirk as I watch Miller's grip on the steering wheel loosen, pride shining in his eyes. Mom completely brightens up at this news. After the night of the auction, she fell for Miller's charm, just as I knew she would. I swear, I've never seen a mother approve of a man dating her daughter quite so quickly.

My phone beeps with an incoming call, and I quickly glance at the screen to see a private number. "Hey Mom, I've got another call. I'll talk to you later."

"Okay, my sweet girl," she says. "I love you. Keep me updated about Brett."

"Will do. Bye, Mom."

"Bye, darling. Wish Miller good luck from us," she says, playing her usual game of never hanging up the phone.

"Okay, Mom. I've got to go, bye," I rush out, hoping I don't miss the other call.

I hang up before Mom can get started on something else and suddenly feel uneasy about who could be trying to contact me, especially from a private number. I hit answer and hesitantly put the phone back up to my ear. "Hello?"

"Hi, Danielle. This is Officer Samuels," she says in her too-chirpy, feminine voice.

"Oh, hi," I say with relief. "How are you?"

Miller turns to me with a questioning raised brow, clearly wondering who's on the line. "Officer Samuels," I mouth to him and pull my phone down to hit speakerphone so he can listen in on the conversation.

"I'm good, thanks for asking. Listen, I have some great news," she starts. Miller reaches over and places his warm hand on my thigh, giving it a small squeeze and smiling at me with encouragement. "We were able to get a confession out of Brett, for both the attempted rape and arson, so he will be going to trial soon. He was surprisingly easy to break."

"Are you serious?" I gasp, wide-eyed.

"Indeed, I am. He will be behind bars until we can get him in to see the judge, which we are hoping will be next week, and then a trial date should be set. Keep in mind, it could be a few months before the trial actually takes place, but just know that we're confident he's going away for a very long time."

Relief fills me, and I let out a shaky breath as I continue listening. "So, with both your statements and his confession, it will be an open and closed case. During his confession he slipped up and admitted that fire was an attempt on your life, so it looks like he will also be going down for attempted murder," Officer Samuels says with pride. "God, it is great to get scum bags like that off the streets and where they belong."

"Wow," I say, not really sure how to respond. After all, this was a guy I dedicated myself to. I was in love with him. Though considering the beatings, attempted rape, burning down my home, and apparently, the attempt on my life, I guess he's going exactly where he belongs. "That's great," I say as Miller grins over at me and squeezes my leg once again.

"Indeed, it is," Officer Samuels says. "It would be good for you to be present in court next week, both yourself and Miller."

"Okay sure," I tell her. "Anything you need."

"Excellent. I'll be in contact with you when I know further details."

"Great. I'll wait for your call."

We say our goodbyes, and I end the call, placing my phone down in the center console and glancing up at Miller in shock. "He's actually going away," I breathe in disbelief.

Miller studies my face and slips his hand into mine, placing them both on the gear stick so he can keep shifting. "You good?" he asks.

"Yeah, I think I am. I feel like a huge weight has finally been lifted and I'm truly free," I tell him. "I'll never have to worry about him hurting me again."

"You have no idea how happy that call has made me," he says, sparing me a glance before returning his gaze back to the road, and I realize he must be feeling the same relief that I am, knowing he doesn't have to continually be on the lookout for my safety.

He glances back at me, and I suddenly begin feeling very hot. "You better concentrate on the road, Mr. Cain," I tell him. "Cause if you keep looking at me like that, you're going to miss your game."

"Is that a promise?" he asks, his eyes darkening with hunger as that deep tone does wicked things to me.

My cheeks flush, and I clench my thighs. "You know it is."

"Fuck," he hisses. "Baby, don't tempt me. I can't miss this game."

"Okay, I'll be a good girl from now on," I smile, innocently batting my eyelashes at him. "But just know, when I get you home tonight, I plan on being a very, very bad girl."

Miller almost swerves off the road and gapes at me before trying to shake whatever image resides in his head. "You're such an ass," he laughs as he finally pulls up at the ice rink.

I go to make my way out of his SUV when his hold on my hand tightens and he pulls me back. "Wait a minute," he says.

I glance back at him with my brows furrowed, unsure what could be keeping him. Usually, he can't wait to get into the rink on game night. "What's up?" I ask, hoping everything is okay.

He gives me a brilliant smile that makes my heart skip a beat and then releases his seatbelt to turn and face me. He reaches into the back seat with his other hand still firmly placed in mine and I wait, wondering what the hell is going on.

Miller pulls a box out of the backseat and hands it over to me. I take it from him cautiously, trying to read the expression on his face. "What's this?" I ask as I flip the box around, trying to gauge a clue as to what the hell it is. I turn more in my seat and face him front on to decipher his reaction.

He smiles at me once again with that amazing sparkle in his eye. "Open it," he instructs.

He releases my hand so I can open the mysterious blue box, and I glance up at him to find him studying me intently, looking slightly nervous and sick. "Are you alright?" I tease, my hand hovering over the lid of the box.

"Shut up and open the damn thing," he demands, a stupid grin stretching across his handsome face.

Putting him out of his misery, I open the box and glance down to find a brand-new camera staring back at me. I suck in a gasp, my heart racing.

What. The. Hell?

"Are you serious?" I squeak, looking up at him. This thing must have cost a bomb. "I can't accept this."

"You can and you will," he tells me. "I know how much you loved your old one, and I couldn't stand the look on your face when you saw what was left of it. I promised myself that I would do anything it took to never see you so down again. I know this will never replace the one you lost or the images you'd taken. Hell, I don't even know if it's the right brand, let alone a good one, but the guy at the store assured me it was."

"Miller," I breathe, unable to find the words as tears well in my eyes. I put the camera down and climb across the truck until I'm straddled in his lap. Miller wraps me in his strong arms and holds me to him as tears spring from my eyes. "Thank you so much. It's perfect."

"It's my pleasure." He smiles as he kisses me. "It's all set up and ready to go so you can use it during the game," he tells me, reaching up and wiping the tears off my face.

I beam down at him. "Seriously?"

"Of course. Anything for my girl," he says. "You lost everything in the fire, and I nearly lost you. I know there's still heaps of stuff that we need to replace, but I wanted to help you start to rebuild that."

"God, I don't know how to thank you," I say, turning into a blubbering mess once again at his use of the term *we*. "I love it, and I love you so damn much."

"I know a few ways you can thank me," he jokes as his hands wind down my body and grab my ass.

"Oh, I plan to," I say, giving him a seductive smile.

Knowing if we don't make a break for it now, I'll end up bent over the back seat, we scurry out of his SUV and make our way into the ice rink, parting when Miller turns off for the locker room. I spot Sophie up in the grandstand in our usual spot and make my way up to her, flopping down into the seat next to her with a satisfied sigh.

"What's up with you? You look all floaty and happy," she gasps, feigning horror.

"Shut up," I laugh, smacking her shoulder. "I'm just having a really great day." I beam at her, holding up my new camera.

"What the fuck?" she screeches, gawking at the device in question.

"Yeah, that's what I thought," I laugh. "Miller got it for me. He wanted to replace the one I lost."

"Holy shit. He must have spent a bomb on this thing," she gasps, taking the camera from me and inspecting it from every angle before proceeding to take a few shots. "Fuck, this is nice. That boy must be head over heels in love with you."

"Yeah," I smile. "He is."

We sit and fiddle with my new camera for the next forty minutes, watching as the crowd around us fills every last seat, waiting to see if their favorite team will make it to the semi-finals; The Frozen Four in Chicago.

I go down to the merchandise store and make sure my girls have everything under control, which of course they do. They've been doing this for nearly the whole season. I purchase another jersey with Miller's name on the back to replace the one I lost in the fire, rip it out of the packaging, and pull it straight over my head.

Making my way back up the grandstand, I get stopped at least a million times by Miller's fans, asking how I am after the fire. After politely responding to as many of them as I can, I squeeze past the rest of the spectators and finally flop back down into my seat beside Sophie, making her jump at my sudden reappearance. "Fuck," she shrieks.

"Sorry," I laugh, pulling my feet up on the chair in front and making myself comfortable. I pull out a bag of chocolates, hang my camera around my neck, and get ready for the boys to come out and dominate the ice.

CHAPTER 22

MILLER

Sweat drips down my back as I push myself in what has to be the hardest game we have played all season. Hell, it's the hardest game I've played since becoming a Dragon four years ago, but I keep pushing. There's no way I'm giving up this close to the semifinals.

The Dragons deserve it. They've been working their asses off all season, and if I'm not doing it for these guys, then I'm doing it for our fans. The very same fans who have supported us all season and who have currently filled our grandstand to maximum capacity. We're going to make it. I just know it.

There are ten minutes left in the game, and we're neck and neck with the opposing team. Coach calls a timeout and we all skate over to the boards to huddle around him. A bottle of water hurls toward my face from who the fuck knows where, but I don't hesitate to grab it. I squirt it into my mouth and over my face then concentrate on every last word coming from Coach's mouth.

He's red in the face from yelling at us during the game. I know he feels just as exhausted as we do, which is exactly what we expect from an amazing coach like him. With only thirty seconds on the clock for our time out, he lays out a new plan of attack, gives us a pep talk, and sends us on our way with refreshed motivation to kick the other team's asses.

Tank and I butt heads and clap each other on the back as we skate into position, the crowd roaring around us, excited for the final deciding ten minutes of the game. I glance up to find Dani watching me with a look of pride on her face, and I know she feels it right there along with me. This game is ours.

The referee blows his whistle and the game is on.

Tank and I push forward as we dominate the puck in perfect sync with each other. Hell, even Jaxon is in with us tonight. Well, I suppose that's not fair. Jaxon has been working his ass off a lot lately. I think he might have even grown enough to take over as captain next year, but we'll see how he does during the rest of the season.

Two skaters charge at me, and I shoot the puck to Tank who sends it straight to Jaxon as he comes up the center. I dart to the left to narrowly avoid being slammed into the wall and come up behind Jaxon in case he needs assistance. He won't, though. He's lined up perfectly. He won't miss.

Jaxon rears back with his stick, shoots it forward, and just as expected, sends the puck sailing straight into the back of the net.

The crowd flies to their feet, roaring their support and practically shaking the stands beneath them. Hell, if this place wasn't built so great, I'd be worried it would come down on us at any second.

Jaxon turns back and looks at me, and I realize he's searching for my approval. I skate up to him and hold my fist out. "Good work, kid," I say with a nod as he bumps my fist with pride in his eyes and a grin the size of Texas across his face.

I watch him in surprise as he skates off. Out of all of us fuck-ups, who would have thought Jaxon Payne would be the one to surprise me?

He skates past the rest of our team hanging out over the barrier to clap him on the back as he passes. I come up behind him and meet Coach's eyes. He gives me a quick nod telling me to keep it up. Like I'd plan to do any differently.

The next eight minutes are both the slowest, the fastest, and the most painful eight minutes of my life as I take in every detail of the game. Watching every player's footwork, their positions on the ice, and where they move while also keeping an eye locked on the puck.

Tank and I take charge of the game. The opposition has been wearing down since halfway through the last period, which gives us the perfect opportunity to show them who owns this ice. Tank and I give the audience a show, demonstrating just how we got dubbed the Dream Team, and pull the scores even further apart.

The final buzzer sounds, and I couldn't be prouder of my boys.

We've made it to the semi-finals. The Frozen Four in Chicago. The place where we're going to annihilate any team that stands in our way of winning the championship.

The audience is once again up on their feet as we line up in the center of the ice to shake hands with the opposing team, all of them grunting at us in frustration and disappointment.

We head off the ice and down into the locker room with Coach Harris following behind. "Good work, boys," he states as he walks into the center of the room to be seen by everyone. "You kicked their asses tonight. It was close for a moment, but you brought it home. You worked as a team and showed them whose house this is," he says, getting a loud cheer from all around the room.

"Get yourselves cleaned up, celebrate tonight, and be back here again tomorrow for training. We're off to The Frozen Four in six days, and you all need to be ready." He gives us a nod before turning and making his way for the door, then doubles back to glance at me and Tank. "You two," he says. "You've got press wanting to meet with you. Don't fuck it up, and most importantly, don't embarrass me."

We each nod and wait for him to exit, then turn to each other with wolfish grins. We fucking made it.

I quickly shower, get dressed, and walk out with my boys. The crowd is still strong as they wait for us to exit, and I search through the crowd and spot a mop of golden hair facing away with my number and name across her back. As if sensing me, Dani turns around and gives me a beaming, brilliant smile.

"Congratulations," she says, jumping into my arms and planting a huge kiss on my lips. "You were amazing."

"Thanks, babe," I say, winding my arms down her body to give her ass a firm squeeze. "You up for the celebratory party tonight?"

"Is it okay if I skip tonight?" she cringes. "It's been a huge week. I was kind of hoping for an early night."

Damn. I should have known. As if she would want to party after the week she's had. "Do you want me to come back with you?" I ask.

"No, don't be stupid," she laughs. "Go and celebrate with the boys. You can wake me up when you get home," she smirks with a wink.

"Fuck, baby, I plan to," I murmur in her ear.

She giggles and gives me another kiss as she tightens her arms around me in a warm hug. She pulls back and looks at me with nothing but awe and pride, making me want to put that look on her face every damn day. "Here," I say, digging into my pocket and pulling out my keys. "Let me put my shit in the SUV and you can drive it home."

"Thanks," she smiles, taking them from me.

I walk her out to the parking lot and throw my hockey bag in the back of the SUV. I tell her about the press interview on the way, which has her asking a million questions. I help her up into the SUV and watch as she drives away before heading back into the stadium to find Tank.

I find him leaning against the wall of the merchandise shop as Sophie helps the girls finish up. "Hey, man," I say, getting the guy's attention. "You ready?"

He nods at me with a wide grin. "Yeah."

We squeeze our way through the lingering crowd and make our

way back down the hallway that leads to the locker room. Instead of heading right, we go left toward the conference room. We find the door and push our way through to discover a few people sitting in front of a long table with two chairs behind it.

Once inside the room, I take a moment to quickly look around. There are two women holding notepads and a man with a camera. Coach Harris stands in the back looking as though he's about to start shitting bricks. We take our seats and they jump straight into it.

We stay for at least twenty minutes, with both the women asking numerous questions about our season, our team, what we hope for the future, and most of all, our relationship as the Dream Team. I even get asked who I think would be a good captain for next season. I let them know that I believe Jaxon should be put up for the role, looking at Coach as I say it. He raises a questioning brow at me but gives me a slight nod, and I realize that Coach has seen the same hard work and improvement coming from Jaxon that I have.

We finish off our interview and meet with Coach right outside the door. "Fuck, that was awesome," I say to Tank, who grins back at me.

"Yes, you both handled yourselves well. Keep it up because there will be a lot more of that in Chicago," Coach tells us, and I momentarily wonder if it will be televised. I know my family would get a kick out of seeing me on live television. You know, apart from the actual hockey games, which they have seen millions of times.

Tank and I head out, bypassing the merchandise store to pick up Sophie, who floods us with questions about the interview.

The boys wanted to head out to a club tonight, so we drive straight past Micky's. Tank pulls up at the club a few minutes later and takes Sophie by the hand, leading her inside. I hang out front for a moment, pulling my phone out to let Dani know how it went, when I see a missed call from Mia from earlier this afternoon and a few missed calls from Mom a bit later on. She probably wanted to congratulate me.

I give Dani a call, giving her a quick rundown of the interview and promising to give her all the lengthy, boring details in the morning over breakfast. She wishes me a good night and I end the call, wishing I could be with her. But it's important to be here with the boys.

Pressing a few buttons on the screen, I pull up Mia's number and hit call. The phone rings out, and I leave her a message telling her to call me back when she can and remind her that she's a brat. Next up, I dial Mom.

She answers almost immediately, which isn't surprising because she hates making people wait. "Hello," she says, her voice hardly recognizable.

"Mom, hey. Sorry, I missed your calls. I was busy on the ice getting my team to Chicago," I tell her, the pride swelling through my chest.

"Oh, honey," she whimpers with a cry, and I realize this isn't a cry of happiness. It's sorrowful and heartbreaking. She lets out a heavy sob that has me wondering what the fuck is going on.

"Mom?" I question, my brows furrowed as concern grips me, refusing to let go. "What's wrong? What happened?"

"Baby, I'm so sorry," she sobs, barely getting the words out. "I don't know how to tell you this. It's Mia."

My concern quickly morphs into terror over what could have the strongest woman I know turning into a sobbing mess. "What is it, Mom?" I rush out as my stomach sinks with unease. "What's wrong with Mia? What happened?"

"There was an accident," she cries as she struggles to breathe, completely distraught. "She's gone, Miller. My baby is gone."

I don't hear what she says next as I fall to my knees in the middle of the walkway, my heart sinking deeper than my despair. How could she be gone? My baby sister? Little Mia.

Dead.

CHAPTER 23

DANIELLE

I'm startled awake by a loud ringing that has me nearly falling out of bed. Groaning, I roll over and reach for Miller, but when I realize he isn't home yet, I sit up a little to see the alarm clock on his bedside table.

Crap. It's two in the morning.

Where the hell is he?

As the ringing continues, I reach for my phone to silence it, but when I see Tank's name flashing on the caller ID, an odd feeling settles in my stomach. Hitting accept on his call, I bring the phone up to my ear. "Hello?" I croak through my sleepy haze.

"Babe, hey. It's Tank," he shouts over the sound of what must be a bar or club.

"Uh, yeah," I hesitate. "What's up?"

"I'm sorry to ask, but do you mind coming out to get your boy? I just found him at a bar and he doesn't look good."

"What?" I ask sitting up in bed. "What do you mean you *found him?*"

"He bailed early on. I figured he went home to you, but apparently, he wanted to drink alone in a bar."

"Oh, umm . . . okay," I say, a little confused as to why Miller would bail on his team, especially tonight. I mean, he's supposed to be celebrating. "Where is he? I'll come now," I say, throwing the blankets off while I run around the room to find a pair of jeans and a shirt.

Tank gives me the details of where to find them as I rush down the stairs and grab the keys to Miller's SUV.

"Hey," he says, pulling my attention back to the conversation. "Could you hurry? He looks off in the distance like there's something on his mind. Something bad. I've never seen him like this."

"What do you mean?"

"I'm not sure," he says. "Just . . . get here."

I rush out the door, throwing myself up into his SUV and kicking the engine over. Hitting the gas, I speed off down the road, following the directions Tank gave me. Twenty minutes later, I pull up to an old, worn-down bar, far away from the college population. A place where you would only go to be alone.

I hop out of the truck and make my way to the door, swinging it open to find Sophie and Tank sitting at a table just inside the door. Sophie jumps up immediately and makes her way to me, pulling me in for a tight hug. "Hey," she says. "Thanks for coming."

"No problem," I say, pulling back and glancing around the bar in concern. "Where is he?"

Tank comes over to join us and nods toward a dark corner of the bar. I follow his gaze and find Miller sitting alone, slumped over the bar, nursing a glass of hard liquor. "You just left him there alone?" I ask, outraged.

"We tried," Tank says. "He doesn't want the company."

I ignore Tank's comments and take a step in Miller's direction only to be stopped by a hand at my elbow. I glance back at Tank who gives me a sympathetic cringe. "Just be careful. He seems angry."

I give him a nod and he releases my elbow. As I make my way over to Miller, I notice his body gently shaking and realize he's sobbing. Rage storms through me at Tank and Sophie for leaving him alone while he's obviously going through some kind of turmoil.

Seeing him like this tears my heart in two and makes me want to do whatever I can to take his pain away. I rush the rest of the way over to him and gently place my hand on his shoulder. His body stiffens under my touch, but he doesn't look up.

"I told you to fuck off," he snarls, tightening his grip on his glass.

I step closer to him so he can feel my body along his. "It's me," I say quietly, afraid to use my full voice for fear of it breaking.

"Dani?" he asks, finally turning to look at me. I gasp when I get a good look at his face. Miller is sporting the red-rimmed bloodshot eyes and wet cheeks of a haunted man. It has me struggling to pull in a full breath. "Dani," he repeats, getting up from his stool and pulling me roughly into his body, wrapping his arms around me like I'm his only lifeline. He buries his face in the crook of my neck and weeps.

I hold him tighter, giving him every ounce of my strength. He wobbles slightly on his feet, and I gently push him back so he sits on the stool. "What is it?" I murmur into his ear. "What's wrong?"

I feel his chest rise and fall with a deep breath as he pulls back to look me in the eye. He searches my face, and I have no idea what he's trying to find, but whatever it is, he finds it there. He lets out a deep sigh as I place both my hands on the sides of his face and lean into him. "Mia was walking home from the store this afternoon. She was hit by a drunk driver. Sh-she was killed on impact," he whispers as he struggles to get the words out.

"Fuck," I gasp, feeling my eyes immediately fill with tears. A violent sob rips from my body, and I crush myself against Miller.

Holy shit.

I know I never met her, but she was the one person Miller loved more than anything in this world. He would talk about her constantly, and I can't imagine, even for a second, the agony he must be going through.

"Let me take you home," I beg, knowing that being here in a rundown bar is not what he needs right now. I've never had anybody close to me pass away before, let alone someone as close as an only sibling. I have no idea what to do or say, and I hope I'm doing the right thing for him. I guess all I can do is be here for him. Be his rock when he needs it.

Miller doesn't answer but allows me to tug on his hand and bring him to his feet. He grabs his drink from the counter and throws back what's left as I loop his arm over my shoulder and struggle to help him out. He leans his full weight on me and Tank rushes in, sliding his arms around Miller and taking his weight, keeping me from buckling to the ground.

Tank helps Miller up into the SUV while I heave myself into the driver's seat. "Why don't you guys get in? I'll give you a ride home."

"Sure," he says, motioning for Sophie to hop in the back. He helps her up before climbing in behind her. "Just take us to your place. You're going to need me to get him upstairs. He's a big fucker, you know," he says, trying to make light of the situation. If only he knew. "We'll walk home from your place."

"Thanks," I say, giving him a tight smile.

"Is everything okay?" Sophie asks, leaning forward in the seat and placing a hand on my shoulder.

I take a deep breath and kick over the engine. "No. It's not," I tell them honestly. "I'm sure Miller will talk to you when he's ready," I tell them both, unsure how he would feel about me sharing his heartache. I glance over at Miller to find him on the verge of passing out, but I have a feeling sleep is going to be hard for him to find tonight.

I pull out of my spot and reach over to him with my free hand, taking his hand in mine and lacing our fingers. He gives me a sad, tortured smile and squeezes my hand gently.

We drive home in pained silence and arrive back at our doorstep twenty minutes later. True to his word, Tank helps me get Miller upstairs. "Thank you," I tell him. "I'll call you guys in the morning."

Tank gives me a curt nod and makes his way back down the stairs.

I lead Miller into the bathroom and begin stripping him. I hear Sophie and Tank let themselves out the front door before hearing the distinct sound of the door being locked. I mentally send Tank another thanks, knowing that it's one less thing I have to worry about tonight.

Miller rests against the vanity as I lean into the shower and wait for the water to warm up. I pull off my clothes and drag Miller into the shower behind me. He wobbles slightly but manages to get himself in the shower.

I focus solely on getting him cleaned up, scrubbing the foul scent of dirty cigarettes and alcohol off his body. Reaching up, I wash his hair and watch as he closes his eyes to allow me to rinse it out. Once he's clean, I press my body against his and wrap my arms around him.

I feel him harden against my stomach and hear him inhale deeply. I raise my head from his chest and press my lips to his. "I need you," he says with a sharp edge to his voice, and I realize that this is something different. This isn't going to be sweet and soft. He isn't going to make love to me. He's going to fuck me, and it is going to be hard, fast, and raw.

Animalistic.

"Okay," I nod, looking up into his eyes so he understands completely. "Anything you need."

He groans into my hair and flips me around so my back is to his chest. His fingers wrap around my hip as he yanks me back into him, crushing my ass against his erection. He places his free hand on my back and bends me over as I throw my hands up against the wall, just in time to catch myself as he slams into me.

I cry out as he pounds into me, over and over again to the point of pain, but I don't dare stop him. I know how desperately he needs this release. His fingers dig into the flesh of my hip, and I know for sure it will leave a bruise, but I can't find it in myself to care. He needs this, and I will do anything to help ease that pain.

His free hand snakes around the front of my body and pinches down on my clit, sending me into an overwhelming wave of pleasure, my orgasm sneaking up on me in surprise. I scream out as he pumps harder, and then finally, he stills inside me as he finds his release.

Miller takes a deep breath as he pulls out of me and lets go of his grip on my hip. He turns me back around and pulls me firmly against his body.

"Come on, let me take you to bed," I say, turning off the water and stepping out of the shower. Dragging him along, I grab a towel, quickly drying us off before leading him to our bed.

I skip the whole dressing thing, deciding that would be way too hard, and put him straight to bed before rushing to the home office, finding a trash can under the desk. Coming back to our room, I place the trash can down beside the bed, ready and waiting in case he needs to throw up.

After placing a glass of water and some aspirin on his bedside table, I finally climb into bed beside him and open myself up for whatever he needs. He rolls over to me and pulls me into his arms, nuzzling his face into my neck. "Thank you," he murmurs.

"It's okay," I tell him. "I just wish I could take away your pain."

"I know," he sighs. "Me too."

With that, Miller quickly falls into a tortured sleep, his head resting heavily on my shoulder. It causes me to cramp up, but I couldn't possibly disturb him. Instead, I wrap my arms more firmly around him as he jumps and frets in his sleep, all the while calling out for Mia to come back to him.

I wake a few hours later, get myself dressed, and pack a few bags for myself and Miller. I'm riffling around in the kitchen to put something together for his breakfast when I hear him approaching from behind. His arms circle my waist, and he pulls me back against him.

"Sorry about last night," he murmurs in my ear.

I turn around in his hold and look up into his bloodshot eyes. "It's okay. You needed it and that's all that matters."

He doesn't reply but holds me closer and lets out a deep breath. When he finally releases me, he takes a look around the kitchen and notices breakfast there waiting for him. He cringes at it and then looks back at me with regret. "Thanks, babe, but I don't think I can handle food for a few hours."

"Yeah, I wasn't sure. Don't worry, I'll eat it," I say, opening the cutlery drawer to pull out a knife and fork.

Picking up the plate, I make my way into the living room and sit down on the couch with my legs crossed. Miller comes and joins me on the couch while I eat, sitting beside me in silence, lost in his thoughts. I'm no mind reader, but I'm certain about where his thoughts have led him this morning.

Finishing my breakfast, I lean forward to place the empty plate on the coffee table, and as I do, Miller grabs me and lifts me onto his lap. I loop my arms around his neck and give him a soft kiss. "I think you should give Tank a call. He's worried about you."

"Yeah, I'll do that this morning," he says, dropping his face to my shoulder. He takes a deep breath before his pained tone cuts through the room. "Will you come home with me? I know it's not the best circumstances to meet my family, or what's left of it," he scoffs. "But I can't do this without you."

I pull him tighter against me. "I've already packed our bags. There's no place I'd rather be than by your side," I whisper. "I figured I could take care of the funeral arrangements if that's okay with you and your mom. It's just one less thing you have to worry about."

"You don't have to do that," he says, shaking his head.

I take his face in my hands and make sure he truly hears me. "Organizing a funeral is hard enough on its own, let alone doing it for your baby girl or little sister. Your mom is already going through enough pain. I just want to do anything I can to make this a little easier for her . . . for you."

"I don't want to burden you with this, but at the same time, I would do anything to make this better for Mom and take away what little pain I can," he says, conflicted.

"It's okay," I tell him as I look deeply into his eyes, hoping he can see just how serious I am about this. "Let me handle this. Talk to your mom. If she's not comfortable with it, then I'll back off."

He takes another deep breath and searches my eyes before giving me a slow, pained nod. "You let me know if it's too much and I'll take over," he says, brushing his knuckles down the side of my face.

"I promise."

Miller holds me for a moment longer when I decide it's finally time. "Come on," I tell him. "Your mom is all alone at home, and she needs you more than ever. Why don't you go call Tank and then we can get going after that."

He lets out a heavy breath and raises us both off the couch before placing me down gently on my feet. He walks to the front door and spots our bags, grabbing them in one hand while digging through his pocket for his phone. I watch him out the window as he loads up the SUV for me and presses buttons on his phone to search for Tank's number.

I do a once over around the house, making sure all the windows and doors are locked, then head back down to the kitchen and wash up my dishes from breakfast. Once I'm finished and ready to go, I grab my handbag off the counter and take a seat in the living room, flicking on ESPN while I wait for Miller to finish his phone call.

The screen lights up with the highlights from the Dragons' game last night, and I listen as the reporter states that it was one of Miller's best games. He comments how it must have been one of the best nights of his life, and I shake my head at the screen, my chest aching.

I hear Miller scoff from behind me. "If only they knew, right?" he murmurs, scowling at the screen before turning his gaze on me. "Are you ready?"

"Yeah, let's go," I say, picking up the remote and turning it off.

I follow Miller out the door and take the keys from him. "What are you doing?" he asks, attempting to take them back.

"After how much you drank last night, I can assure you that you are still way over the legal limit, and considering the circumstances, there's no way I'm letting you get behind the wheel," I tell him, hoping I'm not crossing too many lines with him this morning. I know he's going to have to break at some point. But still, there's no way he's driving today.

He gives in and drops his hand. "Yeah, you're right," he sighs and continues over to his SUV. He opens the driver's side for me and helps me climb up, and even in his worst moments, I can't fault him. He's still the perfect gentleman.

We get on the road, driving the few hours back to his hometown. He points out the frozen lake where he first learned to skate—the very one where he fell in love with hockey and recognized his potential as a player. We continue driving to the next town over, the one they moved to when he was ten. The one that held an actual ice rink with a hockey team for him to join. He continues pointing out different places that hold special meaning to him, like his school and where his friends used to live. Hell, he even shows me the little café where he got his first kiss from some chick named Megan.

Five minutes later, he directs me around some residential streets before telling me to stop in front of a small, beautiful, cottage-style house. "This is it," he says, glancing at his childhood home.

He hops out of the truck and grabs the bags from the backseat before meeting me around the front. Miller takes my hand, and we walk down the small pathway, his gaze roaming over the house, probably remembering all the memories he shared with Mia growing up.

We make it up to the front door, and he takes a deep breath before knocking.

The door opens moments later by a small woman who I can immediately tell is Miller's mom. She gasps the moment she sees him and falls into his arms. Miller drops the bags and catches her with ease as she begins to sob into his chest. He holds her tight and somehow ushers her back inside their home. He leads her to the living room, and I follow behind, bringing our bags in and leaving them by the front door.

I make my way deeper into their home and search out the kitchen. After taking two wrong turns, I finally find it and grab his mom a glass of water before heading back to the living room. The poor woman is trying her hardest to pull herself together.

I hand her the glass of water as she finishes wiping her tears. "I'm so sorry you had to see that, dear. I'm Juliette," she says, taking a sip of water to help calm herself.

"It's more than okay," I tell her. "I understand. I'm Dani."

She flashes me a beautiful smile that's so much like her son's as she and Miller both stand. "It's a pleasure to meet you," she says, stepping forward and taking me in her arms. "I've heard wonderful things about you."

"Thank you," I say. "I'm so sorry for your loss."

She holds me a little tighter then pulls back to study my face. She lets out a pained sigh. "I bet you and Mia would have been amazing friends," she tells me with sincerity.

"I would like to think so, too. I regret that I never got the chance to meet her, but from what I've heard, she was an absolute force to be reckoned with."

Juliette giggles at that and gives me a thoughtful smile. "That she was."

CHAPTER 24

MILLER

The days following my arrival back home are easily the hardest days I have ever endured in my life. I've been to hockey camps that exhausted me physically and mentally, and up until the last few days, I thought they were the worst things I could have suffered through. But being back home in a house full of my sister's memories, seeing her beautiful, smiling face plastered all over the walls in every available picture frame, and knowing it's a face I will never see again, it haunts me.

As promised, Dani has been my rock. She has taken care of everything. She organized the most spectacular funeral for my baby sister, and she made sure Mom and I didn't have to worry about a thing. She shooed away the people who came to the door and took care of the cooking and cleaning while Mom and I were breaking down. She even called Coach Harris to explain what was going on to save my ass from getting kicked off the team due to my unexplained absences.

As I said, she has been my rock. Particularly during the middle of the funeral when one of Mia's very drunk friends got up and decided then was the time to air all Mia's secrets. Dani quickly got up and shut that shit right down like the fucking queen that she is.

I wasn't sure if I'd be able to stand at her service and talk about what she meant to me. I spent the days beforehand sitting in my childhood bedroom ripping up every word I wrote. Hell, I even went as far as to say I wasn't going to do it. Mia knew how I felt about her. Why should I have to share that with a bunch of dickheads I've never met before?

But come time for the funeral, Dani asked me to get up and say a few words. Not something generic that I would have written down, but something for everybody, something that came from my heart. So that's exactly what I did.

I shared stories of my childhood and told the congregation how I loved my sister so fiercely, despite how she loved to be the bane of my existence. I hardly made it through the funeral without breaking down, but I'm happy I did it. I would have never forgiven myself if I hadn't gotten up there and shared a bit of Mia with everyone. A bit that nobody but me, as her brother, had the chance to experience.

Which brings me to now.

I stand here by myself on a mountaintop in the national forest behind my childhood home. The exact mountaintop that Mia and I used to climb every summer. I hold her ashes close to my chest as I remember a night about five or six years ago. There was a huge storm and Mom had been out of town visiting her sister, so it was just me and Mia at home.

The storm was like nothing I'd ever seen, and Mia was scared. She must have only been eleven or twelve. We were sitting in the living room watching some ridiculous movie she chose when thunder cracked so loudly right as the power went out. The house fell into darkness, and she screamed and cried as the front window broke from the wind, sending a raging gust through the house.

I ran into Mom's bedroom, grabbed the blanket off her bed, and covered Mia in it. Come to think of it, the blanket did nothing to protect her from the storm, but somehow, it managed to calm her. I rifled through the house looking for flashlights while trying to use the shitty light on my phone.

I did my best to board up the window, and after deeming the house secure enough, I went back and joined Mia in the living room. She forced me into a game of *Would You Rather* to get her mind off the storm, and I remember her asking me the most ridiculous questions that I was shocked an eleven-year-old could come up with.

We played for ages, asking stupid questions like would you rather eat dog food for a week or go streaking through a movie cinema with all your friends there to watch. The game took a turn when she asked if I would rather be buried or cremated.

I looked over at her in question, trying to figure out why she would even be thinking about it, then she scolded me for not answering her question in a timely manner. "Well?" she asked, crossing her little arms over her chest.

"Well, I don't know. I guess I've never really thought about it," I told her. "Have you?"

"Yep," she announced, proudly. "I want to be cremated."

"Okay," I said, a little confused. "I'll bite. Why would you want to be cremated?"

"Because I don't want my body to rot in the ground til the end of time. I want to be free when I die. I want to be cremated, and you know that mountain we climb every summer? I want my ashes to be scattered there, right at the very top when a big gust of wind comes so I can fly one last time."

That was the moment I realized my little sister wasn't so little after all. She was growing up, and quite frankly, that scared the shit out of me. "Well," I said with a smirk, playing off my emotions. "That's never going to happen because you're going to live forever, annoying anyone who stands in your way."

She laughed up at me and snuggled closer to my side. "I love you too, big brother," she smiled.

So here I am now, standing at the top of this mountain in the very spot she had told me all those years ago, holding her ashes to my chest and not wanting to let go. Mom and Dani wanted to come up here too, but I knew Mom wouldn't be able to make it all the way. After all, it took me two hours to get here and to tell the truth, this is something I wanted to do for my sister. Just me and Mia, one last time.

I feel a strong breeze coming along and begin to unscrew the lid.

"I hate that you left us, Mia, but I know you had no choice in the matter. I love you so much, baby sister. You've left this huge, gaping hole in my chest and it hurts so bad," I tell her as I begin to break down and cry. "I'm going to miss you like you wouldn't believe, but I'll see you again one day. So you better be ready for me when I come."

I feel the wind strengthen around me, and I know it's time to let her go. I tip the ashes out into the wind and watch as she floats through the sky, flying one last time, just like she wanted. "Goodbye, Mia. I love you."

I fall to my knees as I watch her ashes disappear into the wind, finally free.

I can't find it in me to go back straight away, so I sit here at the top of the mountain for another few hours, remembering my sister. Remembering the times we had come up here together.

Picking up a rock, I walk to the highest tree and carve her name into the trunk so she can forever leave her mark on this world. So everyone who comes to this mountaintop will know that Mia was here.

CHAPTER 25

DANIELLE

We arrive back at Miller's place late on Wednesday evening. We would have stayed another night with his mom, but the Dragons are putting on a benefit skate night for the Denver Youth Hockey Program tomorrow. This is the team's big chance to present the youth group with the check from the fundraising we've done this season. Then early tomorrow morning, we have to fly out to Chicago to kick off The Frozen Four. Those few days will be paramount in determining if our boys will remain undefeated and win the championship.

I sit up in bed and plug my phone into the charger. "What if I don't go?" Miller asks as he climbs into bed beside me and begins studying his hands all too closely.

"What are you talking about?" I ask, dreading where this conversation is going.

"The Frozen Four. The NHL. All of it. I pushed myself this hard because Mia was the one who wanted me to go all the way. She was the one who said I could do it. I don't know. It just feels wrong without her here," he says, dropping his head into his hands.

I snuggle into his side. "Do you think you would have still tried to make it to the NHL if Mia hadn't suggested it herself?"

He's thoughtful for a short while before looking up at me. "Yeah, I guess. It's every little boy's dream to be in the NHL. I just didn't think it was possible until Mia convinced me it was."

"Do you love playing?" I ask.

"Yeah."

"Now, do you play because you love it or because Mia wanted this for you?"

"Both," he admits.

"Would you want Mia to give up on something she loves because you weren't around anymore?" I ask, climbing up over his hips to straddle him, giving me a perfect view of his face.

He places his hands down on my thighs. "Of course not."

"Then, assuming she was as stubborn as you are, I think she would have been mighty pissed if she knew you were even considering giving up. If you truly love hockey and it's your dream to be in the NHL, then you need to go for it. Do it for Mia, but mostly, do it for yourself."

He lets out a deep breath and pulls me down to him. "You're amazing."

"I try," I say, then grind my hips down on his, desperately needing his touch. The last time I had him was the rough night in the shower. "I've missed this," I tell him as my lips come down on his.

I feel him harden beneath me. "I know. I'm sorry. Let me make it up to you," he promises, and make it up to me he does.

"C rap, it's early," Sophie yawns as we meet the rest of the team at the airport.

"No, it's not," I laugh. "You just couldn't get your ass out of bed."

We had the Skate Benefit Night last night and it was huge. There were kids everywhere in their little hockey skates and Dragons jerseys. It was amazing. They had the time of their lives when all my boys came out to skate with them, and I must say, it was great to see Miller enjoying himself, even if it was just for a little bit.

My favorite part was when Coach Harris asked me and Sophie to come up and present the huge novelty check, for $150,000.00, to the Denver Youth Hockey Program. He even gave us a special mention, saying none of this would have been possible without us.

Even Professor Whitaker came along to support the boys, and she let me and Sophie know just how proud she was of us. But after still celebrating at the ice rink until 1 a.m., Coach finally sent all the boys home to get some rest.

Which puts us here at the airport, tired as fuck, as we wait for our flight to be called. My phone rings deep in my pocket, and I pull it out, finding a private number.

"Hello," I say, curious as to who would be calling me.

"Danielle, hi. It's Officer Samuels," she says. "I tried to call you a few times, but there was no answer."

"Oh sorry. We have had quite a busy week," I explain. I called her a few days ago explaining why we wouldn't be making it to court. She understood, sent her condolences, and said that our statement alone should be enough to get things over the line.

"Yes, that's right. Anyway, I wanted to call and let you know what happened at court."

"Oh, of course," I say, getting up and walking over to a quiet area of the airport so I can hear every damn word she says.

"It was a success. The trial has been set for three months from now. Brett will remain behind bars, without bail. If all goes well at trial, he'll be convicted of abuse, attempted rape, arson, and attempted murder. He will be going away for a long time," she assures me.

"Wow, that's great," I say with relief. "Is there anything you need from me?"

"No, that's it. It's all over. You are free to get on with your life," she tells me.

"Holy crap," I sigh. "Thank you so much."

"It was my pleasure. Have a good day," she says, then ends our call.

I glance up to find Miller's questioning stare on me and rush over to throw myself into his strong arms, telling him the good news. His body visibly relaxes under me as if a huge weight has been lifted off his shoulders.

Wanting to put my parents out of their misery, I give them a quick call, and the minute I hang up, I find Sophie hovering right behind me. "Did I just hear what I think I just heard?"

I give her a bright smile. "Damn straight you did," I tell her, getting up off Miller's lap and wrapping my arms around her.

"Thank God," she sighs.

"Tell me about it."

Thirty minutes later, we board our flight, and I freak out when the plane takes off, gripping the armrest and praying we survive, only to promptly fall asleep as exhaustion catches up with me.

Coach gives us the rundown of how things are going to go, and it's basically a huge press conference before the games start, with a shitload more meetings and interviews in between. I must admit, I'm nervous about it as word of Mia's death has now gotten around, and they're bound to ask Miller how he's holding up. But I've assured Coach Harris that he will be fine. Or at least, I hope he is. If not, that's what I'm here for.

I wake an hour before the plane is due to land and pull my head up off Miller's shoulder. "Good sleep?" he asks.

"No," I grumble and look up to find Miller smirking down at me. "What?" I ask, narrowing my eyes at him.

He looks around quickly then leans down to me. "You want to join the Mile High Club?" he murmurs in my ear.

"What?" I whisper-yell as my eyes widen in shock. "You can't be serious?"

"Oh, I am so serious," he tells me with a sexy smirk.

I glance around the cabin to find the majority of the team fast asleep, and the ones still awake are certainly not paying attention to us. I bite my bottom lip, knowing this is a bad idea, but honestly, who could say no to this man? "Okay, you're on," I smirk back at him. "How's this supposed to work?"

"Go down to the bathroom. I'll come and join you in a few minutes," he tells me.

I give one last nervous glance around before finally nodding and standing up. Making my way down the aisle to the bathroom, I'm almost certain every last person knows what I'm doing. The second I get inside the tiny space, without a damn person even glancing my way, a wave of relief washes over me.

Twenty minutes later, I can proudly say that I am now a member of the Mile High Club, and to say having sex in an airplane bathroom is difficult is the biggest understatement I've ever heard. But my man can make anything work. What's even better is that no one knows our dirty little secret. Or at least, I hope they don't.

"You ready for this?" Miller asks a few minutes out from landing. "It's going to be crazy in there. Heaps of fans and press."

"Yeah, I'll be fine. It's you they want," I laugh.

"Don't doubt for one second that they aren't going to hound you too. You're my girl. They're going to want to meet the woman who finally tamed the famous Miller Cain," he smirks.

"I can handle myself," I tell him as the plane begins to descend. I grab his hand in a death hold, squeezing it until I'm sure I've cut off the circulation.

"I thought you could handle yourself?" he teases, flipping his hand over so that I can hold it properly.

"I can," I snap. "I just don't like to fly."

"Okay, okay," he says, holding his other hand up in surrender. "No need to get your panties in a twist."

"How can I get my panties in a twist when you won't give them back?" I hiss under my breath. Miller smirks back at me and gently pats his pocket where my black lace thong currently resides. "Jerk," I mutter.

The plane takes its sweet time landing, and when we finally make it into the airport, we find it filled with press and fans, everyone calling out, desperate for the attention of their favorite Dragon. I know I might be slightly biased, but I swear I hear Miller's name being called far more often than the rest of the boys. Though I can't blame the fans for their obsession. Miller Cain truly is a star.

After getting through security and surviving the masses, we finally make it to the hotel. The boys are given a good half an hour to get changed into their suits for the first press conference. I watch as Miller strips off and gets himself suited up, and man does he look good.

"Stop looking at me like that," he scolds as he pulls on his suit jacket.

"I can't help it," I say, continuing to mentally undress him.

He walks over to me with that cocky, signature smirk and runs his fingers down my body, starting at my shoulder and trailing down my waist, sending shivers over my skin. My body reacts to his touch and he doesn't miss a thing. "Fuck, baby. I wish I had time to give you what you need right now," he murmurs into my ear.

"I know you do," I say, reaching forward and palming his hard cock through his pants.

"Don't get me started on something I can't finish," he warns, taking both my shoulders in his hands and stepping out of my reach. "I have to go."

"I know, Captain," I sulk. "You'll be great. I'm going to go down to Sophie's room to watch you guys on TV and order room service."

"Okay," he grins. "Don't wait up for me, though. I'll probably be late."

"K," I smile, stepping back into his arms. "Just be prepared. Someone, whether it's today or in three days, is going to ask about Mia."

"I know," he says, letting out a shaky breath. "But it's going to be okay. I'm ready."

I look up into his eyes and realize he is. Wanting to send him off in the right way, I reach up onto my tippy-toes and give him a deep kiss. "Go get 'em, Tiger," I mock.

"You're such a smart ass," he laughs as he grabs his phone and wallet off the table and slides them into his pocket. He walks with me down to Sophie and Tank's room, and as I slip inside, Tank comes out. Sophie and I watch in awe as our sexy boys strut back down the hallway, looking as handsome as ever in their team suits.

We make ourselves comfortable on the couch as we check out the competition on ESPN while ordering room service. The other teams look pretty good, but we know they have nothing on our boys. But maybe that's just my ego talking. For them to have made it this far in the competition means they're really fucking good, and these next few games are going to challenge my boys like never before. But they're ready. They can handle this.

An hour later, the Dragons are introduced, and my man's face appears on the screen with his ranking and stats. I squeal out as he smirks at the camera and mouths, "Love you, baby." Pride surges through me, and I must admit, I tear up just a little.

Next up is Tank, who holds up his hands to make a heart and gives the camera a sexy smirk while Sophie screams out that she's so horny for him. The rest of the team follows, and eventually, the full team sits behind the longest table I've ever seen, each with their own microphone and little nameplate.

It doesn't take long for the press to jump straight into their questions, starting with Coach Harris and then moving on to the boys. All the regular questions are thrown around.

"How did you prepare?"

"Do you think you're ready?"

"What has your training been like?"

Blah, blah, blah.

Before I know it, they start to get personal, and a wave of nerves settles in the pit of my stomach. The boys are asked about the fundraising event with the calendar and the auction, which managed to get national attention. Miller pipes up and answers these questions, making sure to mention Sophie and me in the process. He then goes on to tell them about donating the proceeds to the Denver Youth Hockey Program.

On and on it goes, question after question until a small brunette stands up and makes herself known. "Hi there, my question is for Miller Cain," she announces. There's a slight pause as the camera pans back to Miller, and he indicates for her to go on with her question. "Hi, Miller," she starts. "I don't mean to be insensitive. However, it's well known that your younger sister, Mia Cain, has recently passed in a tragic accident. What we would like to know is, how is this going to impact your performance tomorrow?"

Miller smiles back at the woman. "I was wondering how long it would take for Mia's name to be mentioned," he smiles fondly. "She always used to bug me about giving her a shout-out at one of these. It's a shame that it's under such awful circumstances. But as for my performance? Mia always had faith in me that I could do anything I put my mind to, including taking out the championship. When I get on that ice tomorrow, I'm skating for her. So, no. My performance is not something I'm concerned about. If anything, I know I'll be skating my absolute best."

Holy crap. That's my man.

I wipe tears from my eyes as pride surges through me, and for the second time in twenty minutes, I realize that every word he has just said is as true as it could possibly be. Tomorrow he isn't skating for himself or his team. He's doing this for his sister, which is how I know the opposing team won't stand a chance. Miller will come out on top, even if it kills him.

A few hours later, I'm fast asleep in bed when I feel a familiar warm body crawl in beside me and scoop me up. "You did amazing. I'm so proud of you," I murmur in my sleepy haze.

"Thanks, baby," he says, planting a soft kiss on my temple. "Go back to sleep. We have a huge day tomorrow."

CHAPTER 26

MILLER

Just as I promised to the nosey bitch of a reporter, I kicked ass and skated every moment of the semi-finals with Mia in mind. It was a hard game, one of the hardest I've ever played. But I kept on and, in the end, we won it for Mia.

The boys all stopped me in the locker room before heading out to let me know that they were all skating for Mia too. It nearly brought me to my knees seeing how the boys had turned into men over the space of the season. I couldn't have been prouder of them.

I thanked them all and got out on that ice, and as a team, we pushed our way right through to the final, where we'll be skating for the championship. We just happen to be up against the L.A. team that beat us last year, but I won't let that happen again. Not on my watch.

These boys have worked too hard to let it slip through our fingers once again.

We celebrate in the locker room with a quick speech from Coach Harris before getting back into our suits to head out for the after-game reporters.

Following our duties and strict instructions from Coach Harris, Tank and I find our girls and head back to the hotel. "Coach isn't letting us leave the hotel tonight, so I was hoping you'd join me for dinner in the hotel restaurant?" I ask Dani as we step into the elevator.

"My, oh, my. Miller Cain, are you asking me out on a date?" she says in a flirty tone, one that makes me want to bend her over the hotel bar and fuck it out of her system.

"And if I am?" I smirk, willing my cock not to harden in front of our current company. I'll never be able to live that down.

"Oh, I don't know," she says, stepping out of my arms. "I have a boyfriend back home, and I'm not too sure how he would feel about me accepting a date with a superstar."

"What's your boyfriend going to say if he found out the superstar is going to be feasting between his woman's legs tonight?"

Her eyes widen and she gasps as her face goes bright red. "I can't believe you just said that out loud," she scolds.

"Is this an open invitation?" Sophie asks from beside us.

"What?" Dani screeches as Tank looks over at her with curiosity.

"Ahh, what?" I ask.

"Get your mind out of the gutter," Sophie scolds. "I meant the restaurant, not the feasting between my best friend's legs. But just putting it out there, I'm down for an orgy gang bang if you guys wanted to find a few of the boys. Maybe Jaxon and Bobby?"

I look down at Dani as Tank shakes his head, more than used to his girl's kinky quirks. "What do you think, babe?" I ask Dani.

She gapes up at me. "About dinner or the orgy gang bang?"

"Dinner," I laugh.

"Why not?" she says, visibly relieved. "It's a hockey trip though. You should be with your team as much as possible. After all, you're graduating soon, and this is the last college semi-final you'll ever be a part of. You may as well make it count."

"Alright then. I'll see if a few of the boys want to join us," I tell her.

"Make sure you invite Coach Harris. I don't want him to feel left out."

"Yes, boss," I mock.

"Shut it."

I go to pull my phone out of my pocket when Sophie glances between us with a raised brow. "Where are we at with the gang bang?"

Dani rolls her eyes just as Tank locks his arm around Sophie's waist. "You want a gang bang?" he says. "I'll give you a fucking gang bang. Now, where are those toys you brought?"

An hour later, we find ourselves down at the all-you-can-eat buffet restaurant meeting the team as Sophie whines about Tank's one-man gang bang show. Apparently, it wasn't the kind of orgy she was hoping for, but either way, she came out of that room more than satisfied.

All the boys appear over the next few minutes, and before I know it, we're all digging in. Even Coach Harris is going hard on the buffet. Dani sits to one side of me, my hand on her lap, with Tank hungrily annihilating his dinner on my other as I down my plate. I'm just about ready for seconds when the captain of the L.A. team makes an appearance behind me with a few of his teammates.

Just great. The biggest douchebag on the planet wants to interrupt my dinner. Wonderful.

The whole table quietens down as every eye turns in their direction, trying to figure out what the fuck they want.

"Miller," the douchebag says, holding a hand out to me.

I get up out of my seat and reluctantly shake his hand. "Trent," I scoff, letting him know just how much I don't appreciate him. "What do you need? My boys are trying to enjoy a nice dinner together."

"I just wanted to come and wish you luck with the championship game tomorrow."

"That's bullshit. Why are you trying to make a very public show?"

He smirks over at me as he looks up and down the table. I notice Tank standing beside me with Dani now also on her feet, looking between us and clearly aware of the tension radiating off me.

"I heard about your sister," he says with a sick smirk. My back stiffens, and I thank God this dickhead didn't actually use her sweet name. Why the fuck is he even talking about her? "A picture was posted of her today," he explains. "It's a damn shame, I would have liked to test out that pussy. I bet she was real tight."

I see red and storm toward him with my fists outstretched. How dare he? Tank wraps his arms around me and tries with everything he has to hold me back as a few of my teammates get up to help him out.

Dani gets up in my face and tries to get my attention. "Get out of my way. I don't want to hurt you," I snap at her, the rage like nothing I've ever experienced before. I almost feel Tank let go of me, more than on board with me beating the shit out of this motherfucker.

"NO," Dani demands, grabbing my face and forcing my attention to her. "This is what he wants. You knock him out now and you're suspended for tomorrow's game. You'll lose the championship and you can kiss the NHL goodbye."

"Dani. Move."

"No. He's scared of you. He's chicken shit. He knows you're going to kick his ass tomorrow, and he's doing whatever the fuck he can to eliminate the competition. You're not throwing your future away because of this piece of shit," she seethes, indicating the dickhead behind her.

"Come on, man," Tank says to me. "She's right, and you know it."

"Fuck," I yell, finally able to see reason. Tank pulls me back one more step, and I reach out to take Dani in my arms when she holds her hand up to me with a scowl.

Dani turns her back on me, and I cringe, realizing this is the first time she's ever been upset with me. She looks up at Trent, and I so desperately want to pull her away from that piece of shit. "You're a real fucking big man, speaking ill of Mia like that," she spits, looking at him in disgust. "But if anything, you're the biggest fucking idiot. You've just sealed your loss tomorrow because I know for a fact that Miller will not stop until he has defeated you and made you look like the absolute fool that you are. Every single one of them will. They will humiliate you. You will be the laughingstock of ice hockey by the end of that game, and when that final buzzer sounds, you better watch your fucking back."

Dani goes to walk away when Trent laughs at her back. "Ooh, I love a fierce woman. Why don't you come home with me tonight?"

Dani turns back around to him, rears back, and punches him square in the nose with everything she's got. I hear the distinct sound of Trent's nose being crushed beneath her fist, and I stare at her in shock, knowing damn well I'm rocking a semi. Only it quickly fades away at the look of sheer pain ripping across her face.

Trent roars out in pain as blood gushes from his nose, then being the fucking idiot that he is, he lunges for my girl.

Not on my fucking watch.

I grab Dani and pull her out of the way, and lucky for that fucker, his boys finally get a hold of him. I see fucking red for the second time in a few minutes. First he comes after my sister, and then my girl? He should consider himself lucky that I now have enough control to battle it out on the ice. Dani was right. I'm going to deal with this motherfucker man to man, and when I do, not even the little leagues will want him.

His boys drag him out of the restaurant as we laugh at his expense, but I only have one thing on my mind. I turn to look at my girl, my gaze roaming over her body, making sure she's alright.

"Fuck," she cries, shaking out her hand with tears of pain in her green eyes.

"Shit, babe. I can't believe you just did that. Let me look at your hand," I ask, reaching out to her.

"No. No fucking way," she snaps, pointing a finger at me, tears streaking down her face, but she's too fucking angry to cry. "How dare you almost throw away your future on that piece of shit!"

"Babe, I'm sorry," I say, reaching out to her again. "Please, let me see your hand."

"No. Don't fucking touch me," she snaps again before checking over her hand and trying to ball it into a fist. "Fuck, that hurts."

Ignoring her demands, I step into her and take her hand in mine, looking it over to find it already swelling. "I think you might have broken something," I tell her. "Let me take you to the emergency room. You need to get it checked out."

"No. I'm sorry, Miller," she says, the tears still in her eyes, each one of them silently killing me. "I love you, but I'm too fucking angry with you."

My jaw drops, and I gape at her in horror. "The fuck, babe? Did you not hear what he said?"

"Yes, I heard it. It was terrible, and I hope to God you deal with it later, but you were so ready to throw it all away and that pisses me the fuck off," she rants. "I swear to God, if you had touched even one hair on that asshole, I would've broken your nose instead."

"She's not wrong," Coach Harris says, suddenly beside me. He reaches for Dani's wrist and glances over her swollen hand with a frown. "Definitely broken," he says, glancing toward Sophie. "Take Dani to get checked out, and Tank? Take this dickhead upstairs and knock some sense into him before I'm forced to do it. I've had enough of this bullshit for one night. I'm going to bed. All you girls be ready for a 5 a.m. training session," he snaps, then turns on his heel and stalks out of the restaurant.

Fuck.

Sophie moves into Dani's side, and I lean in to kiss my girl, relieved when she kisses me back. She's never been this furious with me before, and I've got no fucking idea how this is going to play out. I just hope to God she's not the kind to break up after one disagreement. I wouldn't survive if she walked away from me now.

Dani turns and leaves with Sophie while Tank drags me upstairs. "What the fuck are we going to do about Trent?" he asks as we step into my room, just as riled up as me.

"I don't know, but there's no way that fucker is getting away with disrespecting Mia like that," I growl.

"I agree, but promise me that whatever goes down, it happens under the radar and after the game," he says.

"Yeah, man. Mia would hate me if I threw it all away like that. Dani was right," I tell him as I sink down on the bed.

"That she was," he says. "But I'm pretty fucking impressed with your girl, man. Did you see the way she put that fucker in his place then socked him? Fuck, I didn't know she had it in her."

"Yeah," I laugh. "She was fucking awesome."

With that, Tank bails, and with nothing left to do, I crash, waiting for Dani to text me to let me know how she is. The hours tick by, and it's just after midnight when I hear her key card slotting into the room door.

She walks into our room and strips out of her clothes before crawling into bed with me and moving right over into my arms. "Hey baby," I murmur, pulling her tight against me. "You still pissed at me?"

"Kinda," she sighs, turning in my arms to face me. "You were an idiot."

"I know. You were right," I admit. "How's your hand?"

"I broke my pinkie for your stupid ass," she murmurs.

Shit.

I bring my hand up, trailing my fingers down her arm and back up again. "Damn. I'll have to teach you how to throw a proper punch."

She gapes up at me, her brow arched. "You mean you weren't impressed with my performance?"

"I was definitely impressed," I say, a smirk on my face. "Seeing you like that had me hard as fuck."

She laughs and scoots up in bed to kiss me. "I'd jump you right now, but my hand hurts too much and you have to be up early," she tells me.

"Okay," I say as I take her bandaged hand and give it the gentlest kiss I can possibly manage. "I'll consider it an IOU."

Dani laughs before resting her good hand against my chest and closing her eyes. "You're going to win the championship tomorrow, Superstar," she murmurs with a yawn.

"We sure as fuck are," I say, pulling her in and pressing my lips to her temple, more than ready to prove her right.

CHAPTER 27

MILLER

It's the championship game.

The goddamn championship game and I'm the one leading my team out. Fuck, it feels good.

"Just get out there. Kick those motherfuckers' asses and bring home that damn trophy," Coach yells as we huddle around the locker room, waiting for our team to be announced. Coach focuses his gaze heavily on me. "I shouldn't be saying this, but any chance you have to humiliate Trent Daniels, do it. Just keep it legal."

We know this is going to be the hardest game of our lives, but there's no way that's going to stop us. Hell, we've skated in much worse circumstances.

We hear the L.A. team introduced and the crowd roars. We all put our hands in and begin our chant to drown out the noise of the crowd. Our door opens and an official tells us it's time. We all grab our sticks, and the boys fall in line behind me.

"Alright boys, this is it. I don't need to remind you that there are scouts out here and tonight's game will be a huge deciding factor for them. So, no fuck-ups and no fights, you hear me?" Coach warns, giving me and Tank a nod. "Jaxon, show me what you can really do, then we can talk about next season."

"Yes, Coach," he says with all seriousness.

I lead them out of the hole, down the corridor, and out into the open arena. I look up into the crowd and find the whole right side of the arena in Dragons' colors, then spot my girl and Sophie as they stand up and scream for us. "You see them, man?" I ask Tank, who's walking behind me.

"How can you miss them with those big ass foam fingers waving in the air?" he laughs.

The announcer calls us to the ice, and our fans roar in support. We tune them out, just like we're trained to, and get on with business. We stick to our half of the ice as we do a quick warmup, and before we know it, the referee blows the whistle to get the championship game started.

I stand dead center of the ice, facing a smirking Trent Daniels, and I can't wait to wipe that look off his face. Which is exactly what I do as I demand ownership of the puck and shoot right up the ice, surprising their deadbeat goalie and scoring within the first eight seconds of the game.

The crowd is on their feet, and I hear my name being chanted over and over again. "Fuck, yeah," Tank shouts, grabbing my head and smashing his helmet against mine. "This game is ours," he says as the rest of the team comes to clap me on the back. Coach Harris is almost beside himself with glee.

I glance up to find Dani on her feet with her camera pulled to her face, and I know without a doubt, she's captured that moment just perfectly. Hell, it'll be played on ESPN highlights for years to come.

After coming back to the center with a smirk, I stand before a sullen Trent Daniels. "Look who's laughing now, jockstrap." He doesn't comment, but his scowl deepens, and I realize that humiliating him is going to be so much easier than I thought.

Trent gets frustrated and attempts to slam me into the walls over and over again, narrowly missing me each time, which only proves to frustrate him further and throws his game off. Though he clearly isn't the talent in his team. The rest of his boys make up for what he lacks, giving our team a serious run for our money, but it's nothing I haven't trained my boys to handle.

Trent is thrown in the sin bin ten minutes into the first period, allowing the rest of us to get a proper game in. I push forward with Jaxon and Tank hot on my heels. I recognize one of Trent's boys from last night coming at me with everything he's got, and I nod to Jaxon who cuts across me while I pull back and dart to the left. Jaxon does what he's best at and body checks the dickhead into the wall, leaving their goaltender wide open. I shoot and score my second goal of the night.

The first and second period continues in a similar way, with me and Tank, the Dream Team, doing our thing. Though I must admit, it's fucking nice to have Jaxon keeping up with us again tonight. We might have to come up with a new name to include him. Hmm, Triple Threat? No. That sounds weak. I'll have to keep thinking about it. Right now, I have shit to handle.

The game is close, with us just slightly ahead, and I know we have to keep up our momentum. The opposition has been focusing on me, Tank, and Jaxon, realizing that we're the best players, but they play fucking dirty. They have had three skaters thrown in the sin bin so far, but I know my boys can win this and keep it clean in the process.

I grab a quick drink, take a deep breath, and head back out for our third and final period. When the whistle blows, I dive straight in. I shoot the puck over to Bobby, who forces his way up the ice. When two guys come at him, he shoots it to Tank. The puck is intercepted by the opposition and stolen to the other end of the ice.

Tank charges at the guy with me right on his heels. He does a little fancy footwork that has the guy fucking up his moves, leaving the puck wide open for the taking. I get the puck out from under him and take it back up the other end. I look the goalie dead in the eyes, just so he knows I'm coming for him, and shoot it hard into the back of the net. I loop around the back of the goal to avoid slamming into it when Trent springs out of nowhere. With his gloves already on the ice, he grabs me by the back of my jersey and throws me hard up against the barriers, causing my head to bounce back.

"This is my fucking game," he snaps, getting right up in my face as the crowd goes nuts with the anticipation of a fight.

I give him a hard shove to get the fucker off me as my head spins. "Your game was over before it fucking began," I taunt, knowing exactly what he's about to do, but I let it happen anyway. He rears back and throws a punch, but with my helmet and padding, it really has no effect apart from sending me flying onto my ass. Yeah, it pisses me off and is humiliating as fuck, but I smile at him instead as the referee throws him into the sin bin for the third time tonight. Sometimes, you have to take one for the team.

I get to my feet and search out Dani to find her looking down at me with wide eyes. I give her a slight nod, letting her know I'm fine, before skating over to Coach, who demands to check me over. "I'm good," I tell him as I pull off my helmet.

"I don't give a shit. I'm taking a look whether you like it or not. He got you pretty hard there," he tells me, taking a moment to feel over my head. "Looks like you'll have a nasty bump back here, but you'll be right."

"Good," I say. "Let's get this done."

The last fifteen minutes are excruciating, and I probably should have sat down for a while for my own good, but there's no way I'm sitting out the last minutes of the championship game.

Tank notices I'm lacking and does what he can to be right on my defense, but luckily, my slightly lacking is still better than these fuckers at their best.

Together, Tank and I own the ice, giving it our absolute all for our last college game. For Dani and Sophie, for our boys, and most of all, for Mia.

The other team gets another goal, which we immediately make up for with one of our own, refusing to give up our lead.

The final few seconds count down, and by now, we're just playing with them. We can tell the other team gave up two minutes ago when we scored yet another goal, and they realized it wasn't physically possible to beat us.

The buzzer sounds, and we throw our sticks down.

We fucking did it.

I look up to Dani, who blows me a kiss with a huge grin on her face, and I skate over to Tank. He pulls me in, slapping me hard on the back. The rest of our boys join us, throwing us both down to the ice in the process and jumping on top. The crowd cheers and chants as we are announced as the National Fucking Champions.

The red carpet is laid out and a ceremony is held on ice as we're presented with our trophy. We celebrate, cheer, and go fucking nuts while the photographers and media try to do their thing.

After what feels like forever, we're finally free to celebrate as a team. We make our way back down the long corridor and into our locker room, breaking into chants and whoops while giving high fives and back slaps, but the celebration is far from over.

We fucking did it.

I somehow hear a commotion from down the hallway that sounds suspiciously like Dani and Sophie screaming at the top of their lungs, and I poke my head out the door to find our girls being held back by security. "Babe," I grin, then focus my attention on the security guard.

"Let them pass."

He drops his arms to let them through, and Dani sprints ahead and jumps right up into my arms. "Congratulations, Superstar," she beams as Sophie passes us and heads straight into the locker room. Dani crushes her lips to mine as I walk us back into the locker room. "Fuck, you did so well. You kicked their asses."

I can't help but grin back at her. "I love you," I tell her as all the boys grin and make comments about being pussy whipped.

"I love you, too," she says, then turns her glare on my boys. "Shut up, fuckers," she scolds as they laugh. "What happens now?" she asks, looking back at me.

"Well, there will be another press conference today, and probably a shitload of interviews and meetings after that. Then we can do whatever we want. It's up to you," I say, then lean into her ear. "As long as I get to fuck you at the end of the night, I don't give a shit what we do."

She grins up at me. "How long will all that take?"

I look over at Coach Harris with a questioning eyebrow. "I imagine you seniors will have a few meetings with scouts following the press conference. So, I assume your ass will be stuck here for at least another three hours," Coach explains.

"Fuck. Sorry, babe," I cringe.

"That's okay. You do what you need to do. Sophie and I will head back to the hotel and get ourselves all dolled up, then you guys can come back and take us out. And don't worry, I plan on finishing this night with you deep inside me," she tells me.

"You've got yourself a deal."

"Okay, Superstar," she says, unwinding her legs from my waist. "I'll see you when you're done."

I give her a long, lingering kiss and send her on her way.

Best. Day. Ever.

Two hours later, we finish up in the press conference when Coach Harris pulls Tank and me aside. "Follow me, boys," he tells us in a tone that suggests we shut up and do what we're told.

We follow him down a hallway and into an empty meeting room. He motions for us to take a seat, which is exactly what we do. "What's up, Coach?" Tank asks.

"You'll see," he says with pride in his eyes. "Just don't sign anything straight away. You've got three of these meetings tonight," he casually mentions as the door opens and two men in suits walk in. One of them is the owner of the Chicago Raiders that Tank and I met a few months ago.

"Gentlemen," he starts as he takes a seat before us. "You did an amazing job tonight."

"Thanks," we say in unison.

"I know you must be tired, so, let's cut right to the chase. We want to offer you each a four-year contract," he starts as he slides a pack of official looking papers in front of us. We both grab one and ask a string of questions as we flip through the pages. After another ten minutes, they get up and make way for the scouts from Colorado, followed by the men from L.A., each offering us four-year contracts.

They make their exit, leaving us with more questions than when we started, and I look over at Tank and Coach. "Fuck," I say, breaking into a wide grin.

"I knew you boys could do it," Coach says with pride. "The fucking NHL."

Tank's grin nearly rips his face in half. "Did you see how many zeros followed that dollar sign?" he laughs, running a hand through his hair.

"Sure did, man," I say. "Now, let's get out of here. I promised my woman a night out."

CHAPTER 28

DANIELLE

Sophie and I are finishing off another glass of champagne when my phone rings loudly throughout the hotel room. I grab it off the counter and look down to find Miller's name on my caller ID.

"Hi," I grin.

"Hi, to you too. We're coming up," he says, sounding extremely happy. It makes me wonder if he's started drinking already. "Are you in our room or Sophie's?"

"Sophie's."

"Okay, see you in a bit," he says before ending the call.

By the time I've finished refilling our glasses and tell Sophie that the boys are back, they're pushing through the door.

"There you are," I grin as I sashay over to him. "Where the hell have you been all my life?"

"Waiting for you," he murmurs in my ear as he tosses a stack of papers on the desk by the door then loops his arms around me and lifts me off my feet, giving me a tight squeeze. I let out a girly squeal and demand he puts me down, which of course, he doesn't.

Sophie rushes out of the bathroom and wobbles slightly on her heels as she throws herself into Tank's arms and instantly latches her lips onto his.

"How much have you been drinking?" Miller asks, clearly having seen Sophie's wobble.

I grin up at him. "We just finished off the bottle."

"Have you eaten?" he asks with a questioning eyebrow.

"Nope."

"Alright. How about we take you out for dinner? We can tell you everything that happened tonight and then we can party," he grins.

My returning smile is wide. "Sounds good to me."

"Me too," Sophie mumbles against Tank's lips, making both me and Miller roll our eyes at their display of affection.

"Let's get out of here," Tank says, finally coming up for air.

Sophie and I grab our things and before we know it, we're being seated in an Italian restaurant.

"So, did you sort out Trent?" I ask as we flick through our menus.

"Nah," Miller says, "I figure after your beating and making him look like a fool on the ice tonight, he's learned not to fuck with us," he explains. "And after his performance tonight, there's no way he was

290

offered a contract."

I smile up at him. "I'm proud of you."

He gives me a panty-dropping smile, then reaches over the table to take my hand in his.

We all order, and I can't help but notice the cheeky looks Tank and Miller keep passing each other as though they've got some kind of secret. "Alright. What gives?" I ask them both.

"What are you talking about?" Miller smirks as our dinner is put down in front of us.

"You two," I say, waving my finger between them both and narrowing my eyes at them. "Something's going on here, and I want to know what it is."

"Can't we just be happy that we're National Champions?" Tank asks.

"No," Sophie says suspiciously as her eyes flick between the boys and then suddenly widen. "Holy shit. Are you in? Did you get a contract?" she rushes out.

Holy crap. How could I have forgotten? Of course that would have happened tonight.

The boys grin like little schoolboys who just saw their first set of tits. "Yeah, we got a contract," Miller says, watching me for my reaction.

"Fuck," I shout, jumping up from my seat and launching myself across the table at him, almost knocking over the red wine. "Holy shit. That's amazing. You really are a superstar. What team is it?" I ask as I plant a huge kiss on his lips.

"That's not the best part," he warns me.

I sit back on his lap to study his face and see him look over at Tank, who currently has a very excited Sophie straddling his lap. "Spill it," I demand.

"Well . . ." he starts, dragging it out. "We got three offers. Chicago, Colorado, and L.A. They want us as a package deal, but they will still accept us as individuals if that doesn't happen."

"Wow," I say, looking at him in absolute awe as my eyes begin to water. "Congratulations. You did it. Mia would be so proud of you."

He wipes away my tears with his thumbs. "Baby. No matter which team I choose, I want you to come with me."

I look deep into his eyes and search for any sign that this could be a dream. "Are you sure?" I ask.

"Absolutely. You're graduating soon, and I want you with me. I'm going to buy us a house and make an honest woman out of you, and then we can have a million kids if you want. Hell, maybe even a dog called Louie," he grins.

"I love you so much," I tell him.

"Good," he smirks, "because this would be seriously fucked up if you didn't."

I eventually climb off his lap and eat my dinner that has gone cold with all the excitement. "So, where are you planning on accepting?" Sophie asks them both.

Tank watches Sophie closely as he responds. "We were talking about it on the way back to the hotel. I've always dreamed about L.A., so I'll be signing that contract," Tank announces, getting a delighted squeal out of Sophie. She's always wanted to be a journalist in L.A.

"What about you?" I ask Miller.

He studies my face and sits back in his chair. "I'm happy with either Chicago or L.A. So, I guess it depends on where you would rather be."

"What?" I shriek, the pressure dropping onto my shoulders. "No way. You're not leaving this decision up to me."

"Baby. As long as I have you, I don't care where it is. I'm playing hockey. Which city is going to be the best from a PR point of view?"

"L.A., easily. But what's that got to do with hockey?"

"I want you to have everything, Dani. And if a career in PR is what you want and L.A. is the best option for that, then that's where we're going," he declares.

"Are you serious? L.A.? We're moving to L.A., and you're just going to hand me all my dreams on a silver platter?" I clarify.

"Yeah, babe. I'm serious. And as for your dreams, they're mine, too. So, really I'm just being a selfish asshole, asking you to move with me."

"Damn right, you are," I laugh.

"So, that's a yes then? We're going to L.A. and getting a dog named Louie?"

"Yeah, you big bastard. We're going to L.A."

EPILOGUE

DANIELLE

5 YEARS LATER

"I'm sorry, Danielle. We can't wait any longer," Dr. Adamson says regretfully as he motions for the nurse to put my legs up in the stirrups.

"NO!" I scream. "I'm not doing this without him. I can't," I cry as I squeeze down with everything I've got, probably breaking Sophie's hand.

"Fuck," she cries, attempting to pull out of my grasp. "It's okay, babe. I'm here. You have to push."

"AHHH!" I scream as another contraction rips through my body. "WHERE THE FUCK IS HE?"

The door flies open as Miller and Tank rush in. "I'm here," he yells, rushing over to my side and gasping for breath as Tank takes one look around and promptly turns on his heel, flying back out the door.

"About fucking time," Sophie scowls.

"Did you win?" I ask him as I take slow deep breaths and take his hand in mine.

"Come on, babe, you know I would never let a championship game slip through my fingers," he says with a smirk.

"Fuck, it's happening again," I groan, squeezing his hand.

"Alright, Danielle. I need you to push on this contraction," Dr. Adamson explains.

When the contraction comes on, I feel like my body is being ripped in half. I push with everything I've got as the pain consumes me. I gasp for air, tears in my eyes, only to be told to push again. "I can't fucking do this."

Miller leans over and catches my lips in his. "You've got this, babe," he tells me. "I didn't marry a quitter."

"SHUT UP!" I snap. "I fucking hate you for doing this to me," I say, clenching my teeth together, taking a deep breath, and pushing again. "This is all your fault. You and your big fucking dick can go and fuck yourself."

Miller chuckles under his breath, and I clamp down harder on his hand, getting a very satisfying groan out of him.

"Come on, Dani," Sophie encourages from my other side.

"Fuck you, whore. I'd like to see you doing this," I grunt at her.

"Well, you will be . . . in about eight months," she tells me with a grin. "Now, hurry up and get on with it. You're kind of freaking me out here."

"I fucking love you," I shriek, grabbing her by the shirt and pulling her down to me. I plant a big sloppy kiss on her cheek then groan as another contraction comes on. This news is something we will have to discuss afterward.

I give one more big push and Dr. Adamson announces that the head is finally out. I sigh in relief, knowing from all my books that the head is the worst part. Miller can't help himself and takes two quick steps to the end of the bed to get a good look, his eyes bugging out of his head. "Holy fuck, babe," he gasps. "It's like my favorite bar just burned down."

"I'm going to kick your fucking ass if you don't get back up here in the next two seconds," I growl.

"Okay," he grins, holding both hands up in surrender.

"Actually, why don't you stay down here," Dr. Adamson says as he fiddles around with my hoochie. "You can deliver your baby from here on."

The fuck? Is this guy serious?

Miller's face flicks between me and the doctors. "Are . . . are you sure?" he asks with wide eyes.

"Oh, no," Sophie groans under her breath, knowing this could only be a disaster.

"Sure am, but if you're going to do this, it needs to be now," the doctor announces.

Miller practically skips back into position as Dr. Adamson tells him what to do. I give one final push, then just like that, Miller delivers our sweet baby. "Holy shit," he whispers, looking down at our child in awe as the nurse rushes in with a blanket. Miller walks back around to me and ever so gently, places our baby down on my chest.

"It's a girl," Miller whispers, looking down at us together.

"She's beautiful," I sob, looking down into my daughter's face, the complete and utter pain of the last twenty-four hours completely forgotten.

"Wow, okay. I'm gonna cry," Sophie says with a hand resting against her chest. "She's gorgeous. Does she have a name?"

I look up into the beautiful, dark eyes of my husband. "Mia Rose Cain."

Miller leans down and presses a kiss to my lips. "It's perfect," he murmurs as he gently runs his fingers down the side of our baby girl's face. "You're both perfect."

As the doctors and nurses make their way out of the birthing suite, Sophie excuses herself to give us a little privacy.

I do my best to scoot over in the bed, but to be honest, my cooch is fucking hurting. Miller climbs in as best he can, and together we introduce our baby girl to the world around her. Seeing Miller holding our baby in his arms has tears springing to my eyes. "I love you so much already," he tells her. "I will never let anything hurt you, beautiful girl."

He leans back and wraps one arm around me, allowing me to snuggle into his side while he holds Mia in his other arm. "We did good," I murmur.

He holds me a little bit tighter. "We did the fucking best," he murmurs back, leaning in and pressing a kiss to my temple. "I love you so goddamn much."

I smile up at him, my whole world complete. "And I love you, Superstar."

THANKS FOR READING

If you enjoyed reading this book as much as I enjoyed writing it, please consider leaving an Amazon review to let me know. https://www.amazon.com/dp/B0BSDG5NHC

For more information on the Kings of Denver, find me on Facebook –

www.facebook.com/sheridansbookishbabes

Sheridan Anne

STALK ME!

Join me online with the rest of the stalkers!!
I swear, I don't bite. Not unless you say please!

Facebook Reader Group
www.facebook.com/SheridansBookishBabes

Facebook Page
www.facebook.com/sheridan.anne.author1

Instagram
www.instagram.com/Sheridan.Anne.Author

TikTok
www.tiktok.com/@Sheridan.Anne.Author

Subscribe to my Newsletter
https://landing.mailerlite.com/webforms/landing/a8q0y0

MORE BY SHERIDAN ANNE

www.amazon.com/Sheridan-Anne/e/B079TLXN6K

<u>DARK CONTEMPORARY ROMANCE - M/F</u>

Broken Hill High | Haven Falls | Broken Hill Boys | Aston Creek High | Rejects Paradise | Bradford Bastard

DARK CONTEMPORARY ROMANCE - REVERSE HAREM

Boys of Winter | Depraved Sinners | Empire

NEW ADULT SPORTS ROMANCE

Kings of Denver | Denver Royalty | Rebels Advocate

CONTEMPORARY ROMANCE (standalones)

Play With Fire | Until Autumn (Happily Eva Alpha World)

PARANORMAL ROMANCE

Slayer Academy [Pen name - Cassidy Summers]